Condemned Angel

∘ Book Two ∘

Holly Huntress

This book is a work of fiction. Any references to real places or people are used fictitiously. All other names and places are products of the author's imagination.

Front cover created and designed by Emily Lewis
Book edited by Cristine Huntress and James Dushkewich

Published by Kindle Direct Publishing

Thank you to all of my family and friends who have supported me through my journey of bringing this story to life. A special shout-out to my writing community friends who make writing less lonely and have helped to inspire me to keep writing!

Condemned Angel

Prologue

"This isn't right. Lucifer promised Ronan that he'd wait." Gregor rubbed his brow trying to fend off his headache. Mara was nagging him, yet again, for something out of his control. He answered to Lucifer and no one else. Besides, he knew that Ronan would never be able to hold up his end of the bargain, he'd always been weak.

"Don't remind me. If those idiots hadn't lost Wayne and the child…" he seethed at the memory. That had been their bargaining chip and now it was gone. Ronan had made a deal with Lucifer, so his precious daughter was untouchable for two weeks.

"You know it wasn't their fault…" Mara trailed off. "We need to stay away."

Holly Huntress

"Mara, please, don't you ever want to see Kaden again?" He gave her a pointed look. "If you just shut up and help me, you'll get to see him." He saw her wariness fade away. "Good." Lucifer had commanded that they not touch the girl but had never said that Gregor couldn't mess around in her mind.

"What about...Oliva" Mara gulped, and Gregor whirled around. His rage radiated off of him in waves. He knew she could feel it, and she even took a few steps backward, cowering. This made Gregor sneer. The power he had over her and the rest of his followers made him feel invincible.

"Forget about her. I keep telling you, she was weak and worthless," he growled.

"Yes, Gregor." Mara nodded and took his hand in hers. "I'm sorry, I should remember my place."

Gregor ripped his hand from hers and strode off. He took a deep breath, inhaling the marvelous smells of death and decay; they represented the fight he had won. The screams had ceased, and now all he could hear were the sounds of the hounds running to-and-fro, anxiously awaiting their next order.

Gregor snickered to himself as he thought of the angels who had so pitifully begged for their lives. They were not so high and mighty when their wings had been stripped from their backs, and their swords seized. It brought him nothing

Condemned Angel

but pleasure inflicting so much pain onto those who would deem his master unfit to rule the heavens.

"Sir, they have all been dealt with." Trent stood beside him now, covered in blood. It brought a smile to Gregor's face.

"I need you to do one more thing for me," he paused for dramatic effect. He took great pride in his image and the fear he could instill in others. "Put the hounds on Kaden's trail. It's time for a reunion."

I

The Disappearance

Septimus spent the day helping his father organize guards for the next week. It was a shame he spent such a beautiful day cooped up in a tent, but it had to be done. It was also a pity that Malachi took over Andromeda's training again, Septimus enjoyed spending time with her.

He never really thought about being in a relationship before Andromeda arrived. There had been a time when Gabrielle was interested in him, but he hadn't felt the same way. If anything, he'd always felt more drawn towards Seraphina, but was never compelled to approach her before.

Condemned Angel

Andromeda was a breath of fresh air; someone who challenged many of Septimus' own beliefs and thoughts.

Now, Septimus sat with his head on the desk in front of him, his arms crossed aiding as a pillow. His father was still scribbling animatedly across the paper on his desk.

"There!" He finished with a flourish. "Done. Now, shall we get a late lunch?" Septimus sat up and faced him.

"I was actually hoping to meet up with Andromeda if she's finished with training for the day." Septimus noted the spark of disapproval in his father's expression. It was nothing against Andromeda personally, Septimus knew, it was just that his father worried she would endanger Septimus at some point.

"Of course." Ephram's gaze softened and he managed a smile. "Go to her." He folded up the paper in front of him and placed it in a folder. Septimus stood and left the tent. It was around two o'clock in the afternoon and the camp was bustling with angels who were performing their assigned duties. Everyone else was out with a guard.

As Septimus walked past the dining tent, he noticed Bo was eating with Ace, Micah, Gabrielle, Seraphina, and Nathaniel, but Andromeda was not with them. Bo and Ace must have just finished their training. Septimus wondered if Andromeda was still with Malachi. He saw no sign of either of them. He walked into the tent and straight towards Bo. Bo glanced up at him, a little startled.

"Have you seen Andromeda?" Septimus asked.

"No, I assumed she was still training," Bo remarked, appearing worried.

"Yes, I'm sure she is," as Septimus said this, there was a sudden commotion outside the tent. An overwhelming sense of foreboding came over him, and he instantly tapped into the angel network. A cacophony of thoughts came through, but the one common thread was Andromeda's name, something about an attack, and *she's gone*. Septimus' stomach dropped.

Without a word to anyone, Septimus ran from the tent to find Malachi, supported by two other angels, walking towards his father's tent. Septimus followed and entered the tent behind them.

"What's happening? Where's Andromeda?" Septimus asked before anyone else could speak. Malachi flopped into a chair and Ephram stood from his desk.

"What is the meaning of this?" Ephram scrutinized Malachi and Septimus.

"We found Malachi unconscious in the clearing, sir, the girl was nowhere to be found," Michaela, who had helped bring Malachi in, told them.

"Malachi?" Ephram approached him and he lifted his head.

"It was a surprise attack, sir. I didn't see who hit me." Septimus could tell he was holding something back from the strain in his voice. He approached Malachi.

Condemned Angel

"What else? Did Andromeda not react to the attacker? Where was she?" he asked the questions in quick succession. Malachi avoided his gaze.

"Her back was to the attacker as well. We were practicing sword fighting," he said and Septimus knew that this was all the information he was going to give.

"We have to find her." Septimus threw his arms up and turned as if to leave the tent, but his father cleared his throat and it stopped Septimus in his tracks.

"It is unwise to go gallivanting about searching for Andromeda when we have no idea where she is, or who she is with," Ephram said and Septimus sighed, but he knew his father was right. He turned back to face him.

"We can assume it was the demons who took her, they have made their intentions abundantly clear. We just need to find their camp," Septimus pointed out, and his father nodded.

"Yes, the demons may have taken her. But…"

Septimus cut him off. "No buts, father. If we are to find her, we need to leave as soon as possible. We have already lost too much valuable time. We can still track her now."

"You are discounting the very possible reality that she left of her own accord," Ephram's voice rose. "There are things that you do not know about Andromeda, Septimus. It is too dangerous to go after her."

"And what of your promise to Jeremiah to protect her and keep her from the demons at all costs?" Septimus retorted. "If we give up on her now, then you'll have failed. I'm not willing to let you take the fall for this, especially if she left of her own accord."

"Do not pretend that this has anything to do with me and my status," Ephram's voice was calm and collected again. "If you feel that you must go after her, then I will allow it because I know there is nothing I can do to stop you. You have always been too reckless. It is a wonder you have not wound up dead already." Ephram sighed heavily. Malachi was glaring at them from the corner. He did not need to speak for Septimus to know how he was feeling. Malachi had worked his whole life to protect Septimus and make sure that no one ever got in the way of that, as he tried to do for Septimus' brothers.

"I won't go if you give me a legitimate reason not to," Septimus said, and his father raised an eyebrow.

"Fine. If you must know, Andromeda is not who you think she is," Ephram began and Septimus scoffed.

"What are you talking about? You're the one who brought her here, and Jeremiah ordered us to keep her safe."

"That is true. However, I did withhold some information from you. I knew Andromeda's mother, Angeline, before she had either of her children. She was your mother's best friend. So, I know that Wayne is not Andromeda's real father," Ephram revealed.

Condemned Angel

"And?"

"And her real father is Ronan." Ephram watched as this sunk in. All angels knew Ronan, one of the most notorious demons. Septimus sat down beside Malachi.

"So, what does that mean for Andromeda?" Septimus' mind whirled.

"Andromeda is an angel, but she is also a demon. She has the abilities of both beings."

"Why didn't you tell me sooner?" Septimus demanded.

"Wayne requested that I keep the information to myself because Andromeda did not know yet." Ephram appeared as if he may regret the decision to keep the secret.

Someone cleared their throat at the entrance to the tent and they both turned to see who stood there.

"I'm sorry to interrupt, but I wanted to check and see if there was going to be a search party." Seraphina stood in front of the tent flap, looking self-assured. Ephram shifted his eyes to Septimus.

Septimus rose and faced her. "No. Tell the others, no one is to go looking for Andromeda," his voice came out tired and hardened.

"Andy is my friend, and I want to help bring her back," Seraphina protested, standing tall and showing no fear. "I'm sure Gabby, Nathan, and Micah will want to help too."

Holly Huntress

"There will be no looking for Andromeda because she is not lost. More than likely she chose to leave, and we cannot risk our lives trying to bring back someone who does not want to be here," Septimus surprised himself with his certainty. Seraphina nodded, though she did not seem completely satisfied, and left.

"You know they won't be so easily persuaded to stand down, right?" Septimus said as he turned to Ephram, who didn't respond.

Ephram retreated to his desk and started packing up his things. "We are evacuating tomorrow. We cannot properly guard this camp against the demons." He glanced pointedly at Malachi, who had not said a word since he had told his story.

"I will spread the word." Septimus ducked out of the tent. He noticed Seraphina walking back towards the dining tent where the others were still eating. He ran to catch up with her.

∞

It was a beautiful summer day, and the breeze was blowing lazily through the trees, ruffling Bo's hair slightly. He sat on a fallen log with his head in his hands. As soon as Septimus had told him what was going on, he ran to the clearing. Just like everyone had tried to tell him, *she was gone.*

It was hard for him to accept that she had left. He knew her too well: the demons had probably given her some ultimatum, as they had tried before, and she'd agreed to go, to save someone, or everyone. They were supposed to be safe here…

"Bo," Micah's voice broke through Bo's trance. He glanced up and the sun shone through the trees behind Micah, giving him a halo.

"What am I going to do?" Bo croaked.

"We are evacuating tomorrow. The demons have proven they're stronger than our host. We need to join forces with another camp," Micah said, but none of this meant anything to Bo.

"But what am *I* going to do? I don't belong here without Andy." He remembered Andy asking him if he ever felt like he didn't belong …now he understood what she meant.

"You're going to come with us. Whatever you may think, you do belong here," Micah told him. Bo felt a glimmer of hope sparking inside his chest. He wouldn't give up on Andy, but he couldn't search for her alone. There was a chance he could convince the others to help him save her if he came up with a plan.

2

The Evacuation

As everyone hurried to pack up the last of their belongings, Septimus stood leaning against a tent pole watching in a daze. He could not believe what Ephram had told him; that Andromeda was not only an angel but also a demon. He knew it was possible, but had never even considered that Andromeda may be part demon.

He scanned back through all the time he had spent with her and wondered if there had been clues. Ephram said that Andromeda didn't know that she was Ronan's daughter, but still, she must have at least guessed what she was.

Condemned Angel

Septimus remembered when she had been cut while they were practicing sword fighting. Her reaction had been much more severe than it should have been, but he'd figured that was simply because she was part human.

Again, his thoughts wandered, but this time to his mother. She had been best friends with Andy's mother, Angeline. How could she have been friends with someone in a relationship with a demon? His mother had always been a ray of light, giving Septimus and his brothers guidance and love. For her own best friend to have betrayed her kind so carelessly, Septimus could not imagine his mother standing by that decision. Although, his mother was so accepting and tolerant, he knew that she was capable of forgiving anyone.

"Septimus," Malachi stood in front of him with worry plainly displayed on his face. "Wayne is here with Lindy. They were accompanied by a demon. Your father is outside the camp with them now." Malachi had always protected Septimus, and even now he was doing so. He worried about him because of the revelation earlier and guessed at the turmoil it had caused.

"Thank you for letting me know. I have nothing to say to Wayne, or any demon," Septimus' voice was harder and sharper than Malachi had expected, and he took a step back.

"Of course," Malachi nodded to him.

"Excuse me, I need to finish packing." Septimus turned and disappeared into his tent. He had nothing left to pack, but he didn't want to let Malachi see the pain on his face. Wayne had come back with Lindy, but where was Andromeda? Why had she not come back? He'd hoped that Ephram was wrong about her choice to leave, but this did nothing to convince him of that.

Septimus laid down on his cot and closed his eyes. He listened to everyone bustling around outside and let it drown out his thoughts. He stayed in this meditative state until someone cleared their throat outside of his tent. Septimus immediately thought of Andromeda, the day of their first kiss. The memory pained him.

"Septimus." Ephram pulled open the tent flap and stepped inside. Septimus stood up off his cot to face his father. "I need to speak with you in my tent and bring Bo." Ephram ducked out of the tent as quickly as he'd come in. Septimus sighed, knowing that he was about to discover Andromeda's true motives for leaving, and he wasn't sure he wanted to hear them.

Septimus found Bo in his tent chatting with Micah and Seraphina. It was strange to see them all there without Andromeda.

"Bo, if you could come with me, Ephram would like to speak with us," Septimus said. Bo seemed surprised but nodded in response. He followed Septimus out of the tent, leaving the others behind. They walked in silence. Malachi and Ephram sat waiting for them in Ephram's tent.

Condemned Angel

"I assume you both know that Lindy has been reunited with her brother. They have both gone on ahead to the camp in Baltimore to be sure that the demons won't come back for her," Ephram began. "Wayne accompanied Lindy here, along with a demon named Marcus. He had a message for Bo from Andromeda. She wanted to let you know that she's okay, and she's safe. Andromeda did not want you to worry about her." Bo appeared skeptical.

"How am I not supposed to worry about her when she was taken by demons for God-knows-what reason?" Bo threw his hands in the air. Septimus exchanged a glance with Ephram, nodding to indicate that he should tell Bo about Andromeda's heritage. Ephram nodded back.

"Bo, there is something else you should know. I don't want you to be upset with Andromeda, because she didn't know either," Ephram started, and Bo cut in.

"Just tell me," he was clearly agitated.

"Very well. Andromeda's real father is a demon. One of the most influential demons in the world actually," Ephram revealed for the second time that day. It cut Septimus almost as deeply as it had the first time.

"Wayne is a demon?" Bo scoffed. "No way."

"No, not Wayne. Wayne is not Andromeda's real father. Her father is a demon named Ronan." Ephram said and Bo finally seemed to understand. He didn't seem as off-put by the revelation as Septimus had been.

"But she's still an angel, too, isn't she?" Bo glanced at Septimus and then back at Ephram.

"Yes," Ephram said.

"So, I don't understand why who her dad is changes anything. Andy considers herself an angel, so that's what she is," Bo pointed out. "I know Andy, and I know she belongs with the angels."

"It changes everything," Septimus growled and turned on his heel, striding out of the tent. He had not expected Bo's reaction. He'd hoped that Bo would react similarly to himself. Septimus wanted someone to feel the same confusion and betrayal that he was experiencing. It was selfish and stupid, but he didn't care.

Septimus found himself being drawn into the woods behind the camp where he used to take Andromeda for walks when she had her nightmares. This would be the last time he could walk this path.

"Septimus?" He heard a voice behind him, and he turned to see Seraphina standing outside of Andromeda's tent. "I'm sorry about Andy. If it helps, I don't think she left lightly. I don't know her as well as Bo, but I do know that the only reason she would have left was if she thought it would help everyone else. She's not a selfish person." Septimus sighed. He knew that Seraphina was right, but it still didn't change all the facts that were coming to light.

"Thank you." He inclined his head towards her, thinking to dismiss her. But then before he could change his mind, he asked, "would you like to take a walk?" Sera seemed surprised, but she nodded and walked with him into the woods.

∞

Bo watched Septimus leave the tent as he thought about his own words. He'd told Septimus and Ephram that Andy belonged with the angels, but she had told Bo that she felt as if she didn't belong with them.

Bo turned back to face Ephram. Nothing would stop him from fighting for Andy. He would get her back.

"Septimus may be resigned to the fact that Andy is gone, but I will never stop searching for her. I won't give up on her that easily," Bo spoke with conviction. He could tell that Ephram thought these were just words, but Bo meant it. Demons had already taken so much from him; he wouldn't lose another person he loved to those monsters.

"I would advise you to give up any hope of finding Andromeda on your own. As she said, she is safe, there is no reason to worry about her," Ephram said, and Bo knew there was no swaying him on the subject.

"I'll just go finish packing then." Bo left and walked back to his tent. He noticed Sera walking into the woods with Septimus and Micah coming towards him. Micah lifted his head and smiled as he approached Bo.

"How did it go?" Micah was wary of Bo's reaction, unsure whether he would have good or bad news to report.

"Andy is supposedly safe, and I'm not meant to worry," Bo recounted.

"But," Micah sighed, knowing that there was more.

"But I can't believe that she's truly safe with demons. How am I not supposed to worry about her?" Andy was his best friend. He had promised himself that he wouldn't let anything happen to her, and he'd failed. He wasn't going to give up on her now.

"If Ephram said she's safe, I would believe him. He's a great leader, and although he may not show it, he has a big heart. If he thought that Andy was in danger, he would send out a search party. Otherwise, it's just not worth it." Micah realized his mistake as soon as the words left his mouth.

"*Not worth it?* You're suggesting that Andy isn't *worth* saving? Why? Because she's not a full-blooded angel? If it were Sera or Gabby, would you still think it wasn't *worth it?*" The words burst out of Bo. He could not believe that Micah could be so careless about this. Andy had been his friend too. "I need to pack." Bo pushed past Micah to get to his tent.

"Bo, please, you know that's not what I meant," Micah said, but Bo didn't turn back. He went to Andy's cot and grabbed her backpack from beneath. Inside, her gun still rested at the bottom, untouched since they'd arrived in the camp. There were also knives and some rope. Bo closed the

Condemned Angel

bag and hugged it to his chest. This was all he had left of Andy now, and he would not leave it behind.

Bo shoved a change of clothes for him and Andy into the backpack. They barely fit. He wanted to be prepared in case Andy came back to them. Everyone else had already given up on her, so he would just have to work that much harder to find her.

3

The Introduction

"You are not my father. My dad is the man you used against me for leverage. I don't care what you say, you will never replace him as my real dad." Andy's jaw trembled, and her fists clenched at her sides. Jason sat silently beside her.

"I was not the one using your father against you. Kaden saved Wayne from my comrades who only answer to Lucifer and have their own agenda. Do not forget that." Ronan was eerily calm, but a fire burned in his eyes. "Whatever you choose to accept, or not accept, it will never change who you are, my dear. You may be an angel, but there is no denying the fact that you are also a demon." His face shifted from eeriness to almost happiness as he revealed this information. Andy cringed and covered her face with her hands. She couldn't believe this was happening.

It was no wonder she had shown sympathy for the first angels who had fallen and become demons; she was their kin. What would Septimus and Bo think of her now that she was one of the monsters who had taken so many of their family members away from them? She was grateful they weren't there to find out who, or what, she really was.

Jason put his hand on Andy's arm and brought her back into the moment. She gazed up at him.

"Andy, it's okay. It doesn't change anything," Jason spoke with the same kindness in his voice that he always had, and Andy almost believed him. But when she looked into his eyes, there was no getting past the black rings that had replaced the gold flecks that used to shine there.

"Have you seen yourself in the mirror lately?" Andy asked him, grief thick in her voice.

"So, what, Andy? Just because my eyes have changed slightly, does that make me a whole different person?" He seemed hurt.

"I don't know, Jason." She shook her head. "When did your eyes change? What caused that shift inside of you? I watched it happen with Lindy, and she literally was a different person." She searched his face, but everything else seemed to be the same. He gazed past Andy to Ronan, and then, apparently receiving approval to tell the story, flicked his eyes back to her.

"It was different with Lindy; the other demons were actually inside her mind. I made my choice on my own. My eyes changed about a week after I came here. I went out with a legion on my first mission, and when I came back, they'd changed," Jason told her. Andy nodded slowly, and then a thought crept into her mind.

"What kind of mission, Jason?" she asked, unsure that she wanted to hear the answer.

"We killed a group of angels staking out one of our demon camps," Kaden cut in. "Happy now? Can we please let this sob session come to an end? I'm ready for bed." He pretended to yawn, and Andy scowled at him.

"You may leave, Kaden. Thank you for everything you've done." Ronan dismissed him. *Good riddance,* Andy thought. Once Kaden left, Ronan returned his focus back to Jason and Andy.

"You should both get some sleep as well. We have a celebration to look forward to tomorrow." He turned, regarding Andy, and she realized he was talking about her birthday. She'd completely forgotten about it. "You may do as you wish tomorrow morning, but I expect you both here, by my side, at four o'clock sharp for Andromeda's birthday gala." Jackson and Cairn reentered the room and Andy took that as her cue to leave. She couldn't bring herself to look at Jason after what Kaden had revealed. She walked in front of him and let the demons lead her back to her room. She heard Jason say goodnight, but she ignored him.

Once Andy was alone in her room, she broke down. She screamed into her pillow and sobbed until her throat was raw and her eyes were dry. Jason may have been alive, but he was a stranger to her now. The Jason she knew before would have never hurt anyone. All she could think was that the demons must have messed with his head as they'd done with Lindy.

How could she know whether they'd been feeding her lies this whole time? Were there really any other demons trying to get to her, or was it these same demons all along? She began to panic that they were going to do the same thing to her as they'd done to Jason and Lindy. They'd already been in her head before, what would stop them from doing it again?

Her heart began to race, and she couldn't catch her breath. Her damn anxiety was kicking in, full force. She rolled out of bed and made her way shakily to the bathroom, turning on the lights and splashing water on her face.

"It's all in your head," she told herself, scrutinizing her reflection in the mirror. "Don't let them get to you." Her pulse began to slow, and her breathing became normal again. She let out a sigh of relief. As she stared into the mirror though, she was reminded of her breakdown earlier, and the anxiety came rushing back, bringing with it all the traumas she'd suffered since leaving home.

Jason and her mom were alive, she tried to remind herself. There was no reason to grieve them anymore, but she could still feel that grief threatening to come out of its box. She stumbled to the bathtub and sat down, leaning against it.

"What is happening to me?" she choked out as she sobbed. She reached behind herself and turned on the faucet to fill the tub. Baths had always had a soothing effect on her when she was little, she hoped it would help her now.

She closed her eyes while she waited for the tub to fill. An image of her mom fighting off the demon, who Andy thought had killed her, flitted across her eyelids, followed by her brother, sneering at her with his black-ringed irises. In quick succession, the image was replaced by her memory of the time she and Wayne had all their belongings stolen from them by a group of humans. She knelt on the ground with a gun pressed against her temple, but this time, it was not a strange man holding it there, but Jason.

Her eyes flew open as she gasped for air. She'd stopped breathing without realizing it. Her heart began to beat so fast she thought it was going to either jump out of her chest or give out. The edges of her vision were beginning to blur, and she turned to see the tub was ready, so she quickly stripped down and climbed in. The water enveloped her as if it were a warm blanket.

Condemned Angel

She pulled her hair up and twisted it into a bun, using the elastic she always had on her wrist. Taking deep breaths, she leaned back against the small pillow cushion. She dared to close her eyes again, but this time no images appeared.

In case the anxiety tried to creep back in, she resorted to one of her coping mechanisms. She listed off every place she had visited, and happy memories associated with them. But the happy memories soon turned sour. Neither her mom nor her dad ever told her that Wayne wasn't her real father. Why would they keep such a huge secret from her? How could they?

She drifted off into a fitful sleep, her dreams filled with Jason, Ronan, Kaden, Septimus, and Bo. They all blended, and she couldn't tell one dream from the next. She woke up to cold water and pruning fingers. Half in a daze, she climbed out of the tub, wrapped herself in a towel, and stumbled to bed. Sleep took her again, dropping her back into her confusing and ever-changing dreams.

When Andy woke in the morning, she couldn't remember any of the details from her dreams, but she was left with an ache in her heart, the words *"you cannot escape from me"* running through her mind, and fear coursing through her veins.

Andy rolled out of bed and remembered where she was, and what day it was: her birthday. The clock revealed that it was already noon. She'd slept for more than twelve hours. She walked to the bathroom in a haze, still unable to believe everything that had happened in less than twenty-four hours. She found out her brother was not only alive, but also a killer, her mother was alive, but who knew if that was true, and she found out that she was not only an angel, but also a demon.

After returning from the bathroom, someone knocked on the door. Andy threw on her robe and shuffled over, opening the door a crack. She nearly fainted when she saw her mom standing there in the hallway. So, Jason had been telling the truth about that at least. She gave Andy a big grin and Andy rushed into her arms. Any fears that lingered before had now dissipated as Andy felt her mom's arms wrap around her. She felt warm and safe with her.

"It's really you," Andy's voice came out muffled against her mom's shoulder. There were tears in her eyes, and she couldn't bring herself to let go. Angeline pulled away slightly to regard Andy, brushing Andy's hair out of her face.

"Happy Birthday, sweetie," Angeline smiled warmly. "Come on, let's catch up in your room." They stepped into the room and Angeline shut the door behind them, locking it.

Sitting across from her mom on the bed, Andy could not keep the smile off her face. She never thought she would see her again, and now, here she was, as beautiful as ever, sitting right beside her.

Condemned Angel

"You shouldn't be here," Angeline said, as her eyes scanned Andy's body, checking for signs of harm or weariness. "You were supposed to stay far away from here." A single tear escaped and ran down her cheek, but she wiped it away quickly. "I'm so sorry, Andy." Andy's smile faded.

"If I hadn't come, I wouldn't have known you were alive! I wouldn't have been able to help save Dad and see Jason. And on top of all that, I was putting all of the angels in danger if I stayed with them any longer." Andy tried to make Angeline feel better about the situation, but she shook her head.

"I know, sweetie. I was just wishing things could go back to the way they were before the war." She kissed Andy's forehead. "You did the right thing. I wish it didn't have to come to this; to you leaving behind people you care about. Your father, Ronan, can be a very headstrong man when it comes to getting his way."

"Dad's been preparing me to leave people since we first left home…" Andy had left the angels without much reservation when Kaden had come to her. She wondered if part of that was because of her dad reminding her over and over that it was the only two of them left, and they needed to be prepared to leave others behind to make sure they stayed alive. "Why didn't you tell me that Wayne isn't my real dad?" Andy asked the question that ate at her.

"It's complicated," Angeline avoided the question.

"Mom just tell me. How could you not tell Jason and me who our real dad was? Or that we were angels *and* demons?" Andy pressed and Angeline sighed.

"That is a long story for another time. Just know I did it to keep you and Jason safe." She looked away to the window as if lost in a memory for a moment, and then back to Andy. "I want to know about you, Andy," she finally smiled. "I want to hear what you've been learning. Ronan told me that they were training you at the Camp of Jeremiah." Andy decided to let go of her questions for the moment and enjoy being with her mom again.

"Yes, they were. I learned how to use my strength and sight, and how to create a ball of light. I've been practicing sword-fighting, too," Andy told her, wondering if her mom had been trained when she was young, before she'd had kids.

"I'd always hoped to be the one to help you with your training, but I'm glad you've started." Sadness lingered in Angeline's gaze, and Andy imagined she was thinking of all the time she'd lost with her and Jason because of the war.

"I learned how to wield the heavenly fire, too," Andy said, wondering if her mom knew how it affected her differently because she was part demon. Angeline didn't respond but appeared deep in thought. "What have you been doing while you've been here?"

"That's not important, sweetie. We should start getting you ready for your party," she avoided Andy's question and stood from the bed.

Condemned Angel

"I have three hours until I have to be downstairs," Andy protested, wondering why they couldn't keep talking.

"You can't show up to your own party late. Trust me, it's going to take longer than you think to get ready for this gala." She went to the closet and started rummaging through the dresses. There were flashes of pinks, purples, blues, and reds. Some were glittery, others were poofy, and a few were silky.

When Angeline emerged, she held a beautiful, navy blue, sparkling gown. It was a halter top style with a deep V-neck, and it was fitted to hug the body. When it moved the sparkles threw the light around the room. Andy never would have pictured herself wearing such a dress before, yet there she was, about to put it on.

"It's beautiful," Andy said, admiring the dress.

"It used to be mine." Angeline grinned and held it up to herself. "I hope you love it as much as I did. But first, we need to do your hair and makeup, then you can put it on and choose your shoes." She hung the dress from one of the hooks on the closet door. "Come to the vanity." Andy followed her into the bathroom, sat down, and swiveled the chair to face her mom.

"So, what else did you get to do with the angels?" Angeline asked as she started brushing Andy's hair.

"Well, not a whole lot," Andy said. "I was only there for two and a half weeks."

Holly Huntress

"What's this your dad was telling me about a new friend? I think his name is Bo?" Angeline put the brush down and started pinning up different sections of Andy's hair.

"Yeah, Bo. We met him and his parents while we were on our way to the camp. He and I are, or were, really close. I didn't get to say goodbye..." Andy trailed off and tears pricked her eyes. Angeline stopped and crouched beside her, putting her arms around Andy. Andy leaned into her and let her mom hold her.

"I'm so sorry. None of this should be happening." She squeezed Andy tight and then went back to doing her hair.

"So, I assume Dad made it here okay?" Andy asked, wondering why he had not come to see her yet.

"He returned late last night, so he's still sleeping," Angeline said, smoothing back a section of Andy's hair.

"So, Lindy's okay," Andy let out a sigh of relief. "I was so worried about her, but dad offered to go with her back to the angel camp. Before we saved her, I kept having nightmares about her."

"I know. Your father, Ronan, told me. He wanted to try speaking to you through your dreams, and he could see the images that were haunting you. He was never able to get through because he was too far away," she shook her head. "I kept pleading with him to leave you be, thinking he was probably just making things worse, but he has never been one to take orders from anyone else."

"He's a monster..." Andy grumbled.

Condemned Angel

"I know you think that sweetie, and in a lot of ways, maybe he is." Angeline didn't offer any further explanation and continued curling Andy's hair and pinning sections up as she went. "It was the other demons who were giving you the nightmares..." anger flashed in her eyes. "Kaden did what he could to block them from your mind, but because he wasn't with you, it was hard for him to know whether the others were in there or not until he could hear you screaming," her voice choked on the word, and Andy realized how hard it must have been for her mom, not to be able to be with Andy and comfort her like she had when Andy was little. And then Andy realized something else...

"Kaden was inside my mind?" she whispered, slightly horrified. Angeline crouched down in front of her again and took Andy's hands in her own.

"I'm sorry, that was my doing. When Ronan told me about the nightmares you were suffering from, I turned to Kaden...I asked him to block everyone else from your mind. I gave him my permission on your behalf. I couldn't stand to have you experiencing those terrible nightmares anymore." Her eyes were pleading, silently asking Andy for forgiveness. Instead of responding, Andy changed the subject.

"Have you noticed Jason's eyes have changed color?" she asked, and Angeline sighed, going back to finishing Andy's hair.

"Unfortunately, yes. He is very taken by your father. Ronan has been promising him all sorts of glory and status." There was grief in Angeline's eyes again. If she had been with Jason all this time, why had she not stopped him from going on that mission, or becoming a demon?

"Doesn't Jason realize that he's hurting people? He would've never hurt a fly before the war!"

"I know, sweetie. He's not the same brother you knew before the war, though. Just like you're not the same Andy anymore." Angeline finished her hair and picked up a makeup brush. "We've all changed, but you're both still my children, and I will always love you, no matter what."

"You're right. I'm sorry. I love you, too." Angeline smiled again, and Andy let the conversation about Jason go, for now. "I have a boyfriend." Andy's heart fluttered as she thought about Septimus. Surprise came across Angeline's face.

"Really?" she smiled brightly but continued working on Andy's makeup. "Tell me all about him."

"His name is Septimus..." Her mom dropped the makeup brush and gaped at Andy.

"Ephram's son?" she asked. Andy nodded, unsure whether her surprise was a good reaction or bad. "I'm surprised Malachi doesn't have him packed away in bubble wrap somewhere. He was always so protective of the kids when I knew him." She picked up the brush and resumed doing Andy's makeup.

Condemned Angel

"Oh, I'm sure if Malachi had things his way, that's how it would be," Andy laughed. "He's probably celebrating that I'm gone."

Angeline laughed too. "So how did you get past the defenses then?" Andy soaked in the ecstasy of having a normal moment with her mom, chatting about boys.

"Septimus trained me mostly. Malachi took over for a little while, but that didn't last. Septimus also helped me out a lot with my nightmares," Andy said, though she guessed that was not as true as she once believed, seeing as Kaden was the one who blocked her nightmares from returning each night.

Angeline finished Andy's makeup with some lipstick and a sweep of shimmer on her cheeks. She turned Andy back to face the mirror. Andy gasped when she saw herself. She was almost unrecognizable after spending so much time not wearing any makeup or seeing her reflection in mirrors. Angeline had used a shimmering blue around Andy's eyes to compliment her dress and her hair was in a fancy side ponytail. Studying herself standing beside Angeline, Andy thought it was crazy how much they looked alike.

"Alright. Now we can put the dress on." They walked back into Andy's room and she glanced at the clock; two o'clock. She hadn't realized how long she'd been sitting in that little chair. Angeline grabbed the dress from its hanger and held it out for Andy to step into.

Once Andy had the dress on, Angeline helped her pull the zipper up the side to close it. Andy followed her mom into the closet to look at the shoes. Her mom held up a pair of five-inch heels that matched the dress in color and sparkles, but Andy quickly shook her head.

"I can't walk in those." Angeline set them back down. Andy picked up a similar pair that were silver and only about three inches high. "How about these?"

"Perfect," Angeline smiled and helped Andy put the shoes on since Andy couldn't bend down in her dress. "Alright, come over here." Her mom had her stand in front of the full-length mirror and do a twirl.

"I don't think I've ever felt more beautiful," Andy commented, sweeping the skirt of her dress from side to side, smiling at her reflection. This almost made up for the prom that she'd missed because the schools had closed due to the war.

"You're always this beautiful, but I'm glad I could be of assistance today." Angeline fussed with a few of Andy's stray hairs and placed them back where they belonged. "I have to go get ready now, sweetie. Wait here until Kaden comes to escort you." She went to leave, and Andy caught her arm.

"What do you mean, Kaden is escorting me?" There was a fire in Andy's veins again. Kaden may have helped her with her nightmares, but she would rather spend the whole party at Ronan's side than be escorted by Kaden.

Condemned Angel

"Ronan wants Kaden to escort you more as like a bodyguard rather than a date," Angeline explained. "Don't worry, Kaden will take care of you." Andy scoffed at that.

"He is cold and cruel, why does Ronan want me to go with him?" Andy asked, crossing her arms.

"He's not all that bad, Andy. Give him some time. He's had a much harder life than you know, growing up with parents like his," Angeline scowled. "They are the coldhearted ones. I'm surprised Kaden didn't turn out much worse."

"Fine. I will tolerate him," Andy grumbled.

"He helped you get your dad and Lindy back." Angeline fussed with Andy's hair again as she said this. Andy nodded but was still wary of being escorted by Kaden. "I'll see you in a bit." Her mom kissed her cheek and squeezed her hand. Angeline left the room, closing the door behind her.

Andy stood there in front of the mirror for a little while, realizing she couldn't do much of anything in her dress. She walked over to the desk in the corner and sat carefully, so as not to muss up her gown, and started riffling through the drawers. There was nothing of interest, just some paper and pencils. She took a piece of paper and a pencil out and started doodling. She had no actual drawing skills, but she'd always enjoyed it. So, she drew some stick figures and flowers, and it kept her mind occupied so it wouldn't wander like it had the night before.

Before she knew it, there was a knock at her door. Andy glanced up at the clock and realized it was three-thirty already. She walked to the door slowly, not looking forward to spending any amount of time with Kaden, and opened the door.

Kaden seemed surprised when he saw her, but he quickly composed himself, putting his arm out for Andy to take. She rolled her eyes and put her arm through his. He wore a simple black and white tux. He actually looked quite handsome, but Andy would never tell him that for fear of boosting his already gigantic ego.

"This is ridiculous. Why couldn't Jason escort me? Or anyone other than you?" Andy asked as they walked down the hall. She needed to move a bit slower in her heels.

"Ouch. You should consider yourself lucky that you're with me instead of some of the other people around here. They're not all as gentlemanly as I am," he smirked, inclining his head slightly in a 'gentlemanly' manner, Andy assumed.

"Oh god, if you consider yourself gentlemanly, I'm scared to meet anyone else," she joked.

"You should be," he seemed serious, which made Andy wonder if everyone else here was really that bad, and a chill went down her spine.

"I feel like we're going to prom or something. I would be surprised if there aren't a bunch of parents at the bottom of the stairs with their cameras," Andy said as they approached the spiral staircase.

Condemned Angel

"I wouldn't know, I never went to prom. I never even went to school for that matter," Kaden said, and Andy almost felt bad for him. He had missed out on so much, and yet she still couldn't get past his rudeness from the day before.

At the top step, Andy braced herself for the descent in her heels. She put a little more weight on Kaden's arm than she wanted, but she would rather use him as a crutch than fall down the stairs and lose her chance to see her mom and dad again. Thankfully, Kaden stayed silent for once, not mentioning the extra support she was relying on him for.

They made it to the bottom of the stairs without incident and for the first time since Andy arrived, people were bustling around everywhere. She could see they all had the same black irises. Some of them had a coldness in their eyes that she had come to expect from demons, while others were much more *normal*, like Kaden's eyes. They were mostly all headed towards the throne room, but Kaden led Andy towards the dining room.

"Why aren't we going towards the party?" she asked, peering over her shoulder at the hall that led to where they were supposed to be headed.

"I figured you might want something to eat first since you've been cooped up in your room all day," he answered, and Andy realized he was showing that he just might care about someone other than himself.

Holly Huntress

"Oh, well... thank you." They walked into the dining room, which was filled with platters of food. Andy grabbed a finger sandwich and ate it before anyone else saw. "That is so good." She went to wipe her hands on her dress, and then thought better of it and just rubbed her hands together to brush the crumbs off.

"Alright, come on. We can't be late." Kaden led her back the way they came and this time they walked down the corridor to the throne room. There was no one out and about anymore, so Andy figured they must all already be in there. The same two demons who had been escorting Andy the day before were guarding the door.

"Right on time, Miss Andromeda," Cairn said as he and Jackson opened the doors. Inside, the benches had been removed, opening the room up and creating a dance floor. There were buffet tables along one of the walls filled with food and punch bowls. On the other side of the room, there were some tables and chairs which were occupied with demons. As Kaden and Andy walked in, the room quieted. Ronan was sitting in his chair at the back, and beside him stood Jason. Kaden brought Andy to Ronan's other side and bowed to him before he disappeared into the crowd.

"Thank you all for coming here tonight," Ronan began speaking and anyone who had still been talking stopped. Everyone gazed up at Ronan now. "You all know why we are here. My beautiful daughter, Andromeda, has finally decided to join us. Tonight, we are celebrating her birthday and a

Condemned Angel

recent victory over the angels." Everyone applauded politely. Ronan smiled broadly at this, and Andy scowled. "Now, everyone, please, eat, drink, and enjoy yourselves because tomorrow we return our focus to the war." Everyone started chatting again and some people moved about the floor. A small instrumental band in the corner began playing music.

"Where are my parents?" Andy turned to Ronan and he smiled up at her. She held back the urge to grimace.

"They're on their way, don't worry," he gazed out into the crowd. "I remember when your mother wore that dress. You look as beautiful in it as she did." Andy was not sure how to respond to that, and thankfully, Ronan did not expect her to. "Please, go enjoy yourself." He motioned out to the floor. Andy couldn't get away from him fast enough. Hiking up her dress, so she didn't trip over it, she descended the steps and made her way over to the food table. The sandwich from earlier had barely touched her hunger. She found some cheese and crackers and grabbed a handful of each.

"I guess I shouldn't be surprised to find you here," Kaden joked as he came up beside Andy, grabbing a handful of chips for himself.

"I need something to distract me from all of this..." Andy waved her hands to indicate the room around them, "craziness."

"We had a similar party when your brother joined us, but nothing quite as glamorous. Ronan must think you're special or something." Kaden scrunched his nose with fake disdain. Andy was about to respond when the doors opened and her parents walked into the room, arm in arm. Andy dropped what was left in her hands onto the table and ran straight into her dad's arms, letting him squeeze her against him.

"Andy! I'm so happy you made it here safely." Her dad was fussing over her, touching her hair, and inspecting her, making sure she was healthy and whole.

"I'm fine, Dad." Andy grinned widely, feeling elated, being there with *both* of her parents.

"Happy Birthday, Andy," Wayne said, but that was not what she cared about right now.

"Is Lindy okay?" she asked him.

"Yes, Lindy is with Ace, but the camp has been evacuated now. They were packing up when we arrived," Wayne explained. Now she couldn't go back even if she were ever allowed to leave the mansion.

"Did you see Bo?" Andy asked. Wayne shook his head.

"I was not able to go inside the camp. We only made contact with Ephram and Ace, to be sure that Lindy made it to him safely, but I asked them to pass on your message to Bo." He patted Andy's arm reassuringly.

"I am so happy that everyone is okay." Andy hugged her dad one more time.

"I have to go speak with Ronan, he wanted me to check in with him once we got back from delivering Lindy, but I

Condemned Angel

went to bed. Try to have a little bit of fun, despite being where we are." Wayne gave her a half-smile, kissed her forehead, and then walked towards Ronan.

"I should go with him, Ronan's not the biggest fan of your dad." Andy's mom squeezed her hand and then hurried after Wayne. Andy watched them approach Ronan's throne, and she could almost see the tension in the air between Ronan and Wayne.

4

The Party

Andy glanced around the room and noticed some people had started dancing. A few wore dresses like hers and their skirts swished across the floor, blurring together in a whirl of colors as they moved around the space. Andy was mesmerized for a moment, until a tap on her shoulder snapped her back to reality. Turning, she came face to face with a man who hovered next to her. He appeared to be around Wayne's age, but he was taller and lankier. His hair was as black as his eyes, which held a deep, dark coldness within them. A shiver ran down Andy's spine and she took a step back.

"The famous Andromeda," the man sneered, his breath reeking of stale alcohol and cigarettes. "I don't understand all the fuss over a worthless *half-breed*," he spat out the last two words. Andy cringed away from him and hurried towards Jason, who was near the food table. He smiled as Andy approached him.

"Isn't this great?" Jason's grin widened as he shoved a piece of bread into his mouth.

"I guess." Andy glanced back to see the same demon still staring at her. She shuddered. "Who is that over there, the one just staring at us?" Jason's eyes roved quickly to where she indicated and then returned to the food.

"That's Samson. He's a bundle of joy," Jason chuckled. "I avoid him mostly. He doesn't like anyone who is not a full-blooded demon. Everyone here is, except for us. And Mom and Dad."

"So, are people who have given up their souls to Lucifer considered full-blooded demons?" Andy wondered what classified a person as a demon in Samson's eyes.

"Not exactly. Once someone gives up their soul, they are just claimed by Lucifer. Once they die, they can be summoned back to Earth by a person. Only then are they considered demons, otherwise, they just rot in hell," Jason explained with his mouth half full. "Or you can be like us, having demon parents makes you a demon as well." Andy nodded and surveyed all the demons who surrounded them in the room. "Unlike angels who are sent here by God alone, and none of them used to be actual humans, at least, none that I know of."

"Huh. Thanks for the lesson, Jase." Andy stole a cracker off his plate, and he stuck his tongue out at her, making her laugh. For a moment, she forgot what he had become, and was brought back to the days before the war, when they were *normal*.

Kaden walked towards them, and Andy took that as her cue to be anywhere else. "I'm going to find Mom and Dad." She left Jason and headed in the direction of Ronan. Her parents didn't seem to be around him anymore, but she figured they couldn't have gone too far.

"Andromeda," Ronan called to her as she neared his chair. "Come here," he beckoned her over to him and she hesitantly did as she was told, wondering what he could want to talk about. "Are you enjoying yourself, my dear?" he asked, grinning broadly. Andy pushed down the hatred she was feeling for him and put on a fake smile.

"Yes. Thank you." The lie slipped through her teeth, though she wasn't sure why she wanted to please him. He had ruined her family and torn her away from her friends.

"Now, Andromeda, I may not be an angel, but I can tell when someone is lying to me." Ronan waved someone over and soon Kaden was standing beside her. "You like to dance, don't you?" he asked Kaden. "My Andromeda needs a partner. Please escort her onto the dance floor." Andy's fake smile left her face, and she scowled.

"Why do you keep forcing Kaden to spend time with me? It's torture for both of us." Andy crossed her arms and Ronan smirked. Andy could feel the tension rolling off Kaden.

"You may have noticed, there are only a handful of people here your age. I think it's good for you to make friends here, and Kaden may be the only one who can withstand your... strong personality." Andy rolled her eyes and let out a spiteful laugh.

"Strong personality? Is that another way of saying annoying or something? Great." Andy stormed away from them and towards the door. Before she could reach it, though, someone's hand was on her elbow.

"Hold on, Andy," Kaden said, as she spun around to face him. She yanked her arm out of his grasp. "Just give Ronan the satisfaction of seeing you dance one dance with me. He planned this whole party for you. Besides, he has a bit of a temper and I'd rather not be on the receiving end of it."

"Well, I guess I know where I get it from," Andy huffed, turning back to the door, but Kaden took her hand and started leading her in the opposite direction. She turned to pull her hand from his grip, but when he turned his head to look at her and smiled...she let him lead her to the dance floor.

"I want to leave just as much as you, but unfortunately we are stuck here until the end." Kaden pulled her close and placed one hand on her waist, keeping her hand in the other. Andy went along with it, letting him lead her around the dance floor. "Not so bad, is it?"

"I mean, yes, it is. But I'm stuck here, according to you, so I may as well pass the time somehow," Andy sighed. "How did you wind up here?" she tried taking her mind away from her residual anger towards Kaden.

"My parents were once loyal to Ronan," he said. "They followed him everywhere, and so here I am."

"But you could leave now, couldn't you?" If what her mother had said about his parents was true, why did he not leave and find his own group?

"Why would I?" he asked incredulously. "I have everything I need right here."

"I guess." The song ended and Kaden dropped his hands to his sides. For a moment, Andy missed the weight of his hand on her waist, but she shook that off quickly, taking a step away from him.

"I'll relieve you of my presence," he joked and stalked off towards a large group of demons.

Ronan was now standing beside her. He had finally left his throne. It was strange for Andy; he was taller than she had realized. "May I have the next dance?"

"I guess. I have nothing else to do to pass the time here," she sighed, giving him her hand.

Condemned Angel

"Well now, you could be a bit more gracious, I did throw you this glorious birthday party." He swung her around the dance floor. He was a very good dancer, despite being a monster.

"I never asked for this, and you also took away my choice in being here," Andy reminded him. Her blood boiled at the thought of how he had uprooted her entire life and taken her away from people that she cared about.

"You're still going with that theory? I thought we had cleared up the situation. Kaden may have been a bit too vague when he said that you wouldn't be able to return to the angel camp. He really should have said you wouldn't want to, considering your mother and brother are here. But it brought you back to us, which is all that matters," he smirked, this time Andy tried to sense whether he was lying to her, but everything he said seemed to be truthful. "But all is well now, is it not? You've been reunited with your family, and all of your friends are safe."

"But why can't I be reunited with my friends? Am I not allowed to have both?" Andy asked, wishing that she could have Bo and Septimus there with her. Missing them had left her with a constant knot in her stomach that she couldn't seem to dislodge.

"Your friends are angels and are therefore the enemy," his face was serious now.

"What does that make me, then?" Andy asked, cocking an eyebrow at him. He laughed lightly and led her into a twirl. She spun under his arm and then back into position.

"You have the luxury of having a choice. Most people don't even get that much." There was a flash of a strange emotion crossing his face, guilt? Sadness? Andy couldn't tell and it was gone as quickly as it came.

"So, I choose to be an angel over being a demon. It's simple," Andy stated, knowing that this would always be her decision, no matter what he threatened.

"Give it some time, my dear. It is not all as cut and dry as you believe it to be. Give it two weeks, and then if you still choose the angels over the demons, so be it." He slowed down their dancing and Andy noticed that everyone was watching them.

"And if I do, what then? Will you let me, and my family leave unharmed?" Andy tried not to look around at all the faces that were surrounding her.

"We will discuss that more when the time comes. For now, just enjoy yourself." Ronan bowed to her and slipped back to his throne. Once he was seated, everything returned to normal. People filled the dance floor again.

Andy finally spotted her parents and hurried over to them. They had been watching her dancing with Ronan along with everyone else. Andy worried that Wayne might be hurt by her dancing with her real father, and not him.

Condemned Angel

"Where did you guys go?" Andy asked, grateful to be back with them.

"Sorry, sweetie." Angeline brushed a hair that had fallen out of Andy's up-do behind her ear, avoiding the question. "Is everything okay?" Angeline looked warily up to where Ronan sat, and Andy wondered what was going through her head.

"Not really; Ronan told me I have two weeks to decide whether I will side with the angels or the demons," Andy told them. Wayne seemed angry, but Angeline didn't react. Andy figured her mom had seen this coming, she had been close with Ronan at one time.

"He's hoping you will be as naive as I was when I was your age," Angeline sighed. "I know you will do what you feel is right." She smiled, but it was half-hearted. Wayne appeared a little sick, now. Andy wondered how being immersed in this demon culture was affecting him. He was human, after all. It couldn't be what he imagined for himself before he met Angeline.

"I'm going to choose the angels," Andy said. "I'm going to get us all out of here," she spoke with confidence, even though she had no idea how it would all end.

"Just be careful. Ronan is known to keep a few cards up his sleeve to play when you least expect it. He almost always gets his way," Angeline warned, glancing at Ronan sitting on his chair. "But I believe in you, sweetie. You've always been able to do whatever you put your mind to."

"Thanks, Mom." Andy hugged her.

"Your father and I are here if you need to talk about anything, and we will help you in any way we can." Angeline glanced at Wayne who nodded in agreement.

"Like you were able to help Jason?" the words came out almost as a whisper. Andy felt a strange and sudden wave of anger come over her. She knew she should not blame them, but her mom was with Jason the whole time, and he still chose the wrong side. Angeline cringed and Andy realized she had hurt her, but she didn't feel sorry.

"I tried to steer him in the right direction, but Jason had to make his own decision. Ronan can be very convincing. I hope you can be stronger..." tears were building up in Angeline's eyes, but she blinked them away before they could fall.

"*Jason* is strong! He has always been the strong one!" Andy felt like she had been plunged into ice water. Her whole body was rigid and cold with fear. "If he wasn't able to resist Ronan and the demons, how will I?"

"Don't worry about that right now. You have two weeks, let's just enjoy the moment," Wayne said, putting his arm around Andy, trying to calm her down. Angeline looked at the ground. Ever since they were reunited, Andy had noticed something was off with her mom. She was much more melancholy and almost beaten down like she had given up.

Condemned Angel

She was not the same woman Andy knew before she left. Living here with the demons had already changed her just as it had changed Jason.

Ronan cleared his throat and the room fell silent. Everyone turned their eyes to him.

"Thank you all for being here. You may now go back to your normal duties," he announced, clapping his hands together with finality. Andy glanced at the clock and realized it was already seven o'clock. Everyone immediately began filing out the front doors and dispersing to the rest of the house, or wherever it was that they came from.

"I had the cook make you something." Jason stepped up beside Andy. "Come on." He led her through a side door and down a long, narrow corridor. Their parents followed behind them. At the end of the corridor was the empty kitchen. Jason went over to the fridge and pulled out a plate with a small cake on it.

"Happy birthday to you..." Andy's parents walked into the kitchen singing and Andy couldn't help but laugh. They finished the song and Andy blew out the candles that Jason had lit.

"Thank you so much." Andy hugged them all and felt tears stinging her eyes. "I never thought I'd be spending my birthday this way, but I am so grateful that we are all back together again." The strange tension from before was completely gone now. She felt at ease again, and almost happy.

"We wouldn't miss it for the world," Wayne grinned brightly, kissing Andy's forehead.

Kaden appeared in the doorway to the kitchen and cleared his throat. He leaned casually against the door frame with his arms crossed over his chest.

"Sorry to disrupt this family reunion, but Ronan is requesting Jason and Andy's presence," he announced. Jason almost seemed excited, while dread began to spread through Andy's body. She turned to her parents, who were giving each other worried looks.

"Go ahead, kiddos. We'll clean up here." Wayne tried to put on a smile, but Andy could still sense his apprehension.

"Yeah, come on, kiddos. We ain't got all night." Kaden turned and headed back in the direction he came from, assuming they would follow. Jason went first, and Andy followed him hesitantly, giving one last glance back at her parents.

In the throne room, Ronan was sitting exactly where they last saw him, but the benches had all been replaced already. The dance floor was gone, along with all the buffet tables. Andy glimpsed the glass ceiling and saw the moon and stars shining down on them.

"Here they are, Sir," Kaden announced, waving his hand towards Jason and Andy.

Condemned Angel

"Ah, good. Thank you, Kaden. Please wait outside a moment, would you?" Ronan said, and Kaden stepped out of the room. "Good, good. I would just like to request that both of you join me for breakfast in the morning. I have big plans for the day, and I would like you both to be a part of them."

"Absolutely!" Jason responded enthusiastically, his face lighting up. Andy scowled and crossed her arms over her chest. She would not be as easily won over.

"What kind of plans?" she asked, not sure that she would like the answer.

"No need to worry about that now. I will fill you in on all of it at breakfast. So, I will see you both at eight o'clock in the dining room?" Ronan asked, looking at Andy expectantly.

"Yes, fine," she said, and he nodded, grinning.

"Good, good. Kaden!" Ronan called and Kaden reappeared in the doorway. "Please escort Andromeda back to her room, I need to speak with Jason alone." Kaden beckoned for Andy to follow him out of the room and she reluctantly left Jason behind.

In the hallway, Andy caught up to Kaden, though she had to hike up her dress and step carefully in her heels to do it. He was still wearing his tux, which was tailored to hug his muscles perfectly. Andy blushed as she realized that she was admiring him. She shook her head to clear it.

"I can get back to my room fine on my own," Andy muttered, making Kaden laugh.

"You sure you want to walk these halls alone, knowing people like Samson are also walking around?" Andy looked at him in surprise. She'd nearly forgotten about her encounter with Samson earlier, but she didn't realize that Kaden knew about it. "Don't think I didn't notice him eyeing you all night. Let's just say he will take any chance he can get to rough up anyone who is not a demon. Being Ronan's daughter means nothing to him."

"I guess I should thank you, then," Andy said, with no intention of thanking him for anything.

"No need, it gets me brownie points with Ronan," Kaden smirked, and Andy groaned.

"Why would you be helping me for unselfish reasons? I think I'll be fine from here," Andy tried again as they approached the staircase. A girl about Andy's age swung around from behind the staircase and came face to face with Kaden. She had long black hair pulled up into a sleek ponytail and the same piercing black irises as all the other demons. She was grinning widely as she flicked her eyes from Kaden to Andy.

"Babysitting duty again, Kade?" she mocked him and then turned to Andy. "I'm Lily." Grinning, she held out her hand to Andy.

"Andy," Andy introduced herself, eyeing Lily curiously. She was petite but strong. Her arm muscles were probably twice the size of Andy's. She was dressed in tight black skinny jeans, a white tank top, and black combat boots.

Condemned Angel

She must not have been at the party. Andy felt a little embarrassed to still be in her gown.

"Sorry I missed your party. I had some business to attend to," Lily winked. "Happy birthday, though," she seemed sincere, which made Andy curious about whether she had given up her soul or not. Andy found it hard to believe that any demon who had given their soul to Lucifer could have a single good bone in their body.

"Thank you," Andy smiled back at Lily and glanced over to Kaden who appeared to be bored.

"We should be moving along. The princess needs her beauty sleep," he spoke up and Lily turned back to him, leaning in close enough that Andy thought she was going to kiss him, pausing for a second, and then she stepped back. Another girl came around the corner from the kitchen. She had an armful of mini sandwiches. Her bright red hair was braided and came down over her shoulder. She glanced up and burst out laughing as she saw them. Andy noticed the way her face lit up, and how familiar her features were. She had the same slight but muscular build as Lily, but there was an uncanny resemblance between her and Kaden.

"Oh, what a sight to end my night with!" the girl giggled, and it sounded like music. Andy wished that her laugh sounded as elegant as this girl.

"Shut it, Liv," Kaden grumbled.

"Oh, so sorry, Kade. I should introduce myself to this poor girl," she looked at Andy. "I'm Olivia, Kaden's sister. I'm sorry that you had to endure his presence all night," Olivia laughed again. Andy wasn't sure if she should respond, so she just smiled.

"Oh, leave him be, Liv!" Lily cut in, grinning. "Andy needs to be getting to bed, and we need to be checking in with Ronan." Olivia nodded and set down her sandwiches on the small table beside her.

"Crap almost forgot." She hurried across the room back towards where Kaden and Andy had just come from.

"I'll see you later." Lily winked at Kaden and sauntered after Olivia. She waved to Andy as she went.

"They seem nice," Andy commented. "I didn't know you had a sister."

"It's something I wish I could forget," Kaden mumbled. "Besides, we didn't grow up together. My parents considered me burden enough, they gave up Liv to be taken care of here."

"Oh." Andy wasn't sure how to respond to that. She felt sympathy for Kaden, which she had thought was impossible. She decided to change the subject.

"Is Lily your girlfriend?" Andy asked, thinking that it would be unlikely for anyone to be able to stand Kaden's attitude long enough to fall for him, but anything was possible.

Condemned Angel

"No." He shook his head and started up the staircase saying nothing more on the topic, so Andy dropped it. She slowly followed him up the stairs, teetering now and then on her heels. It was easier to walk in them when her feet were not killing her from being on them for three hours.

At the top of the stairs, Kaden led Andy down the hall towards her room but stopped two doors away from her door. "This is my room," he announced. "I trust you can make it safely to your room from here."

"Yes. Goodnight." Andy continued down the hall. As she opened her door, she turned back to wave as Kaden ducked into his room. He paused for a moment and then turned back.

"Happy Birthday, Andy," he said and closed his door, leaving her with his strangely kind sentiment.

5

The Transition

Ephram beheld their new home, the camp of Emmanuel. This camp was much larger than their last camp. There were a few cabins among the tents, one of which Ephram knew was the meeting house.

When they had first arrived, there had been new tents and cots set up for the angels coming from the camp of Jeremiah. The camp of Emmanuel's leader, Evangeline, had been more accommodating than Ephram could have hoped. He knew her from a time long ago, and he knew her to be kind and just. She was Amelia's sister.

Condemned Angel

Malachi stepped up beside Ephram, bringing him back from a memory. "Ephram, we have finished rearranging your tent. You should get some rest; it's been a long day." He put his hand on Ephram's shoulder, but Ephram shrugged it off.

"Not until everyone else is settled in for the night." Ephram couldn't think about sleeping right now, and even if he tried, he doubted he would be able to fall asleep. There was too much on his mind.

"You're worried about the girl, aren't you?" Malachi always seemed to know what was bothering him. Ephram sighed.

"I vowed to keep her away from the demons at all costs. I have failed. The dominions are not going to be forgiving." Ephram knew the consequences of disobedience and they were not something he anticipated enduring. He could only hope that the dominions would show him mercy since it was not entirely his fault that Andromeda had been taken by demons.

"She will return to us," Malachi reassured him. "She may be young and naïve, but she has a good heart and soul." Malachi may not believe his own words, but it was important for *Ephram* to believe them. He needed to be of sound mind to lead his people. Ephram nodded to Malachi in thanks for his support.

"Ephram, I need to speak with you." Evangeline came up to them, her face serious. Something was going on and

Ephram snapped back from his self-pity. "Alone, if you will," she added, glancing at Malachi.

"Of course." Ephram followed her back to the meeting cabin, which was empty besides the table and chairs. Even though the cabin had been there for years, it smelled of freshly cut wood. Ephram breathed in deeply, trying to calm his nerves.

"Come, sit." Evangeline took the chair at the head of the table and Ephram sat beside her. "I've received a message from Emmanuel," she began. "They have given you a day to settle in here, but the Dominions are not happy. They were clear that the girl, Andromeda, was to be protected at *all costs*, and you have failed in keeping her safe from the demons." Ephram nodded. He'd known this was coming and he had no regrets. His people were safe, Andromeda was reunited with her family, and that was all that mattered.

"She decided to leave. I would not force her to stay, and had I tried, my entire camp could have been destroyed by the demons trying to get to her," Ephram explained to Evangeline, keeping his voice level. There was a spark in her eyes, she understood, but she could not voice this.

"Even so, they are not pleased, and they have decided upon your punishment. They are stripping you of your leadership and all of your followers will now report to me." Ephram could tell that Evangeline was not relishing in this, for which he was grateful. He understood that she was only being the messenger and knew she would lead his people well.

Condemned Angel

"So be it. I will accept the consequences of my actions," Ephram said, letting her know that he would not fight her on this, and she relaxed a little.

"And one other thing, they wanted you to let Malachi know that they are watching him very closely." Ephram knew that this was because of Malachi threatening Andromeda. Malachi had told him the full story once Septimus was no longer around to hear. But Ephram was not going to fill Evangeline in on those details. Malachi had always been far too overprotective, it was in his nature, as a former guardian angel.

"Thank you, Eva," he called her by her nickname, recalling the time before when they worked together and were good friends. It was Evangeline who introduced him to her younger sister, Amelia, whom Ephram fell in love with almost instantly. She and Ephram were together for too short of a time before she was taken back to Heaven.

Now, two of their sons were also there with her, along with Ephram's other four sons that he'd had with Sylvia, his first love. In Ephram's mind, he knew that he would see them all again, but their absence that he felt every day filled him with deep grief. He would gladly join them in heaven; however, he was needed on Earth for a while longer.

"You're the only one who still calls me that, you know." There was a hint of a smile on her face, but Ephram could also see a shadow of sadness in her gaze, as she thought about her beloved sister as well.

"I know," Ephram smiled, reaching out to pat her hand reassuringly. "I am going to tell the others that I decided to step down as leader. It will be easier that way, and they will be happier to follow you. You should have no trouble with them, though, they are all loyal and hardworking. I am lucky to have been able to work with them all for as long as I have."

"I understand. I'm sorry it has to be this way." She reached out and placed her hand over Ephram's atop the table to comfort him. The roles were so easily reversed. He took her hand in his and squeezed it lightly.

"As am I. I just have one question; would you have done it any differently? Would you have risked the lives of everyone in your camp for one person?" he was only asking out of curiosity, he held no resentment towards the dominions for their decision, nor towards Eva for being their messenger.

"There is no knowing what we will do until we are placed in the situation. You did what you thought was best, and that's all that matters. Now, the burden is on me to decide what happens next. You should get some rest." Ephram took this as his cue to leave and pushed his chair back, standing.

"I shall try." He left the cabin and Eva behind, heading, not to his tent, but out into the forest, to find some peace and quiet. He needed to go out past the camp's boundaries to finally be alone. He was no longer needed in the camp.

Condemned Angel

Ephram made his way to a small overhang that overlooked a steep hill leading to more giant oaks, and pines. From there he could see out for miles. He had been there once before, many, many years ago, before he met Amelia or Evangeline. Back when his first love still walked the Earth.

Sylvia was so different from Amelia in every way. They were both remarkable rulers, but Amelia was much more kindhearted and loving. Sylvia was headstrong and less likely to put their family first, which was why she ended up leaving Ephram and their boys behind. She had a choice whether to stay on Earth or return to heaven, and she chose the latter.

"Ephram," the voice was carried to him on the wind, and he closed his eyes, breathing in the fresh air. At that moment, he knew that everything would work out as it should. It was as if the knowledge and feeling of this had been planted in him by that beautiful voice. His Amelia...

In his mind, Ephram envisioned Amelia standing next to their twins, Mathias and Thaddeus, watching over him and Septimus. Ephram could only imagine what they were thinking, and he laughed at the bickering probably occurring between Mathias and Thaddeus. Tears came to his eyes, and he opened them to see a figure disappearing before him. It reappeared at his side. Amelia hovered there, but she was barely a wisp of mist.

"Thank you," Ephram whispered to her. She smiled knowingly and disappeared again. Ephram often heard her voice, and felt her presence but, this was the only time that she had ever materialized before. He wondered if maybe he was beginning to lose his mind. He laughed at the thought, knowing that if he were losing his mind, it would not be his pleasant and level-headed Amelia who came to him. If his mind were to turn on him, Sylvia would be the one to come twist him and wrench him away from saneness.

Ephram turned away from the overlook and began walking back to the camp with a new sense of peace and understanding settling over him. As he reentered the camp, Septimus came jogging up to him.

"Father, everyone is settled. They're wondering what will happen next." Septimus looked to him as a leader just as the rest of his people did. He would be disappointed in Ephram to know that he had lost his status as their leader.

"I will come and talk with them," Ephram offered. He had to let them know sooner rather than later that they would now be following the commands of Evangeline.

As they walked towards the tents that had been set up for them, Ephram thought about what he was going to say. He needed to make sure that everyone would respect Evangeline as their leader. He realized as they reached the first tent, everyone was already gathered, waiting on his word.

"Thank you all for understanding the need to relocate at such short notice," Ephram began. He took a deep breath.

Condemned Angel

"As you all know, Andromeda has joined the ranks of Ronan's group. For those of you who do not know, Ronan is Andromeda's father." Several whispers echoed through the small crowd. "I am not telling you this to change your view of her, she is still an angel. I am informing you so that you understand *why* she made her decision to leave. I want no one to hold any resentment towards her." Ephram knew that what he was about to tell them might be twisted and the blame could be placed on Andromeda. He would do his best to ensure that didn't happen.

"As for the fact that I was unable to fulfill my duty to the dominions in protecting the girl from demons, I bear the full responsibility of that failure." Worried looks crossed some of their faces. They guessed where this was going. "I will no longer be your leader." Murmurs passed amongst the crowd. "You will all be reporting to Evangeline from now on. She is a strong and respectable leader, and I expect all of you to get along fine with this change," Ephram's words caught in his throat. He had been leading this group since before the war broke out, and now he was being forced to abandon them. He knew that Evangeline would take care of them, but it stung, nevertheless.

"That's not fair! It wasn't your fault..." someone called out from the back of the group.

"Please, this is the way that I have chosen it to be, there is no disputing the command. Let us move on from this and become stronger for it." Ephram turned away from them and strode to his tent. There was nothing more for him to say. He suddenly felt weary and needed to rest. Malachi nodded to him as he walked by. Ephram knew that he would stand by him no matter what happened next. Nothing was going to be the same for him after this day, and he had to figure out what his new normal was going to be. He hoped sleep would assist him with that.

∞

    Bo listened to the whispers about Andy and how she had betrayed them. Ephram had tried to dissuade that kind of talk, but it was inevitable. Bo couldn't take it any longer, though, and he left the dining tent. He practically ran to the edge of the camp, and beyond out into the woods. There was less worry here about demons lurking in the trees, especially now that they had gotten what they wanted: Andy.

    He found himself on the edge of a cliff that overlooked a vast expanse of trees. The angels said that this camp was in Baltimore, but it was actually east of Baltimore. Bo had never been here before, but he had been to the city, and it wasn't near where they were.

    "Bo?" Micah's voice drifted to him on the breeze. Bo didn't turn. "Is everything alright?" Bo couldn't help but laugh at the question. How could everything be alright? His parents had been murdered by demons, and his best friend was taken.

"No. Everything is not alright," Bo said.

Micah sighed, stepping up to stand beside him. "I know. Stupid question. Is there anything I can do to help?" He reached out to hold Bo's hand, but Bo turned away from him and started back towards the camp. Micah let him leave without following.

Bo kept walking until he was inside his tent that he shared with Ace and Lindy. Andy's absence was like a punch in the stomach. He collapsed onto his new cot. It felt wrong without Andy there. He had been so lonely since she'd had left. Micah had been trying to fill the hole, but it wasn't the same.

"Bo?" Lindy shuffled over to him. He lifted his head to her. "I miss Andy..." she sniffled and wiped her nose. Bo sat up fully and patted the cot for Lindy to take a seat. She climbed up beside him and tucked her legs underneath her.

"I miss her, too."

Ace came to sit beside them. "I never thought I'd say it, but I miss her, too."

"When is she coming back?" Lindy asked. Bo couldn't find it in himself to tell her the harsh reality that Andy may never come back.

Holly Huntress

"I'm not sure, Lindy. I hope she's back with us soon." Lindy smiled at that, and Bo felt a stabbing in his chest as he held back his tears.

∞

Once Andy was in the safety of her room, she locked the door and shed off her dress and shoes. She went straight to the bathroom and hopped into the shower. Washing off all the makeup and hairspray left her feeling refreshed and lighter. The steam hid her view of herself in the mirror which she was grateful for. She wrapped a towel around herself and went back into the room to investigate her pajama selection.

Rummaging through the dresser drawers, she finally settled on a pair of silk shorts and a silk tank top. She was fairly sure silk was her only option for pajamas here. Though she would much rather sleep in a baggy t-shirt and cotton shorts, the silk *was* comfortable.

In bed, Andy laid awake for a while thinking about what Bo and Septimus must be up to. They would have realized that she was gone as soon as Malachi returned to camp. They were most likely both furious with her. She wondered if they had arrived at their new camp yet. At least they were safe. She drifted off into a nightmare fueled sleep.

"Andromeda!" Septimus called her name. Andy searched all around but all she could see was darkness.

Condemned Angel

"*Septimus!*" *she tried calling back, but her voice came out as a whisper. There was movement in the darkness surrounding her. She tried turning every which way to see if there was light in any direction, but there was nothing but blackness.*

"*Andromeda, where are you?*" *Septimus called to her again, but he was farther away now. Andy started running towards his voice, though she couldn't see where she was headed.*

"*I'm here!*" *she tried screaming this time, but it still only came out as a whisper. Hot breath brushed the back of her neck and she heard the awful gurgling noise of the hellhounds. They were surrounding her. She screamed as they began tearing into her.*

Andy jolted awake when someone knocked on her door. The residual effects of her nightmare left her sweating and breathing heavily. She forgot where she was for a moment, but then felt the bed beneath her, and the memories came flooding back in. Her anxiety flared, her heart and mind racing.

She glanced at the clock on the side table and the time glowed back at her. One thirty in the morning. Then came another knock on her door. Who would be knocking at this hour? She groaned, rolling onto her side, and sat up, placing her feet on the cold floor. A shiver ran up her spine. Stumbling over to the door, Andy cracked it open in time to see Kaden walking back to his room. There was a nightlight in the hallway, illuminating everything in a dull orange glow. He turned back to regard Andy as he heard the click of her door opening.

"You're waking up the whole house," he said in a low whisper.

"Sorry..." Andy's face burned with embarrassment. "Nightmares." She ran her hands over her arms, trying to generate some warmth. She had been sweating moments before, but now she was freezing.

"Well, try to keep it down in there." He turned to retreat to his room and then paused. "And don't open your door at night. You're lucky it wasn't someone else."

"I can't be expected to have the best judgment when I've just been rudely awoken in the middle of the night," Andy snapped, trying to keep her voice low so as not to disturb everyone further.

"Right, I'll just let you stay in your nightmares from now on." He stalked back into his room and closed the door a little too forcefully. The bang echoed down the hall. Andy closed her door and hurried back to bed, alone again. She burst into tears as she thought back to all the nights Bo would climb onto her cot to comfort her and Septimus would take her mind from her nightmares, sacrificing his own sleep. He would be taking her on a walk through the woods if they were still together. She wished they were both there with her. She hugged herself, curling up into a ball under the covers.

6

The Garden

Andy slept until she was awoken by another knock on her door. This time, sunlight streamed through the window and the clock showed that it was seven forty-five in the morning. Andy jumped out of bed, remembering that she needed to be at breakfast in fifteen minutes. She ran to the door and threw it open.

"I'm here..." Kaden gave her a once over. "Is that what you're wearing to breakfast?" he cocked an eyebrow and smirked. Andy let out an annoyed sigh.

"I overslept, okay?" She put her hands on her hips. "I can be ready in five minutes." He gave her a challenging look and she pushed the door shut, turning back to her room. She threw her hair up into a ponytail and headed for the dresser, finding a pair of skinny jeans, and pulling them on. She also put on a light blue tank top and a pair of ballet flats, then thought better of it and traded for her combat boots, just in case whatever she and Ronan were doing that day would require something a little more rugged. She grabbed her leather jacket and draped it over her arm.

When she opened the door again, Kaden was leaning against the wall with one foot resting up against it and his arms crossed. He pushed himself off the wall at the sight of her and grinned.

"I'm impressed, you managed to be ready in five minutes." Kaden clapped his hands together and then motioned for her to follow him. "I mean, you could have pulled off the PJ's, but this is probably more family-friendly." He gave her a smirk over his shoulder, and her face became hot as it turned red. "Ronan will already be there waiting for you."

As they reached the bottom of the stairs, Jason appeared and smiled brightly at Andy. She was still a little wary of his new black-ringed eyes, but so far, he had proven to be the same Jason she had always known and loved. He took her hand and squeezed it reassuringly.

"You look much more like yourself today, Andy," he commented, and she smiled back.

"Ballgowns really aren't my style," she joked. "But you could do with dressing up more often."

"I do clean up nicely, don't I?" he laughed and patted Kaden on the back. "I can take it from here." Kaden moved off in the opposite direction of the dining room.

Andy and Jason made their way into the dining room, where Ronan sat waiting at the head of the table. He smiled brightly at them both as they walked in and Andy couldn't help but smile back for real this time.

"Good morning." He motioned for them to sit down and they sat on either side of him. "So glad you could both join me this morning." Pancakes and fruit were brought out on platters and set in front of them on the table. Ronan made the first move, and then they all dug in.

"So, I promised an itinerary for today," Ronan began. "I have two things," he shifted his gaze to Jason. "Jason already knows what I need him to do. But, Andromeda," Andy looked up from her plate as he said her name. "I need you to be my right-hand woman today. We're going to go visit one of my camps and check in on things."

"Okay." Andy knew she had no say in the matter, so it was easier to just go along with him for now. Besides, she was curious to see another demon camp. She wondered if they were all mansions like this one, or if this was the exception.

"So, when we finish up here, we'll go." He clapped his hands together in finality and continued eating.

After they all finished eating, Jason left to get ready for his mission, and Andy followed Ronan outside an SUV with blacked-out windows waited for them. It reminded Andy of one of the SUVs from the president's motorcade.

"After you, my dear." Ronan motioned for Andy to walk ahead of him. Cairn stood ready to open the door for them. He nodded to Andy in greeting.

"Thank you," Andy said as he opened her door. She climbed inside and slid to the opposite side of the car. Ronan got in behind her.

"Thank you, Cairn," Ronan said as Cairn shut the door. Andy looked around at the all-black, leather interior.

"This is a nice ride," she commented.

"Yes." Ronan glanced around as well. "Unfortunately, we do not have the luxury of having wings like you and your angel friends."

"Well, I haven't gotten my wings yet. The jury's still out on whether I ever will." Andy picked at her nails, not as concerned about her wings as she once was.

"Ah, yes. Further proof that you are truly my daughter," he smiled. "Your mother received her wings on her sixteenth birthday, which was a very lucky coincidence. Usually, the wings' appearance does not directly coincide with a birthday."

Condemned Angel

"I've never seen my mom's wings," as Andy said this, she was reminded of how much her mom had been hiding from her and Jason. That anger that simmered in the tightly sealed box Andy had created, rose slowly, but she pushed it back down.

"I figured as much. She was wrong to hide this side of the world from you and your brother. See how it has left you so unprepared for this new life?" Ronan shook his head. "But I promised to stay out of her life and let her and Wayne raise you both away from angels and demons."

"Why did you promise to stay away?" Andy asked, curious.

"It was what your mother wanted. Contrary to what you believe about demons, Andromeda, we do have hearts, even the soulless demons. We are capable of being compassionate." Andy's face reddened.

"Okay, but I still don't understand. Did you not want Jason and me?" her voice wavered. Even though she loved Wayne, there was a tiny part of her that felt abandoned now that she knew her real father left them, or as he said, 'let them go.'

"My father decided it was time to step down and I took over his place as leader of the North American demons." Andy couldn't help but let out a small gasp. He chuckled. "It sounds like a lot, and it is, but I have commanders stationed everywhere whom I delegate to."

"So, you chose leadership over your own family?" Andy's voice came out sharper than she intended.

"The demons are my family as well, Andromeda. I chose not to allow a foundation to crumble. I chose to let your mother live the life she truly deserved, with a man who could be there for her and you kids. I did what I thought was best at the time." Ronan's tone was defensive. Andy understood what he said, but it didn't negate the fact he had abandoned them.

"What about mom…" how could he leave her if he had truly loved her?

"She was better off without me; besides, your mother's family didn't approve of us anyway. They warned her that there would be consequences, even though all she had done was fallen in love." The look on his face told Andy that he really had loved her, and maybe still did.

"With a demon," Andy added.

"Yes, with a demon," he grinned. "In her defense, I was very charming in my younger years." Since demons, like angels, didn't age past their twenties, Ronan still appeared as a twenty-eight or nine-year-old man. He was handsome, and now that Andy was studying him, she could see Jason in him. He had the same nose and brow. Jason inherited their mother's hair and eyes, just as Andy did.

"And you're not charming anymore?" Andy prompted, wondering what had changed in him since the time he'd spent with her mother.

Condemned Angel

"I cannot afford to be charming now. I have to lead my people and they need a strong, reliable figure to follow," he explained, turning away from Andy, but not before she saw sadness fill his eyes. "Charming does not fit into that bill."

"Do you ever regret leaving us? Would you ever consider doing it all differently if you could?" She felt like she was interviewing him, but these were answers that she felt she needed, she *deserved*. He owed her that much.

"So many questions." Ronan chuckled and relaxed again. "Yes, I've considered it. But, to regret it is not something I can do. It does nothing for us to dwell on things we cannot change. It's a waste of time and I don't have the luxury of spare time." The car came to a stop. "Oh good. We're here. Come along, my dear. It's time you meet some more of your kind."

Cairn opened the door for them again. When they stepped out, Andy realized they were at a camp very much like the Camp of Jeremiah, except there were no angels here. This camp was filled with demons, and stationed at the entrance, she gulped, there were hellhounds. She stuck close to Ronan as they passed them, but they didn't even look at her. She was not the hounds' target.

As Ronan strode through the camp, with Andy trailing behind him, everyone gave him a slight bow as he passed. They approached what Andy assumed was the meeting tent and they ducked inside. Three people sat at a round table inside. Andy noticed with a shock that two out of the three of them did not have black eyes, but blue with black rings just like Jason.

"Andromeda, this is one of my commanders, Xavier." Ronan gestured to the one person who was fully demon. Xavier grinned at them. Andy shivered under his cold gaze.

"It's nice to formally meet you, Andromeda," as he said this, Andy realized that she recognized him. He was the same demon who broke into her house and whom she thought had killed her mother. "I'm sorry we had to meet under such...strained circumstances before."

"I remember you," Andy said through gritted teeth.

"Oh yes, I nearly forgot Xavier's failed attempt at recruiting you," Ronan chuckled, but Andy remained tense. "Anyway, back to introductions."

"I'm Izzy," the woman to the right of Xavier introduced herself. "And this is my sister Annabella." They both had platinum blonde hair. They appeared closer to twenty-six, which was as old as they would ever look.

"They are like you, Andromeda; demon and angel," Ronan pointed out what Andy had already guessed.

"And?" Andy began to feel a little irritated. This was all just one of Ronan's cards that he was playing. Her mom was right. He wanted them to convince her that choosing the demons was the right path for her, just as they had done.

"And nothing. Have a seat. We have to discuss some important matters and I wanted you to witness what it is that I do." Ronan took a seat across from Xavier and, after a few seconds of everyone staring her down, Andy sat beside him.

"So, as I was telling these two, there has been an attack by rogue demons on a nearby camp." Xavier's face was grim.

"Rogue demons?" Andy couldn't help but ask. She had figured all demons were kind of rogue. Without souls, why care about a leader or rules?

"They have been attacking only other demons, as far as we know," Izzy said, everyone seemingly ignored Andy's comment.

"Well, we must find them. We cannot be defending ourselves on both sides, against our enemies and our own kind. We only have so many men," Ronan pointed out. "I will want a scouting group sent out as soon as possible to find these rogues."

"We've been scouting," Izzy said, indicating her and Annabella. "We have a whole group dedicated to finding these rogue demons. So far there has been no sign of them, but plenty of talk about them." Ronan turned to face her.

"Well then, you are not searching hard enough. If they are truly out there, as you seem to believe, then you will find them." Ronan clasped his hands in front of him on the table and closed his eyes. "I will not stand by and allow my people to be killed by our own kind." He opened his eyes, and they blazed.

"We will send out multiple scouting groups right away." Xavier promised and nodded to Izzy, who stood and was followed out of the tent by Annabella. "Izzy will take care of it."

"Thank you, Xavier." Ronan's eyes finally returned to their original calm state.

"So, Andromeda," Xavier began, "how are you doing since we last met?"

"Fine," Andy said. She couldn't help but remember his cruelty from that day he tried to take her from her family.

"Very good. May we have a moment alone, Ronan?" Xavier looked at him knowingly, and Ronan seemed a little unsure.

"Fine. Just a moment. Andromeda, please step outside of the tent, and do not stray far." Andy could tell that he did not trust the other demons not to bother her, and his body was tense.

She could take care of herself. She stepped out of the tent and scanned the area. Demons milled about, and a few of them glanced her way, scowling.

"They'll come around," a voice chirped beside Andy. She jumped at the sudden appearance of Izzy. Her platinum blonde hair shone even more brightly in the sunlight.

"Izzy, right?" Andy eyed her warily, unsure whether to trust her or not.

"Yes. You're like Anna and me, I can tell. I mean, everyone is also talking about it, but your eyes give you

Condemned Angel

away," she smirked. "Mine used to have that same golden glow...before I realized which side I truly belonged on."

"I hope you're not trying to convince me to join the *demons*," Andy scowled. "I know which side I will choose, and my decision will not be swayed." She crossed her arms, trying to appear unbreakable.

The corner of Izzy's mouth twitched. "Just wait. You're still new to all of this. You'll come to find that serving the angels is equally as binding as signing your soul over to Lucifer. Though, you don't need to give up your soul to be a demon. Angels on the other hand, must obey their orders or else be cast out of heaven, and then live among the fallen, or join up with Lucifer. We demons have nowhere left to fall, so we have much more freedom to do as we please." There was a fire in her eyes. Andy wondered if this was what had happened to her. She wouldn't let Izzy's cynicism sway her. "Remaining an angel is a burden."

"I'm sorry you feel that way," Andy responded, trying to show Izzy that her words didn't affect her.

"You'll see, just wait." Izzy walked away towards the entrance of the camp, disappearing behind a tent.

"Another spoiled angel come to see Daddy work?" a drawling voice came from behind Andy. She turned to see a tall, hulking demon swaggering towards her. "Your brother isn't an angel anymore, though, is he?"

"Leave her be, Eban." Annabella popped up beside Andy, making her jump. "She's too good for you." Annabella flipped her hair over her shoulder and leered at Eban.

"Oh, Anna. You know I love to mess with the newbies. Let me have my fun." He bit his lip in a seductive manner, sweeping his gaze over Annabella. Andy felt like she should leave them alone, but when she took a step away from them, Eban turned his intense stare back on her.

"I could turn you. Ask Anna, I can be pretty persuasive." He raised his eyebrows as if daring Andy to make a move.

"Come on, Andy. I'll give you a tour of the camp. Ignore Eban, everyone else does," Annabella flashed one last scathing look at Eban before taking Andy's arm and leading her away from him.

"That was weird, right?" Andy murmured to Annabella as they walked away.

Annabella chuckled. "That was Eban. He thinks he's the hottest and toughest demon around. And he's only half wrong." She winked at Andy, and they both laughed. "But seriously, he's harmless. The ones you have to worry about are…" she trailed off and Andy followed her gaze to a group of demons about ten yards in front of them. They all were glaring at Andy as they sat at a round table playing cards. None of them were like any of the demons Andy had encountered so far, except for Samson. They all wore scowls and scruffy hair with matching unkempt beards.

Condemned Angel

Annabella steered Andy away from the group towards a small building that appeared to have once been a convenience store. "Those are the ones you want to avoid," Annabella whispered as they veered again to the right.

"Shouldn't I be worried about *all* demons, since I'm an angel?" Andy stole a glance back at the group and shuddered when she saw they were all still watching her carefully.

"As long as they know you're Ronan's daughter, you'll be fine. They're more worried about what he'll do to them if they dare even touch you." Annabella led Andy through a grouping of tents. "But those guys back there, they have no regard for their own lives. They could care less whether they were here, or back in hell with Lucifer."

"Well, thanks, I guess. But why are you being nice to me?"

"I was in your position once. I had to choose between being an angel or a demon, and I remember how daunting that was." Annabella shook her head, and Andy saw sympathy in her eyes.

"You chose to give up being an angel," Andy pointed out the obvious.

"Yes, and it was an easy decision. I hope you don't have to go through what my sister and I had to endure," Annabella said. Andy was about to ask her what she meant when Ronan emerged from the tent beside them.

"Ready, Andromeda?" he gave her a reassuring smile. Andy put on a fake smile and nodded. She needed to fast walk to keep up with him as they left the camp. She looked back once to see Izzy and Eban watching her, Eban winked and Izzy punched his arm. Andy stifled a laugh and turned back towards the SUV, where Cairn opened the door for them.

"Why did you bring me with you?" Andy asked as they drove down the road leading away from the camp. The trees turned to a field of overgrown grass and weeds.

"I wanted you to see what it is I have to deal with." Ronan continued gazing out his window. "It's not all about collecting souls or fighting angels. My top priority is keeping my people safe and happy."

"Well, isn't it hard to keep them safe in the midst of a war?" Andy questioned him.

"Yes, but that cannot stop me from trying."

"So, demons go rogue?" Andy asked the question that had been bugging her.

"Yes. Those who have given their souls willingly to Lucifer will sometimes regret their decision and rebel. However, since Lucifer controls their souls, he can easily end their rebellions. But those who are still in command of their own souls, have the free will to do as they please. It is uncommon for them to turn on their own kind, but it's not unheard of."

"Kind of like how the original fallen angels turned on their own," Andy said, and he nodded.

Condemned Angel

"Demons and angels are not so different, unsurprisingly, since demons are descended from the angels," Ronan pointed out. "Demon is simply a label, placed on an angel who has sided with Lucifer." Andy had not thought about it like that before.

"Do you think the rogue demons are hoping to redeem themselves and be regarded as angels again, instead of demons?" Andy wondered aloud.

"That's an interesting thought, Andromeda. It's possible, I guess, but I've never heard of such a thing occurring."

"You can just call me Andy."

"Do you know that I chose your name?" Ronan asked, but then shook his head. "No, probably not. Well, your mother wanted to name you after her best friend, Amelia. I talked her into trying something a little different. I wanted you to have a more fitting name because I knew you were going to be extraordinary." Andy blushed and hated that he told her this. It made him seem that much more human.

Neither of them spoke for the rest of the ride.

Once they returned to the mansion, Ronan brought Andy with him to his throne room. He took his seat and she sat in the chair beside him. She gazed at the rows of empty benches laid out in front of them. She wondered what it would be like to sit up here when they were all filled.

"How does it feel, Andy?" Ronan smiled, trying out her nickname, and gesturing to the room.

"To sit in front of a bunch of empty benches?" she raised an eyebrow but indulged him anyway. "Empowering, I guess. I mean, I've never really liked being a leader, or being in charge."

"You could get over that. I never thought I would like to be a leader either, but here I am, and I enjoy every moment of it. Well, almost every moment." He closed his eyes and leaned his head against the back of his chair. It was weird for Andy to see him like this; almost relaxed and vulnerable.

"Do you enjoy hurting people? Because you do hurt and kill a lot of people." Andy noticed his mouth turn down and he opened his eyes to look at her.

"This is a war. You cannot expect us to lie down and let our enemies walk over us. Angels kill too. If you are to condemn me for the same actions that your angel friends are committing, then you must also condemn them, or else be a hypocrite." He was not angry, but Andy could tell that he had thought this through. He had been anticipating her question.

"Demons kill for fun, angels kill out of necessity, and they only kill demons, not humans," Andy pointed out, she had thought about this, too.

"You have, again, confused the cold and heartless demons with all of the others. I cannot speak for all demons, as you cannot speak for all angels, however, I have never killed for fun. I will admit to killing humans, but again, not for

Condemned Angel

fun. Only out of necessity, as you would say." Ronan stayed on the defense, and Andy decided to let it go, for now. He was right about one thing: believing demons to be bad because they killed was hypocritical of Andy, but she couldn't help but feel that demons were worse than angels.

"There is something else I need to ask you." Andy's mind drifted to Lindy, Ace, and the mystery of their parents. Ronan nodded for her to go on. "Lindy, the little girl that Kaden saved from the other demons; her mother is a demon. Somehow, those other demons had her mother's charm bracelet. Do you know anything about Lindy's parents?" Ronan appeared thoughtful for a moment, and then he nodded slowly.

"I seem to recall her mother, Natalia, marrying a human. Which, subsequently, is how she fell from her status as a ruler of angels."

"Wait, she became a demon because she fell in love with a human?" Andy interrupted.

"No, she abused her power as a leader and fell from grace. After that, she chose to fully transition to become a demon."

"Why would a former angel choose to become a demon?"

"Living among the fallen is almost torture for an angel. You retain your immortality but are forced to live among humans, without any of your former glory or power. Many would rather transition into a demon than stay in limbo forever," Ronan explained. "Though, it is not unheard of for a fallen angel to be accepted back into grace. Now, as I was saying, Lindy's father, he is still very much human. Explaining why Lindy is only half-demon," he continued. "As for Ace, they adopted him thinking they would never be able to have children after years of trying. Lindy proved that they were wrong."

"Natalia and Thomas came to me soon after the war began, but not before they had a run-in with another group of demons, the very same who attempted to take you. I assume that they must have taken the charm bracelet from her then. They are the one group whom I have no control over, for they report directly to Lucifer himself. I sent Natalia and Thomas to a camp on the outskirts of Las Vegas." He laid his hands out in front of him on the armrests and slowly clenched his fists. "There was a skirmish with the angels out there last week and I have not yet received the final death count." Andy's hand flew up to her mouth. After everything that Ace and Lindy had been through, she had hoped she would be able to bring them better, more hopeful news of their parents.

"When will you know?" Her voice wavered.

"Within the next few days. I will let you know when I find out." He promised, and Andy wondered if she could take his word, but she had no other choice.

"Before the war, if an angel fell in love with a human, they must not have told their significant other that they were

Condemned Angel

an angel, right?" Andy asked, figuring that this would be a surefire way to break the rules.

"It is uncommon for angels to be with humans, mostly for that reason. They can fall in love with humans, and have children with them, but whether they should has always been the dilemma. To tell the human would result in being cast out of heaven, and to lie to them wouldn't be fair." Ronan stared at Andy for a moment and then sighed. "I assume you're asking because you are wondering why your mother never told your father about being an angel."

"Well, that is part of it," Andy admitted.

"You will have to talk to your mother about that. I don't know whether she ever thought about telling him, or if she was always set on keeping it to herself."

"Fine. I'm a little hungry. Is there any food I can eat?" Andy changed the subject, hearing her stomach gurgling. It was one o'clock in the afternoon, and she hadn't eaten since breakfast at eight. Her body was growing accustomed to having three meals a day again.

"Ah, you've inherited my appetite. Your mother, being an angel, doesn't need to eat as often. Demons on the other hand were cursed when they fell from heaven to suffer the needs of an average human. Sometimes it's a bit of a burden, I will admit," Ronan paused and then called out, "Cairn!" Cairn appeared in the doorway. "Please escort Miss Andromeda to the dining room." Cairn nodded and waited for Andy to reach him before turning and walking towards the dining hall. As they passed by the staircase, Lily walked into the room from the entryway.

"Hey, Andy," Lily greeted her. "Where are you headed?"

"To get food."

"I can take her, Cairn, if you could let Ronan know I've returned?" Lily patted Cairn on the arm. "Thank you!" She looped her arm around Andy's and led her into the dining room. There was a spread of food all along the table and all the chairs had been removed.

"Do they do this every day?" Andy asked Lily, who was already making herself a plate.

"Every day that there isn't a gathering, meeting, or party of some sort. There are about forty demons who live here, and we have to keep them all fed, or else it can get ugly," Lily laughed, popping a grape into her mouth.

"Forty? Wow." Andy figured the party should have given her some indication of how many demons lived here, but she had assumed some of them came from other camps.

"Yeah. This is the largest demon dwelling in North America. Since Ronan is the leader of us all, he has to be the most protected. All of the other camps are smaller, with a minimum of ten demons and a max of like thirty."

"How do forty people sleep here? I mean, this place is huge, but I didn't think it was *that* huge." Andy wondered if there was a whole other section to the house that she didn't know about.

"Well, you and Ronan are the only two people in the house who have their own rooms. Otherwise, there are four people to a room, with two sets of bunk beds in each room. There's not a lot of room for much else. Most rooms share a bathroom with a few others." Lily explained, and Andy felt guilty that she had that whole giant bedroom and bathroom to herself.

"There are only six rooms upstairs, besides mine," Andy pointed out.

"Yeah, there are seven rooms upstairs and six including Ronan's in the basement. Your parents have one of those rooms as well. They're lucky they don't have to share either," she said all this matter-of-factly. There was no resentment about the fact that she had to share a room, while Andy's family was given special treatment.

"What about Jason?" Andy asked, realizing that a bedroom for him was not included on the list.

"He chose to share with Kaden and his roommates," Lily responded, taking a bite of a scone.

"Ladies." Kaden strolled into the room as if summoned by the mention of his name. He gave Lily a smirk and she winked at him, flipping her hair off her shoulder. Andy held back a gag.

"How did your raid go?" Lily asked him, and Andy cocked an eyebrow at him, wondering if his raid involved killing any angels. He pursed his lips. "Oh, come on, Kade," Lily gave him a little pout and he caved.

"It went great. We all came back unscathed," he revealed, still leaving out any real details, but Lily seemed satisfied with his answer. Kaden grabbed a plate and started piling food on top of it.

"I was just about to show Andy the gardens, did you want to join us?" Lily gazed at him hopefully.

"You were?" Andy asked, surprised by the news. Lily gave her a look that said *zip it*, so Andy said nothing more. Instead, she took a bite of her sandwich.

"I've got nothing better to do," Kaden said, and Lily feigned only slight interest. Andy knew it was all an act.

Lily and Andy finished their plates and Lily led the way out of the dining room, back towards the room with the staircase. Kaden brought his plate with him. They passed the staircase and Andy realized there was a door there that she had not noticed before, it led to another hallway. As they walked down the hall, Lily pointed to a door on the left, turning back to Andy.

"That leads to the basement where the rest of the bedrooms are," she said. At the end, there was a single glass door that led outside and gave a glimpse of the world behind the mansion.

Condemned Angel

Outside, Andy could fully see the gardens. They were beautiful. Rose bushes lined the walkway that led to a ten-foot-tall, three-tiered fountain. Past the fountain was what appeared to be a hedge maze. There were all different kinds of flowers: blue and purple delphiniums, pink begonias, red lilies; a flower in almost every color imaginable. Narrow pathways led off in both directions.

"This is amazing," Andy said, still gawking at her surrounds. She had never seen anything quite like it before.

"Isn't it?" Lily grinned and kept glancing over at Kaden. Andy walked ahead of them and stepped up to the fountain, admiring it. The water was so crystal clear, she couldn't help but reach out and drag her fingers across the surface. Suddenly, she was thinking about the night at the lake with Septimus, and a lump formed in her throat. Lily stood beside her and gave Andy a strange look.

"Are you okay?" Lily asked. Andy nodded and quickly turned away from her to walk around the fountain, but she bumped into Kaden who had stepped up on her other side. Thankfully, he had finished eating and had ditched his plate somewhere, or there would have been a mess to clean up for sure. Instead, Andy lost her balance and fell backward, nearly into the fountain, but Kaden grabbed both of her arms and pulled her back up straight, bringing her face to face with him.

"S-sorry," Andy stammered, her thoughts about Septimus shattered.

"Uncoordinated too? You are the whole package, aren't you?" Kaden joked, letting go of her arms and stalking off towards the hedge maze. Lily strolled casually after him.

Neither of them waited to see if Andy followed before they disappeared into the maze. Andy waited a moment and then decided to go in. Kaden and Lily had veered off to the left, so Andy chose to go right. She needed to be alone for a little while and this seemed like the perfect opportunity.

After a couple of turns, Andy was good and lost. She sat down with her back against the hedges and pulled her knees up to her chest. She closed her eyes and started taking deep breaths, trying to clear her mind of everything, especially Septimus. If she was going to make it through the next two weeks, she needed a clear and level head. Lily was laughing somewhere off to Andy's right and she blocked her out. She had no desire to think about what Lily and Kaden were doing elsewhere in the maze.

Instead, Andy focused on creating a ball of light. She put her hands out in front of her and felt the energy coursing through her body and through her fingers into the light forming between her hands. Andy grinned and continued to put all her energy into the light. Her light went out unexpectedly, but she could still feel the energy running through her. Andy furrowed her brow and shook out her hands to try again when a shadow entered her vision. She squinted up into the sun and saw Kaden standing above her, smirking. He had a ball between his hands, but it was like a black hole instead of light.

"Looks like the darkness wins this time." He dropped his hands to his sides and the black hole disappeared. Andy realized this was what Septimus had been talking about when he said that demons could take away light rather than create it.

"Where's Lily?" Andy peered past Kaden to see if she was nearby, but she was nowhere to be seen.

"I lost her somewhere along the way, she took a left and I went right," he stuck his hands into his jean pockets. "It's easy to get lost in here."

"Apparently I wasn't trying hard enough, because you found me." Andy stood up and strolled back in the direction she had come from, or at least, the direction she *thought* she came from. Kaden let her leave him behind, and she glanced back to see him strolling in the opposite direction.

After a few minutes, Andy knew for sure that this was not the way that she had entered the maze. She took a left, and a right, and a couple other turns and realized she was thoroughly lost again. Her next turn brought her face to face with Kaden again. Andy staggered back so as not to bump into him.

"How's getting lost going for you?" he smirked, and Andy rolled her eyes.

"Can we just get out of here? This place is starting to give me the creeps." It was also getting darker, and Andy didn't want to be stuck in the maze at night. She rubbed her hands over her arms, trying to warm up the goosebumps that had risen on them.

"What's the magic word?" He crossed his arms and Andy could tell he was enjoying messing with her. She groaned in annoyance.

"Please?" she offered, playing along with his stupid game. She just wanted him to get her out of there.

"Close, but I was looking for something a little more... desperate," he winked, and Andy pretended to gag, making him laugh. Andy stifled her laugh; she didn't want him to think that she found him funny. His ego had already been boosted too high.

"Just get me out of here, okay?" Andy crossed her arms to match his stance.

"Fine, take all the fun out of it, but you owe me." He turned and took the first left they came to. Andy followed along as he turned this way and that, and within a minute or two, they were out of the maze. Lily was sitting on the fountain waiting. She eyed Kaden and Andy warily as they came out of the maze together.

"I've been waiting for you guys, what took you so long?" Lily stood and took a step towards Kaden, glaring at Andy.

Condemned Angel

"I got lost and Kaden had to come find me. Sorry," Andy tried for an apologetic smile. She could tell that Lily liked Kaden and didn't want Lily to think that anything was going on between them. Lily seemed satisfied and finally smiled back at Andy.

7

The Runway

Bo returned to his new favorite spot the next day, the cliff overlooking the National Park that they were camping out in. He sat cross-legged in the grass, thinking about his parents.

A twig cracked and he whipped his head around to see Ephram walking up behind him.

"I see you've found the best hideout," Ephram said, smiling down at him. "I've always loved it here."

"I can go, if you want to be alone," Bo said quickly, moving to stand.

Condemned Angel

"No, no," Ephram waved at him to stay seated. "I don't mind the company. Since I'm no longer a ruler, I find my days are lacking purpose and are a little lonely."

"I'm sorry about that," Bo mumbled, feeling partially responsible for not helping to convince Andy that she needed to stay.

"You have no reason to be sorry. You are a great friend to Andromeda and the others here. I have seen the way you interact with them. Not all humans are as kind and accepting as you, Bo." Ephram sat down beside Bo in the grass. This surprised Bo because it made him seem less superior. He always thought of Ephram as some supreme being, holier than any other angel.

"Thank you, though I'm not so sure I've been the greatest friend these past few days…" Bo had pushed away everyone, except for Ace and Lindy.

"You've gone through great trauma these past few weeks, it's to be expected that you would need some time to process. I see it all the time, and you are managing far better than most."

"I'm worried that I'm not managing as well as it seems," Bo's voice caught in his throat.

"Don't worry about that so much, just let yourself feel whatever you're feeling, and eventually, it will all be a little easier," Ephram gazed out over the trees. Bo knew that Ephram had lost six sons and two loves and spoke from experience. Bo watched him for a moment, noticing an aura begin to glow around Ephram. It was a bluish color, unlike the usual golden glow he saw around angels.

"I know that you didn't come out here just to talk to me," Bo said. "What's on *your* mind?" He almost felt like he shouldn't be asking that question, but Ephram had been open with him so far.

"Quite a lot, actually. I'm worried about Septimus, and Andromeda," he said.

"But that's not what's causing you to be…blue…" Bo realized that he may have overstepped when Ephram turned to him with a confused look on his face.

"Blue?"

"I'm sorry, I shouldn't have said anything…it's just, I have always been able to tell how people are feeling. Everyone gives off an aura that I can see most of the time," Bo explained and Ephram surprised him by laughing.

"You're an empath, Bo," he said. "You can sense other people's emotions. It's not common, but not unheard of either. That means that somewhere in your bloodline, you have an ancestor who is an angel."

"But neither of my parents were able to see people's auras. I tried to ask them about it, but they thought I was seeing things," Bo wasn't sure there was anything quite so special about him.

"It tends to skip generations, sometimes multiple generations, so that does not surprise me," Ephram explained.

"Not only are empath's able to sense others' emotions, but they can also sense spirits to some extent. For example, if someone you love who had passed on wanted to communicate with you, it would be easier for them to get through to you. You would also be able to connect with guardian angels, who are normally unseen and unheard by humans." Bo gaped at him.

"You mean, I could talk with my parents?" he felt his heart leap in his chest. "Why haven't they reached out to me yet?"

"It takes time. First, they have to realize they are a spirit, and then, they must learn how to reach out and communicate. Give it time and I am sure that they will reach out to you." Ephram stood up and brushed himself off. "You will be okay, Bo. Don't worry about anything but healing. If you need to talk, I'll be around."

"Thank you," Bo said, but Ephram was already walking away, back towards the camp.

∞

Ronan left the next day to attend to the aftermath of the attack in Las Vegas. He took one of the jets they had in a concealed hangar about a mile from the mansion. This left Andy free to do as she pleased within the bounds of the house.

She decided to spend the day exploring inside and around the gardens.

Andy started by throwing on a sundress since it was an especially hot day and there was no air conditioner in the house. She wondered if it was a demon thing to enjoy the heat.

She skipped shoes, preferring to remain barefoot for the first time in months. She made her way downstairs to the basement where her parents' bedroom supposedly was. Voices filtered out from behind closed doors, but she couldn't make out what they were saying, and she didn't care enough to listen. She continued down the hallway.

The downstairs turned out to be similar to the upstairs, a long hallway with multiple doors on each side leading to bedrooms. The hallway opened at the end to a wide round room with two couches and bookcases lining the walls. A few demons sat on the couches chatting and reading. Andy didn't see anyone she knew, so she turned back before they noticed her. She wasn't sure which room was her parents' and didn't want to disturb the wrong person, so she headed back upstairs.

In the dining room, there were platters of pastries and fruit laid out on the table for breakfast, so Andy grabbed a plateful and headed out to the garden. There was no one else out there, thankfully. Andy took a seat on the fountain and picked at the food on her plate. She almost felt guilty doing nothing, knowing there was a war going on in the world. Septimus, Sera, Gabby, Micah, and Nathan could all be with a guard, risking their lives fighting demons right now. Andy tried to focus on the garden around her.

She abandoned her plate and strolled down one of the paths leading around the outside of the hedge maze. The grass tickled her feet and she laughed, feeling more carefree than she had in a while. There were plenty of roses, geraniums, marigolds, lilac, and lavender. There were also a lot of flowers that she did not recognize.

"What a pretty little thing," a sneer came from behind her, and she froze. She recognized that voice...turning slowly she saw Samson prowling along the path behind her. Andy tried not to let the fear show on her face.

"Hello, Samson," she greeted him coldly. "To what do I owe the pleasure?" He cackled and it set Andy on edge.

"Oh, so brave, little princess." He took a step closer, but then paused and sneered at something over Andy's shoulder.

"Watch yourself, Samson," Kaden's voice growled from behind her. Fear flashed in Samson's eyes, but it changed quickly to annoyance.

"See you around, Princess," Samson said as if it was a threat, and Andy took it as one. He stalked off towards the mansion and disappeared around the hedge maze. Andy turned to see Kaden watching where Samson had just disappeared.

"You shouldn't be out here alone." Kaden strode past her and Andy followed behind him.

"Sorry, I didn't get the rule book yet," Andy snapped.

"It's called common sense," Kaden snapped back. Anger welled up inside of Andy, and she reached out, grabbing Kaden's arm, so he had to turn and look at her.

"Don't talk down to me," she growled, and he dared to smirk. "You are such an ass." She shoved him backward, but he barely moved, and it only made him laugh. Andy threw her hands up in frustration and stormed past him.

"I'm sorry, try it again, and I won't laugh this time, promise." Andy could hear the laughter that he was holding back, and she did not turn around. "You're welcome." Andy slammed the door behind her and went straight to her room. She only came out when Jason invited her to dinner, and then retreated to her room. She did not want to see or hear from Kaden, or anyone for that matter.

Andy could not help but think back to what Annabella had told her about avoiding certain demons. Samson seemed to fit the bill of one of those to avoid. It wasn't as if Andy had gone looking for Samson, though, he seemed to have sought her out.

Anxiety came creeping up as Andy sat on her bed. It started with her heart beating faster, then her palms began to sweat. Those reactions caused Andy to panic, and brought on the tunnel vision, making her think she was about to pass out.

Condemned Angel

"Stop-stop-stop." Andy rocked back and forth, trying to will the anxiety away. She took a deep breath, and closed her eyes, but immediately regretted doing so. An image of Samson sprung up behind her eyelids. She opened her eyes and groaned in frustration. Sleep would not be coming easily that night.

Andy climbed out of bed and paced the room. The deafening silence was something she would probably never get used to after all those nights sleeping in the woods. A floorboard creaked out in the hall and Andy nearly jumped out of her skin.

"It's fine. You're fine," she reassured herself, her heart still pounding. But her thoughts betrayed her. *What if it's someone who wants to hurt you? What if it's Samson? Anyone could be out there. You can't fight a demon. You don't even have your sword anymore, you're helpless.*

Andy tried to push the thoughts away, but they kept barging back into her mind. To try to appease them, she went to the door and opened it. There was no one in the hall. Whoever had been out there had gone into their room. She took a deep breath. *You're fine. It's fine. There's no one trying to hurt you. Unless they're waiting for you to be out of the house. That group of demons at Xavier's camp could show up at any time. They know where to find you.*

Andy slammed her door shut and went back to pacing the room. She needed a distraction, something to take her mind away from the intrusive thoughts. Seeming to answer her silent request, someone knocked on the door. Andy's hand trembled as she reached towards the doorknob.

She paused and called out. "W-who is it?" she cursed herself for stuttering and allowing her fear to be so apparent.

"Kaden," the response was gruff and annoyed, but Andy knew it was truly him. She opened the door and tried not to let her anxiety show.

"What do you want?"

"Nothing. Just making sure you weren't going to continue slamming doors," he looked past Andy into her room.

"That was an accident. I just thought, well, never mind. I won't be slamming doors," Andy cursed herself again for sounding so stupid. Kaden probably thought she was insane, and maybe she was. "I mean, I wasn't slamming doors," she tried to recover but only made Kaden appear more amused.

"I didn't realize it was such a touchy subject. I won't bring it up again," he smirked. He started to turn away but then paused. "Almost forgot, your parents are out doing an errand for Ronan, so they won't be around the next day or two. Jason asked me to tell you if I saw you." He turned away before Andy could respond. She closed the door as he walked away. She collapsed onto the bed and thought about what her parents could be doing for Ronan.

The distraction allowed Andy to fall asleep. That night, she had another nightmare.

Condemned Angel

Evergreen trees surrounded Andy like the ones behind the camp of Jeremiah. Except, there were no angels here. Lurking behind the trees, there were shadows. Andy knew who lurked there, and she tried to stand tall and show she was unafraid, even though she was terrified.

"Andromeda," the voice that had been haunting her filtered through the trees.

"What do you want?" she called back.

"Andromeda," is the only response she received. She took a shaky step forward, and a snarl ripped through the night behind her. It changed to that low gurgling growl that the hellhounds made, and Andy didn't dare move. She slowly turned her head and could see the hellhound out of the corner of her eye. "You cannot escape me, Andromeda." The voice warned, and then the hellhound lunged, and she screamed.

"Andy!" There was a banging on her door and her eyes flew open. She gasped for air, feeling as if her throat had been torn out by the hellhound. Clasping her hands around her neck, she realized, it was only a dream. "Andy!" The banging came again, and she recognized Jason's voice.

"Coming," Andy called out to him. She stretched and rolled out of bed. All her limbs felt heavy and tired as if she hadn't slept at all. Stumbling to the door, Andy opened it weakly. Jason sidestepped her and surveyed the room.

"Is everything alright? I heard you screaming." He looked Andy up and down, making sure that she was unharmed. She nodded and yawned.

"Everything's fine. It was just a nightmare," Andy reassured him. "Sorry I woke you." Andy worried that she may have woken up more than just Jason.

"That's what I tried to tell Kaden, but he said I should come check on you," Jason yawned. "I'll let him know I was right. Well, goodnight." He gave Andy a wave as he slipped back into his room. Andy closed her door and locked it again. Back in her bed, she let herself think about what Jason had told her...Kaden wanted him to come check on her...she shook her head. Probably because she was interrupting his beauty sleep.

As Andy tried to fall back asleep, her anxiety pressed in on her. She took deep breaths and started a new list in her mind; every kindness Kaden had shown her so far...starting with knocking out Malachi.

Andy was back in the forest. This time, sunlight filtered down through the trees, and she could hear the breeze rustling the leaves. She took a deep breath and filled her lungs with fresh air. There were no hellhounds, and no voices threatening her.

Andy took a step forward and realized she could see the gardens behind the mansion through the trees. She made her way towards them and found her way out of the woods. A smile stretched across her face as she took in the sight before her.

Condemned Angel

"Beautiful, isn't it?" Andy jumped at the sudden voice and turned to find Kaden walking towards her through the flowers. He smiled, a real smile that transformed his face from his usual cool indifference, and she felt a twinge in her heart. She could see vulnerability in his features for once.

"What are you doing here?" Andy asked him, and he looked away sheepishly.

"Sorry, I couldn't let you suffer through your nightmares anymore. I can leave, I just wanted to make sure that you were having sweet dreams." He stuck his hands into his pockets and started to turn away.

"Thank you," Andy said to him before he disappeared into thin air. Andy waded out into the sea of flowers and lay down, arms and legs outstretched. She could feel the sun soaking into her skin and everything felt right.

Ronan returned from his trip the next day, but Andy had no obligations to meet up with him or anyone else. She took her time getting ready, choosing to wear a sundress again since she had missed the freedom of wearing a dress for so long.

Downstairs, Andy filled a plate with fruit and headed into the sitting room to eat. She was surprised to see Olivia there. She hadn't seen her since the night of the party.

"Good morning," Olivia greeted her cheerily. Andy smiled in response. "I heard about your unfortunate meeting with Samson yesterday. He is such a creep. Just do your best to ignore him."

"Oh, did Kaden tell you?" Andy blushed as she thought about the others talking about her.

"Yeah, well kind of. He was talking to Lily about it and she's my roommate, so I heard too," Olivia explained. "Unfortunately for me, I get kicked out of my own room way too often because of those two. I guess I should be thanking you for coming along. Since Kaden came back with you, I haven't had to deal with that. Though, Lily's pretty ticked about it." Andy felt her entire body grow hot with embarrassment. This was way more information than she wanted.

"I- erm, you're welcome, I guess."

"Oh, sorry. I didn't mean to make you uncomfortable. Sometimes I forget how fragile angels are when it comes to these topics," Olivia laughed.

"I'm not fragile. I just don't need to know what Kaden does in his spare time," Andy felt defensive.

"Trust me, I really would rather not know either," Olivia rolled her eyes. "But here we are."

"So, are you and Kaden close? I know he said that you were raised separately," Andy changed the subject.

"We're not as close as most siblings, but we've been living here together for about eight years now. So, it's hard not to grow close to someone in that time, especially your own brother," Olivia said. "He did try to distance himself from me at first, but I wore him down," she smirked. "I'm surprised he even told you about our parents at all. He hates talking about them with anyone, even me."

"I'm sorry," Andy felt stupid apologizing, but it slipped out.

"Don't be. I have to head out, but I'll see you around." Olivia left the room. Andy finished her fruit and returned her plate to the kitchen. With no training to get to, and no Bo to talk to, she felt lost. She'd already explored the gardens, and the downstairs, and now she knew her parents weren't around because of some mysterious errand.

"What are you doing?" Kaden's voice drifted to her as he descended the stairs. Andy lifted her head and realized how she must look, standing in the doorway to the dining room, staring off at nothing.

"I wish I knew. I feel useless here," she admitted. At least in the angel camp she was training to be able to help fight in the war.

"And you think standing there is going to help?" Kaden reached the bottom of the stairs and leaned against the railing. He showed no indication that he wanted to talk about that dream he had given her, and Andy wasn't sure she was ready to talk about it either.

"Obviously not," Andy scoffed. "What do you suggest I do?" Kaden pushed away from the railing and motioned for

Andy to follow him. He led her out the front door. "Where are we going?"

"You may as well get a tour of the grounds." He entered a code on a padlock to open the front gate.

"Are you sure I'm even allowed to be out here? Isn't it kind of a liability bringing me around, showing me escape routes?" Andy joked.

"I'm not sure any rules apply when it comes to you. You are Ronan's daughter, after all," Kaden smirked, and Andy rolled her eyes. "Besides, are you really going to run away from here knowing that there are worse demons out there waiting to bring you straight to Lucifer?"

"Fair point," Andy agreed grudgingly. "Though, in that case, you could just let me wander out here on my own, knowing I won't run."

"Ronan would kill me if he knew I let you outside the house alone."

"Whatever you need to tell yourself," Andy smirked. She knew that he was probably right that Ronan would be pissed, but she couldn't help but push his buttons, just a little. "I think you just need to admit to yourself that you like my company," she teased him.

"If you want me to leave you out here alone, fine. I'll go back and let you deal with Ronan." He backed off.

"But then who will I torment?" Andy joked, and added, "besides, we both know that you'll be the one in trouble for leaving me unattended out here. I can do no wrong. After all, I am Ronan's only daughter." Andy fluttered her eyelashes and Kaden rolled his eyes this time.

"So, you admit it." He nudged Andy's arm as he walked forward again and passed her.

"I admit that I share his DNA, not that I consider him to be my dad. That is Wayne and always will be," Andy clarified for him.

"Ronan isn't all bad, you know." Kaden stopped as they reached another gate. He entered another code into a little monitor, and the gate swung open. Andy saw an opening through the trees ahead and a few cars. "After you." Kaden let Andy walk through the gate first, closing it behind himself as he followed her through.

"So, this is where you keep all the cars," Andy said as they walked closer to the lot. Kaden nodded, but then veered off to the right towards a barely visible pathway.

"Come on." He dipped into the trees and Andy reluctantly followed. They walked in silence for a little while, and once they were about half a mile away from the house, Andy decided to try to reach out to the angel network. She focused all her thoughts on reaching out and could almost hear some chatter when she felt a wall go up and silence followed.

"It's not going to work," Kaden said, guessing at what she was doing. "The demons are blocking any angel communication in this area."

"How?" Andy asked, not even trying to hide that this was exactly what she had been trying to do.

"Similar to how they caused your massive headache before, and the same way you communicate in your mind by focusing your thoughts. You could block someone else's communication too if you had enough practice and tried hard enough."

They continued walking in silence again until they came to a clearing in the trees and Andy gaped as she saw where they kept Ronan's jet. There was a runway leading away from the hangar that spanned thousands of feet into the distance.

"Wow," was all she could say. Had she not known that Ronan had a jet, she would have never guessed this was here among the trees.

"Pretty cool, right? I've been up in the jet a few times." Kaden continued walking. He led them away from the hangar and towards another copse of trees. Through there, Andy saw a small clearing filled with tons of little purple johnny jump-ups and buttercup flowers mixed in among the grass. It was beautiful.

Andy became lost in the memory of being with Bo and seeing the hills that were dotted with purple and yellow flowers. She found herself wandering farther into the clearing and wishing that Bo would appear by her side. She spun around. Kaden watched her curiously.

Condemned Angel

"It's quite beautiful, don't you think?" Andy asked him, but he was still gazing at her, his hands in his pockets.

"I guess. I've seen things more beautiful, though," he said. Before Andy could respond, pain exploded in her head and she fell to her knees. Shock came over Kaden's face and he ran towards her. He had not yet reached her, when he stopped in his tracks and gripped his head, his face twisting in pain. He started moving towards Andy again after a moment. When he reached her, he tried to help her up, but the pain was so severe, she could barely move. She thought she could hear laughter somewhere in the back of her mind.

"We need to get out of here," Kaden said through gritted teeth, but Andy was too busy squeezing her head in her hands. "Come on, Andy." She shook her head. "Fine, then let me carry you home." She didn't protest as he scooped her up effortlessly into his arms and started running back the way they came. They got back to the mansion in half the time it had taken them to get to the clearing. Andy's head was still in excruciating pain as Kaden carried her inside. She couldn't even open her eyes.

"You shouldn't still be in pain. I'm taking you to Ronan," Andy heard Kaden say, but it sounded distant. She felt like she had cotton balls in her ears, everything seemed muffled and far away.

"Put me down," even her own voice sounded wrong. Kaden hesitated but did as she said. Andy was standing, somehow. She felt a presence in her mind and started to panic, but she was no longer in control.

"Is the pain gone?" Kaden gave her a strange look and Andy felt herself grinning.

"How rude of you to run away. Stay and chat next time," Andy said, knowing that these were not her words. Kaden gripped her arms, trying to make her focus on him.

"Andy, look at me," he said. "Block your mind to them." Andy closed her eyes and tried to figure out how to do that. The pain in her head was back for a second, and then gone, along with the presence. Andy opened her eyes and Kaden was still gripping her arms, studying her face.

"We should go see Ronan," Andy said, turning away from Kaden and walking towards the throne room, where she knew Ronan would be.

"Are you okay, Andy?" Kaden asked, catching up with her, the concern clear on his face.

"No," she answered truthfully and kept walking.

8

The Maze

Septimus had watched his father announce that he was no longer a ruler. His heart broke for his father. He knew what it meant to him to have that title stripped away. It only made his feelings for Andromeda even more complicated because she was the reason that Ephram had lost his status.

Bo had come to him multiple times asking to talk about Andromeda, but Septimus had refused. He wasn't sure what there was to talk about. She had left them behind without so much as a goodbye.

"Septimus," Bo was like clockwork. He walked up to Septimus who stood leaning against a tree. He had hoped that no one would find him there, but Bo always seemed to find him.

"I still don't want to talk about her," Septimus said before Bo could press him about it, yet again.

"You don't have to talk, just listen," Bo said, and Septimus raised an eyebrow at him. "Your dad was demoted from ruler. If we bring back Andy, there's a chance that he could regain his status. The dominions wouldn't have a reason to be upset with him anymore." Though it was something that Septimus had thought about many times, he knew it was way too risky to even consider.

"Bo – "

"Septimus, just please think about it. I can't stand being here without her. We can help each other. Don't give me an answer now. Give it a day, mull it over." Bo walked away before Septimus could say anything.

∞

Bo knew that Septimus would say no. He had been heartbroken when he learned that Andy was part demon. But Bo knew there was still a part of him that cared about her. He was banking on that part eating away at Septimus until he agreed to help Bo.

Condemned Angel

Bo had been avoiding Micah, but if Septimus agreed to help him, he would need Micah. This was something he couldn't do alone. He felt guilty for pushing Micah away the past few days, but he was finally ready to let him back in.

Bo took a deep breath as he approached Micah and Nathan's tent. He cleared his throat and heard a "come in." Pushing aside the entrance flap, Bo ducked inside.

"Bo." Micah stood up and smiled when he saw him. It twisted the knife of guilt a little deeper into Bo's gut.

"Hi."

Micah became worried. "What's going on? Do you need something?"

"No, I just came to...well apologize. I've treated you horrible these past few days." Bo rubbed his neck in embarrassment. Micah just laughed, confusing Bo.

"You haven't been horrible. You've been grieving. You may not have lost Andy forever, but she's still gone. I understand that you needed time to process that." Micah took a step towards Bo, and Bo closed the gap between them, throwing his arms around Micah and kissing him.

Bo pulled away slightly. "You're too good for me."

"That's funny, coming from you," Micah trailed his hand down Bo's spine, causing him to shudder. "You are the epitome of goodness, Bo."

Bo ducked his head. "Not lately."

Before Micah could respond, Bo heard a rustle and Nathan entered the tent. "Oh, sorry. Didn't mean to interrupt anything."

"It's fine, I was just leaving." Bo pulled away from Micah. "I'll see you later," he said, giving Micah a quick kiss before exiting the tent.

∞

There was a round table set up in Ronan's throne room with chairs surrounding it. Ronan sat facing the door while demons Andy didn't know sat around him in the chairs. She recognized one of the demons, Xavier. She realized that they might be talking about the attack on the demon camp where Lindy and Ace's parents were, but that wasn't what she was there for. Andy approached the table warily and cleared her throat, attracting the attention of everyone in the room.

"What is the meaning of this?" Ronan asked calmly. "We are in the middle of an important discussion, Andromeda." He glanced curiously from Andy to Kaden and back again, waiting for an answer.

"Sir, Andromeda and I were on a walk near the hangar and came across what must have been the rogue demons," Kaden began, because Andy couldn't seem to find her voice with all the demons staring at her. "I put up a block in their minds so they couldn't see us, and we were able to get away. But that's not all..." he trailed off and looked at Andy. She realized this was where she was supposed to pick up the story. She cleared her throat again.

"They were able to talk through me," she said, trying to explain what had just happened to her without breaking down.

"And?" Ronan raised an eyebrow. "We already knew they were out there. Let them come. Then we can end this quickly and be done with them." He remained calm and looked as if Kaden and Andy had just announced that they had encountered a few birds rather than demons trying to kill them.

"And? I guess that's it. Sorry to have bothered you with such insignificant news. I'll make sure to keep it to myself next time someone tries to kill me." Andy couldn't help but be snippy with him. He made her so angry. She turned on her heel and stormed out of the room. Tears stung her eyes and she fought to keep them back. She wouldn't let Ronan get the better of her. She made it to the staircase and took the stairs two at a time.

"Andy," Kaden called to her from the bottom of the stairs, but she kept moving.

"I'm fine," she called back down. At the top of the stairs, Andy paused and took a deep breath. There was so much running through her mind, she could barely think straight. She felt exhausted but jittery. She wanted so badly to get out of that house and as far away as possible, but she knew that was impossible. Whoever was out there would find her, and who knew what they would do to her.

Andy made her way down the hall to her room and paused outside of Jason's door. She thought about knocking to see if he was in there, but then she realized she didn't even want to see him. He wouldn't understand. He seemed to like Ronan and would probably take his side. That wasn't what Andy needed at the moment, though she didn't really know what she needed. Andy turned to go to her room when the door to Jason's room opened.

"Jase-"Andy began but stopped as she realized who stood before her. "C-cory?" Her first thought was it must be a dream. He had been among the demons who attacked the camp that Wayne, Phillip, and Eleanor had been staying in.

"What a small world, Gorgeous." Before Andy could say anything else, he leaned forward and kissed her like he used to. Her hands flew up to her mouth as he pulled away and she was in too much shock to say anything. She couldn't believe he was there, of all places.

"Well, I guess I missed something." Jason's eyes were wide as he watched from his bed, and he seemed like he was in almost as much shock as Andy.

"Andy and I were dating before the war started, I never had a chance to say goodbye before my mom and I left to join forces with the rest of the demons," Cory explained to Jason, keeping one arm around Andy's waist, with his hand placed on the small of her back. It felt wrong. "When I first

Condemned Angel

heard you were here, I didn't believe it, but here you are, just as gorgeous as ever." He looked her up and down. "I've missed you."

"I-I don't know what to say," Andy stammered, still wondering how on Earth this was happening. She tried looking to Jason for help but remembered she never told him what happened between her and Cory, so he had no reason to worry. Jason never met Cory, and Andy had not talked about him much, so there was no way that he would have known that he shared a room with her ex-boyfriend.

"I wanted to talk to you when I saw you before, but your friend pulled you away too quickly." Cory drew Andy into the room with the weight of his arm and closed the door. There was a bunk bed on either wall, two dressers on the back wall side by side, and that was it. There was no room for anything else.

"I assumed you were fighting with those demons who were slaughtering all the humans." Andy put venom into her words and Cory didn't even flinch.

"Nah, I was there delivering a message to Kaden. I figured I'd check out the fight, and fate brought us back together," Cory explained, grinning. Andy finally pushed Cory's arm away from her. He appeared hurt for a second but did not react.

"A lot has changed since we were together," Andy reminded him. "I have a boyfriend now."

"Should I go?" Jason asked awkwardly and Andy shook her head quickly.

"A new boyfriend? You're right, things have changed. I should have known you'd move on. I was nothing to you. I understand that now." Cory grabbed his sword from the top bunk and Andy was scared for a moment, but he stormed out of the room.

"That could have gone better," Andy sighed.

"If I'd known he was the Cory you used to date, I would have warned you he was here." Jason looked apologetic.

"This day just keeps getting better and better." Andy threw herself onto the bottom bunk that Jason was not occupying.

"If you reach under the bed, you'll find Cory's stash. I wouldn't mind breaking into it," Jason told Andy. She rolled over and reached under the bed. She grabbed a bottle and pulled it out. Tequila. Andy twisted the cap off the bottle and took a swig, wincing as it burned all the way down into her stomach. The second sip went down a little smoother. Jason hopped off his bed and came over to take the bottle from Andy. He poured himself a glass, topping it with some lime seltzer from the mini-fridge in the corner of the room. He poured a drink for Andy, handing her the cup instead of the bottle.

"Thanks." She drank greedily from her cup, hoping it would help drown her memories from the day.

"Don't tell mom," Jason joked and they both laughed. It felt so nice and normal to laugh with her brother again. "So, what else happened today?" he asked. Andy didn't want to talk about how her mind had been violated, so she just shrugged. "Ah yes. The standard Andy response."

"Sorry. I just don't want to talk about it right now."

"Well, if you ever want to talk, I'm here," he offered, and Andy's heart swelled. He was proving to be the same brother she knew and loved, despite choosing to side with the demons.

"Thanks." Andy could feel the alcohol beginning to cloud her mind and her cheeks grew warm. She knew it was a temporary and unhealthy solution to her problems, but it also felt nice to be sharing this moment with her brother.

There were footsteps in the hall and Andy worried that Cory was back, her heart beginning to race, but instead, Kaden opened the door.

"Hey Jason, have you seen-" he stopped as he noticed Andy in the room.

"Have I seen who?" Jason asked, and Kaden motioned to Andy.

"Found her. Though I'll admit, I didn't expect to find her in my bed," he joked, and Andy sat up quickly, causing her head to spin.

"Sorry, I didn't know." She tried to stand, and stumbled, catching herself before she toppled to the ground.

"Ten out of ten," Jason laughed at her. Andy stuck her tongue out at him.

"You didn't have to get up, I don't need the bed. But just out of curiosity, what do you have in your cup? Because I can't imagine it's just water." Kaden grinned playfully. Jason shared a conspiratorial look with Andy and then grabbed the tequila bottle from behind his bed.

"Stole this from Cory, if you want to join in on the fun," Jason offered, but Kaden shook his head.

"All set. You know Cory's going to throw a fit when he finds that missing." Kaden walked to his bunk and sat down, stretching his legs out in front of him.

"He's got a lot on his mind right now. I think we'll be okay." Jason glanced up at Andy. "Besides, he's apparently got a thing for my sister, so I'm not worried." Andy let out a little gasp and smacked Jason's arm, causing him to laugh and drop the bottle of tequila.

"Oh, shit," Jason groaned, peering down at the shattered bottle and spreading puddle. "Thankfully, it was almost empty. I'll go get some paper towels."

"You do that." Kaden spread out on his bed and put his hands behind his head as he lounged. Jason hurried out of the room, leaving Andy standing awkwardly between the two beds. "So, you and Cory, huh?"

"Not exactly," Andy took a gulp of her drink. This was not a conversation she wanted to have.

Condemned Angel

"I mean, I'm just surprised, you know, since I thought you were still with Septimus," Kaden said nonchalantly. Andy felt a spark inside her, and anger overcame her.

"You don't know anything about my relationship with Septimus, or Cory for that matter." She finished off her drink and hurried to her room, slamming the door behind her. She took her jacket off and threw it aside in frustration, then unlaced her boots and kicked them off, leaving them in the middle of the floor. She crawled into bed and under the covers to hide from the world.

After a minute, there was a knock on her door. Andy debated getting up to answer it, but instead, she just hollered out, "it's open! Come in!" She didn't even come out from under the covers to see who walked in.

"I thought I warned you about keeping your door locked?" Andy heard Kaden say as he shut the door gently behind him.

"What does it matter? Someone can just control me to open it for them anyway," Andy muttered. "There's nowhere safe. They can all just get inside my head and make me do and say whatever they want." Andy felt a tear trailing down her cheek and she wiped it away with the sheet, still completely under the covers.

"Only really powerful demons can control others like that," Kaden said, which did nothing to ease Andy's mind. "I think Ronan is wrong to brush this off. I was barely able to fool them long enough for us to get away from them." Andy pulled the blankets back enough so that she could see Kaden.

"How were you able to hide us from them?" she asked, suddenly curious.

"I was able to find their minds and put an image of an empty clearing there, so they couldn't see us. I don't have to be able to actually see them to do it. I've had a lot of practice. I used to use the trick on my parents all the time... and when my dad caught on, he taught me how to *really* use the mind tricks." There was disgust in his voice when he mentioned his father. "The other demon used it on you, that night when you were drinking with your angel friends. They made you and Septimus believe they had disappeared, but they were there the whole time. I was about to step in when Septimus showed up."

"That's crazy." Andy shook her head. "My mom told me about how you helped me with my nightmares..." Andy wondered if he had messed with her head any other times.

"I've stayed out of your head since then," he assured her, though she wasn't sure if she should believe him, since he may have just read her mind to answer her unasked question. She eyed him suspiciously. "Other than last night," he corrected.

"Why was I the only one in pain in the clearing today? Why weren't you affected by them?" Andy asked, remembering how she had seen him hesitate only for a moment before continuing towards her.

"I was affected. I was just able to push through it," Kaden shrugged.

"How?" Andy wished she had the same strength of mind that he seemed to have.

"As I said, I have a lot of practice with this kind of thing, and I also had some external motivation. But anyway, I went back out there, and whoever it was, is gone." Andy was surprised to hear that, but it did make her feel slightly better.

"I can help you strengthen your mind to keep people out," Kaden offered.

"Okay, let's do it."

"We can start tomorrow night; I have to go out with a legion in the morning." Kaden leaned back into the chair.

"What's a legion?" Andy asked. Her thoughts were becoming hazier and her insides warm and tingly as the alcohol absorbed into her bloodstream. The tension inside her began to loosen up, and she felt lighter.

"That's just what they call the groups that are sent out to defend our camps," he explained, and Andy realized the legions were the equivalent of the guards at the angel camps. This thought brought Septimus back to the forefront of Andy's mind. Septimus...who she thought had made her feel safe when it had been Kaden taking away her nightmares.

Andy stood up and walked to where she had left her boots in the middle of the room. Now that she was standing, she realized how much she had drunk in such a short amount of time, on top of having an empty stomach. "I'm not much of a drinker..." Andy commented, swaying as if on cue.

"I couldn't tell," Kaden laughed, amused by her apparent drunkenness. "But you have an excuse, you are technically underage."

"There is that," Andy laughed. "But I also never saw the appeal before. Sure, it can be fun, but it can also turn you into a different person... I remember one party I went to before the war began. I was there with a group of friends, and my boyfriend at the time. It was my first party. I was seventeen, but he was eighteen and had been to quite a few more parties than me. He was really into drinking and trying to out-drink his friends." Andy sat on the floor and started pulling her boots on.

"He was a good guy, up until that point, a bit mysterious and intriguing, but that night he was a totally different person." She fumbled with her laces as she tried to tie her boots. "I think I must have said something or done something to set him off...I don't really remember how it all happened; I was a little drunk myself." Andy glanced up and realized Kaden was crouched down in front of her. He gently took the laces from her hands and started tying her boots, which made her laugh at herself, and he grinned.

"You don't have to tell me any of this," he said, and Andy realized that she had no idea why she *was* telling him, but she felt like she needed to finish the story.

Condemned Angel

"I know. He was so upset about something, and I thought it would be a good idea to offer him another drink...he threw it in my face and shoved me so hard I fell backward through a glass table." For some reason Andy found herself laughing again. "It shattered. I mean, it was crazy, there was glass everywhere. Everyone was staring and he acted like nothing was wrong. He walked away. There was no trace of the guy I had known only a few short hours before," Andy finished. "I wonder if that's what it's like when you give up your soul. Does it completely change who you are?"

"Not exactly, but hopefully that's something neither of us will never have to find out. Now, come on. Let's get off the floor." Kaden stood and held his hands out to help her up. Andy put her hands into his and let him haul her up off the floor. They were face to face and Andy felt drawn towards him, but she took a step back.

"Thank you...for helping me with my boots. I swear I know how to tie my shoes," she joked. Her head spun from getting up too quickly, but she also felt bubbly and energized. A giggle escaped her. Kaden grinned and dropped Andy's hands.

"Can we do something?" Andy asked, her eyes wide. Kaden cocked an eyebrow at her, curious.

"Like what?" he asked. Andy walked to the door and opened it, glancing back over her shoulder, and flashing her best devilish grin. She walked out the door and down the hall.

"I think we should keep you contained in your room in your current state."

"And I think you should just trust me," Andy said over her shoulder.

"Fine." At the stairs, Kaden insisted on walking in front of Andy in case she lost her footing. It annoyed her at first, but after stumbling on the third step, she was grateful he was there.

At the bottom of the stairs, Andy paused, unsure of where to go next. "I honestly have no idea where I'm going, I've only been in three rooms of this house," she admitted.

"So much for me trusting you," Kaden laughed, shaking his head.

"I just need...I know." Andy headed towards the back of the house, to the gardens.

"Please tell me you're not going to attempt getting lost in the maze again, I don't know how well that will go," Kaden teased.

"No, I just need to be outside. It's so stifling in here."

Outside, Andy felt much better. The fresh air felt freeing and it cooled her down. She spun around with her arms out.

"This place feels like a prison." She walked towards the fountain.

"We just left the house this morning. You're not exactly trapped here," Kaden pointed out, following behind her, steadying her as she stumbled.

Condemned Angel

"I just wish I could get away from here." Andy sighed, running her hand along the surface of the water in the fountain, creating ripples.

"Has it really been so bad?"

"No, but how do you think you'd feel if you were forced to be here? You choose to be here, so it's different for you," Andy tried to explain.

"I guess."

"Have you ever been away from here for longer than a few days? And not including when you were stalking me."

"Stalking is a little harsh..." he smirked.

"That's beside the point." Andy gave his arm a playful push.

"Fine. No. I spent my whole life with my parents until Ronan took me under his wing. I've spent every minute since then trying to repay him for it." He turned away from Andy and sat on the edge of the fountain.

"Repay him?" Andy asked, wondering what kindness Ronan could have possibly shown to him.

"Yes. I probably wouldn't have survived if he hadn't stepped in when he did. I owe him my life." Kaden observed the gardens, and Andy noticed a darkness shrouding his expression as he was lost in a memory.

"Fine. He has a heart of some sort. A warped, disturbed heart, but a heart." Andy sat beside Kaden on the fountain. She placed her hand over his, and he glanced at her, intrigue in his eyes.

The sun was setting, and the stars began to appear overhead. Andy stood off the fountain and walked to a small patch of grass. She laid down and gazed up towards the sky, which slowly faded to black.

"Now what are you doing?" Kaden sounded a little annoyed.

"Shut up and come lay down beside me," Andy snapped. Kaden didn't respond but did as she said and laid down beside her. She could feel the heat coming from him and his hand brushed her arm as he put his arms up under his head to use as a pillow.

"This is lame," he commented. Andy glanced over at him and realized he was looking back at her. She blushed and turned her face back towards to the sky.

"Just watch." The sun was gone, and the stars filled the sky. "Look!" Andy pointed as a shooting star disappeared. She smiled at the sight.

"Is this what people do for fun? I don't think I've missed out on anything." Kaden faked a yawn and Andy rolled her eyes.

"Fine. You can leave. I think it's amazing. It reminds me that there's so much more out there. It's not all about angels and demons, or this stupid war." A lump caught in Andy's throat and tears escaped her eyes. She wiped them away quickly and sat up.

Condemned Angel

"Done watching the stars already?" Kaden remained on the ground. There was a small flutter in Andy's stomach as she looked at him, and she quickly turned away. She convinced herself it was just the alcohol impairing her judgment.

"Maybe I do want to try out the maze after all." She jumped up and made her way to the hedge maze. She needed to distract herself from the butterflies now multiplying in her stomach. Kaden groaned as he stood up to follow. Andy walked a little faster so she could have a few minutes to herself. Inside the maze, Andy took a left, a right, and another right. She looked back and felt relief when she saw no one there.

"This is a bad idea, Andy," Kaden called from outside the maze. He was probably right, but she needed to get away from him.

"Are you worried you won't be able to find me when I get lost?" she called back, still walking deeper into the maze. Everything started to blur together thanks to the alcohol, and Andy couldn't remember which way she came in, but she wasn't worried. She knew Kaden would find her when she wanted to leave the maze.

"Oh, I know I'll be able to find you, just maybe not before you fall and break something," he laughed.

"You have very little faith in my agility skills." Andy ran her hand along the hedge and felt it prickling her skin.

Kaden didn't respond, and Andy finally felt alone. She took a deep breath and let it out slowly. She couldn't shake the bubbly, dizzy feeling that the alcohol has infused in her. It also seemed to have heightened her paranoia. She kept feeling like someone was watching her, and she saw shadows around every corner.

"Let me know when you want me to come and find you. I'll be out here," Kaden yelled, and Andy was about to answer when a hand fastened onto her arm. She tried to scream, but a hand clamped over her mouth next. Her entire body went cold with fear.

"What's the precious princess doing out here all alone, so late at night? Don't you know that's when the monsters come out to play?" she recognized Samson's voice and felt his hot, stale breath on her neck. Andy cringed away from him, but he had a death grip on her arm. "What's wrong, Princess? Your bodyguard's not here to save you?" In her mind, Andy was in a complete panic. She couldn't make her limbs move to try to escape and his hand was still over her mouth, so she couldn't scream. All Andy could think about was the time she reached out to the angels to find the camp. She closed her eyes and focused as hard as she could on reaching out. She knew the demons had blocked all communication for angels, but she had to try.

Andy screamed in her head, hoping, and praying that somehow, she could get through to someone, but she knew there was little hope. She opened her eyes again and saw nothing but stupid hedges.

Samson's body pressed closer to Andy's as he kept taunting her. She tried to block him out. She remembered her training with Septimus and lifting the log. Focusing all her energy into pushing Samson away from her, Andy felt strength surging through her body. She caught him off guard and was able to shove him aside, but he had inhuman strength as well and was only put off for a moment.

"Well, she does have some fight in her, doesn't she?" he grinned wickedly, but Andy turned and ran before he could grab onto her again. He growled behind her and Andy thought she might vomit, though whether that feeling was from the alcohol or the fear, she wasn't sure.

"Kaden!" Andy called out, almost frantic. "Come find me!" she yelled as she kept running. She knew she could hit a dead-end at any moment, and Samson would be upon her again.

"Come on, pretty Princess! No need to hide!" Samson called, loud enough for only her to hear. He was right behind her. Andy tripped over a root jutting out of the ground and fell hard onto her stomach. Bile rose in her throat. She rolled over onto her back as she tried to scramble back up onto her feet, but Samson was already there. He clucked his tongue. "It was a good effort, Princess," he sneered. Suddenly a strange look came across his face, and he stiffly walked past Andy and around the corner until he was out of sight.

Andy let out a sigh of relief, that was more like a sob. Her whole body shook, and tears rolled down her cheeks. She couldn't find the strength to get up off the ground, so she hugged her legs to her chest.

"Andy?" she heard Kaden as he came from the direction where Samson had just disappeared. "I guess I was right about not trusting your agility skills." He tried to lighten the mood and Andy found herself laughing through her tears. She could finally sit up.

"You found me," she breathed, grinning like an idiot, but she did not even care.

"Yeah, you probably alerted every single demon in a one-hundred-mile radius with your scream." He helped Andy off the ground.

"It worked? I got through?" Andy was shocked she was able to break through the communication barrier.

"I'd say so. But, if you were trying to get through to the angels, you failed there because you were definitely on the wrong network. But nice job." Andy threw her arms around him and felt him stiffen, but slowly his arms came up around her as well.

"I'm never coming out here again," her words were muffled against his shoulder. She pulled away from him. "What happened to Samson?"

Condemned Angel

"I took care of him. He'll have Ronan to answer to now." Kaden took a step away from Andy and rubbed his neck, a blush creeping up onto his face.

"Why did he just walk away, though?" Andy thought about the strange look on his face. "Did you get inside of his head?"

"It's not a happy place." Andy could tell Kaden was keeping something from her. "We should get inside." She grabbed his hand to stop him from turning away from her.

"What aren't you telling me?" she demanded. He sighed and squeezed her hand.

"I could see what he wanted to do to you." Kaden fumed, and Andy took his other hand in hers.

"I could see it too, not in his mind, but on his face," she told him. "But there is no point in dwelling on what might have happened... I can't, or I'll go crazier than I already am. Come on, you're right, we should get inside." He nodded and led the way out of the maze, never letting go of Andy's hand.

9
The Talk

It had been three days since Ephram was stripped of his leadership, and he still couldn't bring himself to accept the fact that the fate of his group no longer rested on his shoulders. He checked in with all of them, making sure that everyone was settling into their new camp well. Whatever happened to them, he would feel personally responsible, even though he no longer called the shots.

Malachi had not accepted Ephram's demotion yet either. He kept coming to him with new ideas to try to convince the dominions to reinstate him as a ruler. Ephram was not sure that this was what he wanted. If they truly did not agree with his decision to keep his whole group safe, rather than keep one angel away from the demons, then maybe he wasn't suited to be a ruler. Ephram would work on helping to keep his people safe from the sidelines now.

"Ephram?" Eva came up beside him, breaking through his reverie. He turned to face her. "I just wanted to check in with you, and make sure everyone is settling in alright." Ephram nodded and clasped his hands behind his back.

"Yes, thank you. Everyone seems to be doing fine," he informed her. There was a time when Eva would have reported to Ephram. Back many years ago, when Amelia was still alive, and Eva and Ephram were still working together.

"I can tell when you're thinking about her," Eva said and Ephram raised his eyebrows. "You were always easy to read when it came to your love for her."

"She was extraordinary," he said. Eva smiled and put her hand on his shoulder.

"I wonder every day if I'm making her proud. She was always better suited to be a ruler, but I'm doing my best." Ephram could tell this was hard for Eva to admit, and he knew that she would never be saying it to anyone else. Amelia was a natural when it came to being a leader, and everyone wanted to follow her.

"I wonder the same thing." Ephram observed the sky and the sun that was shining so brightly. "She must think me a fool for having lost my status as ruler," he chuckled, and Eva squeezed his shoulder.

"You're not a fool, Ephram. You calculated the cost of each decision and chose the path that would end with fewer casualties, just as any of us would do if put in the same position. Have faith Andromeda will come back to our side and maybe then the dominions will reinstate you as a ruler once more," she tried to reassure him. "Until then, trust that I am keeping your group's best interests in mind as well as my own group's. Now, I have a meeting to attend, so I must go." She took her hand off his shoulder and returned the way she came.

Ephram retreated to his tent to lie down for a while. As he closed his eyes, he hoped that he would be able to see Amelia in his dreams; the most beautiful angel he had ever met. If only he had been there to keep her safe when she needed it most.

∞

Ronan's henchmen greeted Andy and Kaden in the hallway. Cairn and Jackson stood with arms crossed, blocking their path, but Andy wasn't afraid. Cairn just seemed worried, while Jackson appeared indifferent.

"Ronan would like to see you now," Cairn announced. He led them to the throne room where Ronan sat alone, waiting. His hands formed a steeple in front of him like he was in deep thought. Once Kaden and Andy were seated, Ronan dropped his hands onto the armrests.

"You seem to keep finding yourself in harm's way today," he said, his brow furrowing.

"So, you care now?" Liquid courage still ran through Andy's bloodstream. "Because I would have thought this would just be another annoying interruption for you."

"Do not mistake my calmness for not caring. I've been around a long time and I have learned how to best deal with these types of situations. If I appear worried, everyone around me will worry. I care deeply about your wellbeing, Andromeda, do not forget that." Andy felt two inches tall as he glared at her, but she still couldn't stop her mouth from spewing out her thoughts.

"Brushing me off doesn't help anyone either. I would have never been in the maze tonight if it weren't for me trying to drown out all the thoughts in my mind. I needed *you* to tell me that you were going to do something to help me." Andy didn't know why it meant so much to her that Ronan wasn't acting more like a father when she didn't even want him to be her father.

"I'm sorry you feel that way, but I will not change the way that I lead my people because it is not agreeable to you," Ronan said. "But that is not why I asked you to come here. I wanted to let you know that Samson will no longer be a threat to you. I sent him somewhere else, where he can learn to have some respect for his own kind."

"And, what about the rogue demons? Are you still going to do nothing about them?" Andy pushed him, she needed to know that *something* was being done. She could not have her mind invaded by them again.

"We have search parties on the lookout for them. You were at that meeting if I remember correctly," he reminded Andy. "Once they are found, they will be dealt with accordingly. I have assigned Kaden to your safety for a reason. As he has displayed many times today alone, he is very capable of handling himself against any threat."

"Thank you, Sir," Kaden spoke up, and Ronan nodded to him.

"If there is anything else that I can do to make you feel safer, I will do it, but I think it's unnecessary," Ronan said.

"Fine. I guess that's enough for now." Andy crossed her arms over her chest.

"And, as for your question the other day, Lindy's parents are alive and well. They are on their way to Xavier's camp now." Andy's heart leapt at the knowledge that Ace and Lindy's parents were alive, just as their Uncle Tim had suspected. She would not have to bear the weight of that possible bad news any longer.

"Thank you, Ronan." A smile permeated her cold mask from before. She stood and turned to leave.

"I have not dismissed you," Ronan's voice was just as calm as ever, but it had an edge to it. Andy turned back to him and crossed her arms once again.

"If you ever want me to even *consider* choosing to stay here, instead of going back to the angels, you need to start treating me less like an inferior and more like an equal, or an actual *person*. I don't need to be dismissed; I will leave if I want to leave. I will never choose to stay somewhere that I feel like I'm a prisoner," she told Ronan, and without even blinking he stood and gave her a slight bow.

"If that is your wish, Andromeda. Just remember, with more power, comes more responsibility. If you want to become more of an equal, you will perform the same duties as everyone else." He turned to Kaden. "She will accompany your legion tomorrow. Let Jason know."

"But, Sir, she's never been in combat against angels before," Kaden protested, but Ronan shook his head.

"I don't wish for her to engage in any fighting, I simply want her to be a witness to what it is that we are fighting for." Ronan clapped his hands together. "Now, I am going to bed, and I suggest the two of you do the same." Andy turned to leave.

"Sir," Kaden said, and Andy turned back to him, "I just need a minute alone." Kaden glanced over at Andy and she turned away, heading towards the doors. Ronan turned back to Kaden as Andy closed the doors behind her. She stood with Cairn outside and he smiled down at her.

"You look so much like your mother, you got lucky," he winked, and Andy found herself laughing with him. She hadn't really talked to him before, but he seemed nice enough.

"They were too powerful..." Kaden's voice drifted through the doors. "My parents...I understand...rogue... of course." Andy caught snippets of what he was saying, but she couldn't hear Ronan. She could have focused a little and heard them clearly, but she decided to respect their privacy.

"How long have you known my mom?" Andy asked Cairn, trying to make conversation.

"I met her when she was your age," he began, but Kaden opened the door behind them before he could continue.

"I'd like to hear the story sometime," Andy told Cairn. He nodded and smiled. "See you later."

Kaden and Andy walked upstairs in silence. When they reached his room, Andy paused. "I guess this is goodnight, then." She turned to face Kaden.

"I guess. I'll see you in the morning." He opened the door and Jason popped up from inside.

"I thought I heard you guys out here." He grinned and looked from Kaden to Andy. "You disappeared before."

"Sorry, we went for a walk through the gardens," Andy lied.

"Well, you're back now. Want another drink?"

Condemned Angel

"Yes please!" Andy bounced into the room, tripping over her laces, which had come untied, and fell to the floor laughing. "Someone here sucks at tying shoes. Not naming names."

"Hey, at least I was able to tie them," Kaden pointed out. He and Jason were both laughing at Andy now. Kaden sprawled out on his bed while Jason went to the mini-fridge to make more drinks.

"Your sister is a bit of a lightweight," Kaden remarked, and Jason nodded in agreement. Andy still sat on the floor, playing with her laces. She felt pressure pushing on the edge of her mind. Anxiety started to creep in, and her heart began to race as she realized what that might mean. She took deep breaths and edged towards Kaden. He sat up and concern crossed his face. Andy shook her head trying to indicate that she didn't want Jason to know what was happening.

"Jase, can you, uh, get me some water, please?" Andy asked him, trying to get him to leave the room. "I don't feel so good." It was not entirely a lie.

"Yeah, sure. I'll be right back." He left the room, closing the door behind him. Kaden stood up off his bed and sat on the floor in front of Andy.

"Just keep breathing deeply," he instructed her. She tried, but her anxiety worsened, forcing her breaths to come in short gasps, and her vision narrowed.

"I can feel someone, or something, pressing." She mimicked the feeling with her hands, pressing them against her head. "I don't know if it's real, or if... I don't know," she started to panic.

"It's okay. Close your eyes for me." Andy did as Kaden said and kept trying to slow down her breathing. "Now, focus all of your thoughts on putting up a barrier. Imagine a wall in your mind." She imagined a wall going up around her head. "Keep it up. Push it out as far as it can go." As she did this, the pressure lessened, and it became easier for her to relax and stay focused.

"It's working," Andy said, keeping her eyes closed.

"Good. You can open your eyes now," Kaden murmured. She did and Andy realized that she was gripping his hand in both of hers. She released it, blushing. She pulled her knees up to her chest and wrapped her arms around them.

"Thank you," Andy's voice came out as a whisper. She could hear Jason's footsteps coming back down the hall towards them. Kaden reached out and brushed the hair that had escaped Andy's ponytail behind her ear. Then he was up off the floor and collapsing back onto his bed. Jason entered the room and looked suspiciously at them both.

"There is some definite tension in here..." he handed Andy the glass of water. "I'm not even going to ask."

"I'm going to bed," Andy announced, standing up and heading for the door. "I'll see you in the morning." She waved to Jason, but didn't look back at Kaden. She could feel his eyes on her as she left the room.

    Alone in her room, it was all Andy could do not to have a complete meltdown. After everything that had happened that day, she found herself jumping at every creak and shadow. She turned on all the lights in the room and bathroom. She took a quick shower, and every time she closed her eyes, Samson's face loomed closer.

    After Andy made it through that ordeal, she put on one of the silk slips that were a poor excuse for pajamas and climbed into bed.

    It was too quiet. Andy kept peering around the room expecting someone to pop out from behind something. Her anxiety took over and kicked her senses into overdrive. She felt like the walls were beginning to close in around her, and her blood roared in her ears. Then came a knock on the door, and everything stopped. Andy had locked the door this time. It gave her a small sense of security. She hesitantly got out of bed.

    "Who is it?" she called through the door.

    "I'm glad you've finally taken my advice on the whole door locking thing," Kaden said, and the tension in Andy's body faded away. She unlocked the door and opened it a crack.

"Are you just here to pester me about my lock?" she joked, grateful for his presence because it took her mind off everything else.

"No, I wanted to check and make sure you're okay." His features softened and he seemed worried about her. She let the door open fully and shook her head, feeling like all her emotions might start pouring out of her.

"I'm surprised you didn't send Jason again," she smirked, and Kaden cast his eyes down. "All I can see every time I close my eyes is Samson, and all I keep thinking is that at any moment someone can take over my mind and... and I don't even want to think about what might happen," her words tumbled out all in a rush. Kaden stepped into her room and closed the door behind him, locking it.

"You don't have to worry about Samson ever again," he reassured her.

"Because Ronan sent him to another camp?" Andy scoffed. As if that would be enough to keep Samson away if he truly wanted to get to her.

"Because Ronan sent him to hell," Kaden clarified. "Samson is dead, Andy. He's not coming back, ever." Andy felt relief flood over her, and then guilt that someone had died because of her. But it still didn't stop her from being relieved that he was gone for good. "And, as long as I'm here with you, I won't let anyone take control of your mind. Just remember what I taught you earlier, about the wall. If you feel that pressure again, imagine the wall," he instructed, helping to ease her anxiety.

"Okay, well, I'm at least going to lie down, so that I *might* fall asleep." Andy walked back to her bed, extremely conscious of the paper-thin silk slip that was the only thing covering her. She crawled back under the covers. "You can turn off the light switch, I think I'll be okay with just this light on." She gestured to the lamp on the side table. Kaden flipped the light switch. It was still bright enough to be able to see every part of the room, so nothing could sneak up on Andy, but dark enough that she could fall asleep if her mind let her. Kaden sat on the desk chair that was still pulled up next to Andy's bed from earlier.

"Just let me know if you want me to leave," he said, and she felt a twinge of fear at the thought of him leaving.

"Please don't leave me alone." Her anxiety crept back in as she imagined being alone again. "Even if I fall asleep, I don't want to wake up alone."

"Okay." He eyed her curiously for a moment. "I noticed when you were in the angel camp that you didn't like to be alone…" he trailed off, blushing slightly. Andy felt herself doing the same. "Sorry, it's just, I *had* to keep an eye on you for Ronan."

"Don't be sorry. You saved me on multiple occasions and helped me with my nightmares. But you're right, I don't like to be alone. It's just that…" she paused wondering if she wanted to dive into this with him, but for some reason, she felt comfortable enough to tell him everything. "I've been having a lot of anxiety ever since that day when I thought my mom and Jason were killed. It seems to get worse when I'm alone."

"Have you tried talking to anyone about it?"

"No, I haven't had the time." She avoided his gaze. "It's not that big of a deal anyway, there are more important things going on right now." Andy tried to push aside her issues, as she always did.

"Well, you have some time now. Talk to me," he offered.

"Um, okay. I'll try, but I don't know where to start." Andy looked away from him, tucking her hair behind her ear.

"How did you feel when you thought your mom and Jason were dead?" he asked. Andy closed her eyes and remembered the crushing grief that she had forced into a box and never fully confronted for fear of spiraling into a depression. The tears surfaced now.

"Hollow," she whispered. "Like I had this hole ripped in my chest and I'd never be able to fill it again." She let a sob break loose as the lump that had formed in her throat became unbearable. She felt Kaden's hand close around hers and she opened her eyes to smile at him, though it probably came out as a grimace.

"And how did it feel when you found out they were alive?" His voice lowered to match the volume of Andy's.

"I felt...pure joy." The lump in her throat eased slightly thinking of the moment she saw Jason on those stairs. "And the hole filled up a little."

"But not completely," Kaden didn't phrase it as a question because he already knew the answer, but she answered him anyway.

"No. Not completely," Andy admitted.

"How come?" Kaden pressed.

"I guess, a part of me feels...betrayed." Hearing the words aloud made Andy realize the truth in them.

"Betrayed, how?"

"They let me believe them to be dead," she voiced her thoughts. "They let me hurt, and grieve, and suffer," she choked the last word out.

"They didn't know you thought they were dead, Andy," Kaden said, but it did not quell the heat now coursing through her. "They didn't know the pain that you were feeling." Andy turned on him suddenly, and her vision blurred from the tears in her eyes.

"But you did. You knew," she accused him, and he leaned back, guilt clouding his gaze.

"I didn't know the extent to which it ate you up inside, Andy. You hid it too well. I never pried into your mind, I only helped you with your nightmares." His voice sounded cooler, and Andy realized she had too quickly turned the blame onto him. "I was instructed not to intervene unless absolutely necessary."

"I'm sorry. You're right," Andy sighed. "I just needed..." she stopped because she didn't know what she needed.

"You needed an outlet to vent some of your anger. I understand, but there are more constructive ways to do it."

"Like drinking," Andy scoffed.

"There you go again," he groaned. "No, not like drinking. After we go out on our legion tomorrow, I will show you what I mean." He settled back into the chair and crossed his arms over his chest. Andy couldn't help wondering how he was going to sit in that chair all night. It couldn't be that comfortable.

"You know, you're pretty good at this talking thing."

"Marcus taught me," he said. Andy recalled the demon who had helped them rescue Lindy and Wayne was named Marcus. The same Marcus who had watched out for her before she reached the angel camp.

"This bed is huge; you can lay down if you want to," Andy offered, hoping he didn't think she was trying to make a move or anything.

"I'm fine," he insisted.

"The offer stands." Andy laid down, resting her head on her pillow. "So, what are we doing tomorrow?"

"With the legion?" he asked, and she nodded. "There is a group of angels that were spotted staking out one of our camps about thirty miles East of here. We have to deal with them."

"You mean kill them." Even though she had suspected it, she was still horrified that she had to take part in it tomorrow.

"It's a war, Andy. Kill or be killed," Kaden justified.

"Whatever helps you sleep at night," she said, and Kaden rolled his eyes.

"I've never seen anyone stand up to Ronan like you did earlier," he changed the subject, which Andy was grateful for.

"I'm tired of him thinking that he has any control over me and my actions. He played no role in raising me and I'm not going to let him think he can step in now and change who I am." Andy never wanted anyone to think that they had control over her, especially after someone *literally* controlled her earlier.

"Well, I think he got the message. You really should get some sleep, though. Tomorrow is going to be draining." They stopped talking and Andy attempted to fall asleep.

10
The Legion

Bo went with Ace and Lindy the next day to meet with Evangeline. She seemed nice enough. The interaction was kept short and sweet, with a simple introduction and talk of expectations. They would have chores just like all the angels, but they also had the choice to leave and rejoin human society if they wanted. Ace and Lindy had both looked to Bo when she had given them that offer.

"No thank you. We would like to be reunited with Andy before we make any decisions on relocating," he responded, and Evangeline nodded in understanding. She had dismissed them after that, and they all trudged back to their tent. Bo was surprised to find Septimus waiting for him when they returned.

"I thought about what you asked," Septimus said, and Bo ushered Lindy and Ace into the tent. Ace protested but gave in under Bo's commanding glare. "Come. We can talk elsewhere." Septimus strode off, Bo hurrying to keep up behind him.

They stopped when they reached the overhanging cliff. Bo kept quiet, expecting Septimus to elaborate on his earlier statement.

After a few minutes of silence, Bo spoke. "So, what did you decide?"

"It's a terrible idea to go after Andromeda."

Bo sighed. "That's what I was afraid you'd say."

"It's a terrible idea, but I am willing to help you," Septimus clarified. "I know the general area where Ronan's camp is located, and we should be able to pinpoint it once we are in the vicinity." Bo felt his hope soar as Septimus spoke. Not only was Septimus willing to help, but he knew where to go! Bo was thrilled.

"Thank you so much! When do we leave?" Bo was ready to leave right then and there.

"Tomorrow. I must talk to my father, and we need to recruit a few others. I'm sure you can take care of that." Bo nodded quickly. "Good, then it's settled. Tomorrow we will set out to find Andromeda."

∞

Andy opened her eyes and she was surrounded by hedges. Fear seized her as she realized she was back in the maze. Whirling around, she tried to find a way out.

"Princess!" Samson's voice called out to her. Andy's heart started to race as she tried to determine which way to go. She started moving sluggishly away from his voice. Every time she tried to move faster, it seemed like she slowed down, as if she was trudging through quicksand. He was getting closer. Then, there was a voice inside her head.

"Andromeda. We're coming for you. You cannot escape us," the voice said. The same voice that had haunted her for weeks now.

"Get out of my head!" Andy yelled, and suddenly Samson stood in front of her.

"Boo!" He cackled and Andy screamed.

Andy opened her eyes and realized Kaden was shaking her shoulder.

"Andy," his voice cut through the haziness of sleep. "Wake up, you're dreaming." Andy's eyelids fluttered open and she saw his face. He was still in that chair.

"Sorry," she mumbled, stifling a yawn. "Did I wake you?"

Condemned Angel

"I couldn't sleep," he admitted. "Too much on my mind, I guess."

"Well, if you want to talk about anything, I'm awake now." Andy sat up so she would not fall back asleep. Her eyes were still heavy, and she blinked them rapidly to try to chase away the sleep trying to settle in.

"I'd rather not." His face remained guarded, and Andy knew he was holding back from her.

"Fine. We can sit here in silence." Andy folded her hands in her lap and looked around the room.

"I know you're not capable of doing that," Kaden smirked. "Tell me about your dream."

"It was a nightmare," Andy clarified. "But I was back in the maze and Samson was there. I was hearing voices, too. They were saying that they're coming for me."

"It was just a dream," Kaden pointed out, though this did nothing to take away the residual fear still weaving through Andy's mind.

"But what if it wasn't? What if they were really in my head? Demons have been messing with my dreams for weeks now, who's to say the rogue demons can't do it too?" She felt helpless. She couldn't even feel safe while sleeping.

"They already sent their message; they don't need to invade your dreams," Kaden rationalized.

"I guess you're probably right," Andy sighed. "It just felt so real, you know?"

"I can imagine. I never dream, so I can't really relate." He picked idly at a string on his shirt. Andy gaped at him.

"What do you mean you don't dream? Doesn't everyone?" she asked, unsure how dreams really even worked.

"I guess not. Or, at least, I never remember dreaming." He didn't seem too upset or concerned about this fact, but Andy was not willing to let it go so easily.

"So, you just go to bed, and then nothing? Not even a glimmer of some dream or nightmare?"

"Nope."

"Well, aren't you the lucky one? I would love to never have another nightmare. I've had them almost every night since the war began." Andy could do without her nightmares, but she might miss her dreams.

"I can help if you want me to. Like I did before, when your mom asked me to, I can manipulate your dreams away from the nightmares," he sounded unsure, not of himself, but of how Andy would react.

"I don't know..." she wondered if she wanted him in her head while she slept.

"I can just block the images for you if you want," he offered.

"Maybe...if I can even fall back asleep."

"You should try. You can get at least another two hours or so in before we have to be up and ready."

Condemned Angel

"Alright, but only block the nightmares, no other shenanigans." He laughed and agreed.

When Andy woke up again at seven, she felt fully rested. She'd had no more nightmares or dreams. Kaden was asleep in the chair, so she got up quietly and headed to the bathroom. She grabbed an all-black outfit to change into.

When she came back out, Kaden was awake. He seemed on edge but relaxed a little when he saw Andy.

"I'm surprised you were able to fall asleep in that chair," she said, pulling her hair up into a messy bun.

"We should get going, I'm sure the others are already waiting downstairs." He left the room and Andy followed. He stopped outside of his room and opened the door. "I'll just be a second, I need to change real quick," he said, disappearing inside and closing the door behind him.

A few minutes later he reemerged wearing black jeans and a tight black t-shirt that showed off every muscle. Andy blushed and thought that maybe it hadn't been the alcohol giving her the butterflies before. Thankfully, Kaden didn't seem to notice.

"Let's do this." He led the way downstairs to the dining room. Jason and Lily were already there eating breakfast.

"Good morning." Jason looked up coolly. "Someone disappeared last night, and now he reappears with my sister..." he eyed Kaden suspiciously. Andy noticed jealousy flicker across Lily's face, but she quickly regained her composure and let out a dainty laugh.

"That explains why he didn't show up in my bed last night." She cocked an eyebrow at Andy as if challenging her, and Andy ignored her.

"I'm going to get food." Andy walked past them into the kitchen, her face feeling like it was on fire. She kept telling herself that she didn't care if Kaden and Lily were together, but she couldn't help but feel a small little twinge of jealousy. Though, Olivia had said that they hadn't been together since Andy got to the house. *You are with Septimus,* Andy reminded herself. *There is no reason to care if Kaden is with Lily.*

"You gonna grab some food, or just stare at it?" Kaden came up beside Andy and took a bagel and bacon. He eyed her curiously. She brought herself back into the moment and grabbed some fruit, ignoring him, and walking back to the dining room. Andy sat next to Jason.

"Am I going to have to start guarding your door at night or something?" he joked, but Andy knew there was some truth behind it. He had always been protective of her.

"Please, Jason. Nothing happened. I have a boyfriend anyway." Andy threw it out there not just for his sake, but Lily's as well. Lily brightened as Andy said this. Andy didn't look at Kaden.

"Oh, that's juicy. What's his name?" Lily gushed. She was doing this purely to start something. Kaden seemed unfazed as he continued to eat his breakfast next to Lily. She reached out and grabbed his hand under the table but made sure Andy saw it. He didn't make a move to pull it away.

"Septimus," Andy answered, throwing it almost like a dagger. She tried to keep her anger in check, she knew she had no logical reason to be upset.

"He's super broody and romantic," Kaden said, making a joke of it all. Andy glared at him, but he avoided her gaze.

"I'm sorry, do you have a problem?" Andy asked, her fists clenching on top of the table.

"You can date whoever you want, Septimus, Cory, Samson."

"Oh, screw you!" Andy was about to go off on him, but Jason cut in.

"This is all news to me," he interjected. "I'm going to need to approve of this guy." He shoved a forkful of eggs into his mouth.

"That'll be a conflict of interest; he's an angel," Kaden said, and Andy turned her glare on him again. Jason tsked, disapproving.

"Even juicier!" Lily grinned, eating up the drama, and it took everything in Andy not to reach across the table and slap the grin off her face.

"Let's not talk about this anymore," she snapped. Everyone finished their breakfast in silence, but Lily wore that stupid grin the whole time.

After breakfast, they headed outside. Jason led the way to where all the cars were kept. There were ten cars in the dirt lot. He walked up to a silver sedan and hopped into the driver's seat. Andy got stuck in the back seat with Lily.

She tried to avoid talking with Lily, but once they were out on the road, Lily grabbed her hand to get her attention away from the window. Andy slowly turned to her and saw that Lily was giving her an apologetic smile.

"I'm sorry about earlier. I didn't realize that your boyfriend was a sore subject, but I should have known. I want us to be friends, as long as you're here." Lily seemed sincere, but Andy had known plenty of girls like her before, who liked to keep their enemies close.

"It's okay," Andy managed to say through her anger. "We *are* friends," she lied. Kaden watched them in the rear-view mirror, and Andy gave him a scowl, which he rolled his eyes at and turned to stare out his window.

"Oh good." Lily seemed satisfied. "If you ever need to talk about Septimus, just let me know." She gave Andy a convincing fake smile, and Andy simply nodded in response. Andy turned to look out her window, hoping that Lily would leave her be for the rest of the ride.

They drove for about forty minutes, and then Jason pulled off the road. He turned off the car and they all climbed out. Jason popped the trunk open, and out came the weapons. They each had their own swords and daggers.

"Here, Andy. Ronan wanted you to have this back, to keep." Jason handed Andy her sword. Having it back gave her a renewed strength. She felt like she could finally protect herself again. "It's a little different than before, we had to make sure your weapon was forged in hellfire, the holy water would have done you no good in any of our fights," Jason said all of this so casually, as if it wasn't a completely different sword with a whole new purpose. Andy inspected it, but it appeared to be exactly like her old sword.

"I thought I wasn't fighting today, just watching?" Andy gulped, not ready to test out the fighting skills that she'd learned. Though they had served her well against demons, she wasn't sure she would be able to use them against angels.

"You *are* just watching, but if something goes wrong, you need to be able to defend yourself," Jason explained, which only made Andy feel a tiny bit better. "Come on, let's get this over with." He led the way into the woods. Andy prayed that whomever these angels were, she wouldn't recognize any of them. Everyone remained silent so as not to alert anyone to their presence. They were all so stealthy, Andy felt like every move she made was ten times louder than their movements.

"Stay here," Kaden murmured in her ear. She jumped, not realizing he was behind her. "And stay quiet." She did as he said and stayed hidden behind a tree, while the three of them continued towards the angel camp that was in sight. A small group, maybe three or four angels, sat around a fire pit, chatting. They had not set up a tent or anything yet, there were just sleeping bags on the ground. Andy turned away because she couldn't bear to watch what was about to happen.

There was a commotion and then the sound of swords clanging. Andy stole a glance back at the fight and saw Jason thrust his sword through an angel's chest. Andy saw the pain on the angel's face before he crumpled to the ground, and then he disappeared in a beam of light. Andy felt bile rise in her throat and she crouched down behind the tree trying to keep it down. Tears welled up in her eyes and she couldn't believe what was happening. If Ronan had expected her to enjoy or understand any of this, he was wrong. Andy heard one of the other angels cry out with grief and then a large rustle sounded in the trees above them as she took off into the sky. The rest of her group was dead. Andy threw up her breakfast into the bushes.

A hand rested on her back as she retched. She wiped away her tears and turned around to see Kaden there. Jason and Lily were already walking back to the car as if they had not just murdered those angels.

"Come on, Andy. It's time to go," Kaden said, but her whole body went rigid. Andy could feel the angel's presence

Condemned Angel

before she saw her. The angel who had appeared to have fled, landed, and stood with her sword raised directly behind Kaden. As she swung her sword down, Andy shoved Kaden with all the strength she could muster, and unsheathed her sword in the same movement, blocking the angel's blow. Andy's arms rattled with the force of the strike. Kaden was back up on his feet in an instant with his sword drawn.

"Go, Andy. I'll take care of this," Kaden growled as he blocked the angel's sword from cutting Andy in half. She did as he said and ran to catch up with Lily and Jason. Andy stopped and turned back to see Kaden sheathing his sword and the angel lying at the base of the tree Andy had been hiding behind. Her wings were splayed out on either side of her, and then there was a sudden burst of light that shot up into the sky. Andy turned and ran.

She didn't run back to the car. She didn't want to see Jason or Lily. She needed to breathe and get away from the brutal scene she'd just witnessed. She knew the others would be annoyed, or maybe even worried about her, but she needed some space.

Andy came across a stream running through the woods and bent down, splashing water on her face. It was cool and slightly shocking. She sat on a rock next to the stream and took deep breaths, trying to slow her heart rate and clear her thoughts.

The sound of the water running down the stream was calming. Andy closed her eyes and felt as if she could fall asleep. She remembered how she had feared the woods only two weeks ago. Now, she felt as if there was nothing more to fear. She had joined the monsters who haunted the woods.

The angel that Andy watched Jason kill, entered her mind, and his face swam behind her eyelids. Her eyes flew open, and she turned over the side of the rock and threw up the rest of her breakfast into the bushes.

"Andy," she started at the voice, nearly falling off the rock. Kaden stepped up beside her. "What are you doing?" Andy re-balanced herself on the rock, wiping her mouth.

"I need to clear my head." She closed her eyes and saw that angel's face again. She cringed.

"Jason and Lily are waiting," Kaden pointed out what Andy had already assumed.

"They don't need to wait for me. I can walk back." She wouldn't mind a nice, long, walk...alone.

"It's like, an eight-hour walk," Kaden sounded a little annoyed.

"Look, I'm sorry I'm inconveniencing you." Andy opened her eyes. "None of this is okay. I have no idea why Ronan ever thought this would make me more likely to choose to be a demon over an angel, but it has had the complete opposite effect. I want to get as far away from everything to do with demons as soon as possible." There was hurt in Kaden's

Condemned Angel

eyes for a moment, but it disappeared before Andy could be sure it was ever even there.

"I know you think you are the most righteous, holier than thou, being, but you should know that those angels killed one of our night watch legions yesterday. Two of those who were killed were close friends of mine. If you think the angels are any different than us, then you're a hypocrite." Kaden crossed his arms and turned away from Andy to toss a rock into the stream. It skipped three times.

"I've been called a hypocrite a lot since I've been here," she admitted. "I get it. Maybe I am a hypocrite. Or maybe, I don't want to be on either side of this war. I don't want to have any part in it. I want to get away from demons, but I want just as badly to get away from angels. I will never be able to kill anyone just because we're not on the same side." Andy stood up and threw a rock into the stream too, but hers just plopped in without skipping, dropping to the bed of the stream.

"That's not an option. You are a part of this war whether you want to be or not." Kaden sat down on her rock, pulling one knee up to his chest.

"Why did you tell me Lily wasn't your girlfriend?" Andy changed the subject, catching Kaden off guard.

"She isn't my girlfriend," he said. "I don't have girlfriends."

Andy scoffed. "That's stupid." She sat on the ground and placed her hand in the stream, letting the water run around it and between her fingers, creating little ripples.

"Why did you save me? You could have let that angel kill me." Kaden nudged Andy with his boot. She gazed up at him and furrowed her brow.

"Why would I do that?"

"You said you don't want to take part in this war, yet you were willing to fight that angel." Kaden stared into the water.

"I may not want to take a part in this war, but I also don't want the people that I care about to be hurt."

"So, you care about me?" He cocked an eyebrow and smirked. Andy rolled her eyes, caught in her admission.

"I'm regretting my decision to save you more and more by the second." She scooped a handful of water from the stream and threw it at him. He was shocked for a moment, and then they both laughed. Kaden kicked up a small wave of water which landed in Andy's lap, soaking her pants thoroughly.

"Really? I mean, I barely got a drop on you, now I have to explain that I didn't pee myself to the others," Andy tried splashing Kaden again, but he swung himself around to the other side of the rock. The water missed him completely and splashed harmlessly to the ground.

"Sorry." He smirked and stood up off the rock. "But we should head to the car before they send out a search party." Andy shifted into a crouch beside the stream.

"Wait, just come look at this for a second," she put as much intrigue into her voice as she could. When he stood right beside her, she sent a small wave of water at him. "Ha!" Andy pumped her fist in the air. "You're too easy." She laughed, sticking her tongue out at him. Kaden picked her up and waded into the stream. Andy laughed so hard, she couldn't even protest.

"You're lucky this stream is so pathetic." Andy looked down to see that the water in the stream just barely reached his knees. He put Andy back onto her feet. The water soaked into her boots and seeped through the only part of her pants that had still been dry. She turned her gaze to Kaden, now only inches away, and felt the butterflies in her stomach again. He was still laughing, giving her that genuine smile she'd only seen in her dreams and Andy realized that she may care about him more than she should.

"What are you guys doing?" Jason appeared from behind the trees. Grateful for his interruption, Andy made her way out of the stream and tried to shake some of the water out of her boots.

"I fell in," she said, which was an obvious lie. Lily came up behind Jason and gave Kaden and Andy a reproachful look. A blush crept up Andy's neck.

"Yeah, your sister is really clumsy, Jason," Kaden joked, walking up beside her and putting his hand on her lower back. Andy felt her face burning, and the butterflies started going crazy in her stomach. Lily did not miss the gesture and Andy could tell she was fuming on the inside by the fire burning in her eyes.

"We need to get back and give our report to Ronan," Lily snapped, turning on her heel. Jason waited for Kaden and Andy to walk past him before he followed.

Back at the house, Kaden and Lily went to report on their mission to Ronan. Jason and Andy headed into the small sitting room beside the dining room to wait for them. Andy's pants and shoes were still wet.

"You need to be careful with Kaden," Jason warned Andy once they were settled on the couch. Andy feigned confusion, pretending not to know what he was talking about.

"I told you, I have a boyfriend," she countered.

"Yeah, well, either way, you just need to watch out for yourself. Kaden has a history with girls." Jason had always been overly protective of Andy and it didn't surprise her that he still was.

"He told me he doesn't have girlfriends, so there is no need to worry," Andy repeated Kaden's words.

"That's because the last two girlfriends that Kaden had were killed. He hasn't dated anyone since the last girl over a year ago," Jason explained. This brought up so many questions, but Andy didn't want Jason to think anything was going on with her and Kaden, so she kept them to herself.

"Again, I have a boyfriend, so it won't be an issue," she repeated instead, trying to make Jason believe her, though she wasn't sure if that was even true anymore.

"Okay," Jason sounded skeptical, and she didn't blame him. Kaden and Lily came into the room.

"All set," Lily announced. She seemed to be in a better mood. "Kaden and I are going out to run an errand for Ronan," she added, for Andy's benefit only.

"Have fun." Andy gave Lily her most genuine smile to show that she was not getting to her. Kaden just gave a small wave and they turned to leave.

Jason and Andy went their separate ways for the day. Andy stopped in the dining room and grabbed a plate of food before retreating to her room to change out of her wet clothes.

∞

Septimus approached Ephram's tent. He knew that his father was not going to be happy that he had decided to go after Andromeda. It was something he needed to do. If he did nothing, he would never forgive himself. As much as he had tried to tell himself that he didn't care for Andromeda any longer, he knew it was a lie.

"Septimus, I know you're there. Come in," Ephram called out to him. Septimus stepped through the entrance and saw his father sitting in a chair, pulling on his boots. He must have just gotten out of bed. It was strange that he was not already out and about, organizing their fellow angels into guards.

"I have decided to go after Andromeda." Septimus decided to get straight to the point. Ephram stopped what he was doing and gazed up at Septimus. There was no surprise on his face, he had seen this coming.

"I was wondering when Bo would convince you to go after her," he sighed heavily. "I will not stop you. If this is what you think is right, then do as you wish. I am no longer your ruler. It would be wise for you to consult Evangeline before you leave. Or you may seek absolution once you return."

"I don't care about Evangeline's advice or permission."

"You should. If you seek my advice, then it is to go to Evangeline. Also, despite the stories you have heard, Ronan can be a reasonable man. There is a reason that Andy's mother fell in love with him. Do not fear him – fear the other demons who may be lurking in the confines of his territory." Ephram continued tying his boots and stood up. "Good luck, my son. Do not try communicating on the network while you are out there, it can be intercepted once you're out of angel territory."

"Thank you, father." Septimus followed him out of the tent, where they went their separate ways. He decided he

Condemned Angel

would heed Ephram's advice and seek permission from Evangeline to go after Andromeda.

That night, Septimus met up with Bo in the dining tent. He had Micah, Seraphina, Gabrielle, and Nathaniel with him.

"I see you found our rescue guard," Septimus said.

Bo nodded. "It was easy, they all wanted to go after her the day she disappeared."

"I talked with Evangeline earlier and she approved our mission. It took a bit of persuading, but Ephram was on our side, so that helped," Septimus explained. It had taken more than a *little* persuading. Evangeline thought it was stupid and reckless for them to go after Andromeda but understood why Septimus felt he had to.

Bo grinned, excited that they were finally executing his plan. "Great. So, what's next?"

Septimus exhaled. "We pray that we can get to Ronan's camp undetected and find Andromeda without being killed first."

11

The Dream

In her room, Andy peeled off her soaked jeans and tank top and threw on a summer dress. This one flowed out more than the last one and was plain white. She pulled the armchair over to the desk and took a seat, curling her legs up beneath her, and started picking at her lunch.

She must have fallen asleep at some point because the next thing she knew, she was back in that angel camp from earlier.

Condemned Angel

People screamed all around Andy. She couldn't tell how many, but the sound pierced her ears. She turned this way and that, but she couldn't see anyone. She ran forward, past the sleeping bags, and then she stopped. The screaming ceased, and dead silence replaced it.

Andy glanced down and realized that the sleeping bags were bleeding. No... it wasn't the sleeping bags. She staggered back in horror as empty, golden eyes stared up at her. There was a flash of light, and everything disappeared. Andy was left all alone.

Andy's eyes flew open and she gasped for air. She ran to the bathroom and threw up into the toilet. Her stomach muscles screamed in protest. Tears streamed down her face, both from the memory of her dream, and the pain.

She sat on the floor for a while, nothing else coming up, until someone knocked on her door. She thought about getting up but couldn't find it within her to pick herself up off the floor.

"Come in," Andy called out, her voice hoarse.

"I just wanted to check...." she heard Kaden begin, but he stopped, and she assumed he'd realized she wasn't actually in the room.

"I'm here," she rasped. Kaden came into view and Andy wondered what a sight she must be. Her hair pulled back into a messy bun, so it wouldn't get in the way while she vomited, and her dress spilled out on the floor around her as she sat cross-legged against the wall in front of the toilet. Kaden appeared concerned as he took it all in.

"I'm sorry..." he nearly whispered it. "I just wanted to check and see if you were okay, after earlier..." He took a step into the bathroom but didn't come any closer. Andy assumed it must smell horrible, and she cringed at the thought.

"I'm just peachy," she laughed bitterly, but it turned into a cough, her throat protesting at the effort.

"Do you need anything?" Kaden ran his hand over his shaved head, and Andy could tell he was uncomfortable.

"You don't have to pretend to care about me. I'm sure you'd rather be elsewhere, with someone else." Andy looked down at her hands in her lap and pretended to be interested in a string on her dress.

"I have nowhere else I need to be." He took another step towards her. "Tell me what's happening." Andy looked up at him and sighed.

"I fell asleep and dreamt about those angels that you all killed today... their faces are burned into my mind, and the blood..." the bile rose in her throat again.

"It's a hard reality of war. The first time I remember seeing someone die, I was eight." Kaden leaned against the vanity.

"*Eight?*" Andy gaped at him.

"My parents were not exactly the nurturing type. They took me with them on all their...hunting trips, as they called them. I probably witnessed more deaths before, but the first I recall was while they were still working for Ronan. The woman they killed was another demon, but one who had just been summoned back to Earth to collect someone's soul. She failed and ended up accidentally killing the person whose soul she was to collect. Her punishment was to be sent back to Hell – a life for a life." He told the story, and Andy saw no emotions on his face. He seemed to have detached himself from the memory.

"You watched them kill her?" Andy's voice remained hoarse, and quiet. She felt small, sitting on the floor, while Kaden towered over her.

"Yes. They'd stolen a sword blessed with holy water from an angel and used it to torture the woman. Ronan had told them to make the death quick, but they had their own plans. They've always enjoyed causing pain." Distress flashed in his eyes, but it was gone quickly. He did a good job of masking his own emotions. "They made me watch every atrocity they committed because my dad said to shield me from any of it would only make me weak."

"I'm sorry," Andy murmured, not sure if that was what he wanted to hear, but she didn't know what else to say.

"It's my life. I'm used to it," he sighed. "It doesn't make killing any easier, though. The first time I ever killed someone, I spent the next day in the same position you're in now. Even after all those years of watching my parents end lives, it still affected me more than I ever thought it would when I did it myself."

"I'm sorry," Andy repeated herself. "I mean, I didn't even do any of the killing today, and... look at me," she laughed shakily.

"You grew up with parents who actually cared about you and shielded you from the horrors of the world as they should. Don't be sorry for me, but don't feel like there's anything wrong with you either," Kaden urged. Andy nodded absentmindedly.

Imagining all the horrors that Kaden must have witnessed and experienced as a child made Andy understand him much more. It also amazed her that he hadn't turned out to be a monster like his parents. It made her think about all the times he had lashed out at her when she mentioned his parents, and she felt sorry that she had pushed him so hard.

"You know, before I came here, I thought all demons were as you describe your parents," Andy admitted. "I think it was easier to think of demons that way. That there was good, and there was evil. No in-between."

"I'm sure I helped solidify that for you," Kaden laughed.

"Actually, you're the main reason I realized I was wrong. I mean, you can definitely piss me off, but no more than anyone else," Andy smirked, and Kaden looked a little sheepish.

"I'm sorry about what I said this morning, about Cory and Samson. That was a low blow. I shouldn't have said it," he ducked his head and Andy could tell he was being truthful.

"You know that story I told you about the ex-boyfriend who pushed me through a table," Kaden nodded, and Andy went on. "That was Cory." Kaden whipped his head up and Andy saw the anger flare in his eyes. It surprised her.

"Are you kidding me? That makes what I said this morning so much worse! I'm such an idiot. Andy, please never forgive me," Kaden shook his head, but Andy laughed.

"Too late. I forgave you when you pretended I'd tricked you at the stream earlier and let me splash you," Andy smiled and Kaden chuckled.

"Caught on that easily, did you?"

Andy was able to stand up off the floor, using the bathtub as leverage. She smoothed her dress out and took a step towards the sink.

"I'm just going to..." she motioned to the sink, and Kaden moved out of the way so Andy could step up to it and brush her teeth. He seemed lost in thought as he stared ahead at the wall, still leaning against the vanity, with his arms crossed. Andy finished up and turned to him. "Thank you for checking on me, I think I'm okay now." Andy sounded unsure even to her own ears. She didn't know if the images would come back, and if they did, she didn't know how she would respond the next time.

"Sorry about the stream, you know, getting your pants and boots wet," Kaden smirked, and a mischievous light sparked in his eyes. Andy started to walk past him, into the bedroom, but she paused and faced him, only inches away, as they had stood earlier in the stream.

"I didn't mind." She bit her lip and winked at him, playing into his game. He hesitated and then leaned forward slightly, but Andy turned and continued into her room, leaving a crackling tension to dissipate. When she reached the middle of her room, she glanced back over her shoulder to see Kaden still lingering in the bathroom doorway, looking amused.

"You promised to show me how to more constructively vent my anger." Andy cocked her eyebrow at him. "Or are you just going to stand there all night?" Kaden laughed and strode towards her.

"Only if you're into that kind of thing." He sauntered past her but stopped short of the door, and she blushed. "Come at me."

"Excuse me?" Andy raised her eyebrows in confusion causing him to laugh.

"Try to land a punch," he instructed, and Andy shook her head.

"Are you crazy? I don't want to hit you." Andy had no idea how this was going to help her.

"You need a way to work off some of your pent-up emotions. I'm offering for you to try to hit me. Do it," he challenged her, and Andy rolled her eyes, but lunged forward and tried to throw a punch. Kaden caught her fist in his hand and moved it aside, smirking.

"Now try harder." He let go of her fist and took a step back. Andy took a deep breath and tried to punch him again, this time aiming a little lower. He stopped her again. "You're too predictable."

"I've never exactly learned how to punch someone properly, sorry," she said, annoyed. "I only practiced sword fighting."

"And what would happen if you lost your sword while fighting an actual enemy?" Kaden pointed out and Andy felt another wave of annoyance.

"I guess I'd be dead, wouldn't I?"

"Or you could learn to defend yourself without your sword so you could stand a chance at staying alive."

"Fine. Teach me how to defend myself," Andy said through gritted teeth.

"Well, first," Kaden stepped forward until they were only a foot apart, "your stance is a little off. It's fine if you're sword fighting, but now you have no sword. You need to change it up a little. May I?" Andy nodded and he pivoted her legs into a more stable positioning. Her right foot in the lead position, her legs slightly further apart, but not so much that it depleted her ability to move swiftly. Andy's skin tingled under his touch and she blushed again.

Kaden stepped away and Andy almost leaned forward to be close to him again, but she caught herself and snapped back to her senses.

"Now try again," he instructed. He led Andy through the motions of throwing and landing a good punch. He also helped her learn how to use her elbows and kicks for more versatility. They went slow at first, just going through the motions, but as Andy became more fired up, she started moving faster. She felt a release of energy and emotion with each movement and it felt amazing. She was sweating and nearly panting by the time Kaden told her to stop. "Not bad. I must say, I was worried that the dress would slow you down, but you seemed to have no problems with it." Andy looked down, remembering that she was still wearing the sundress.

"I've got shorts on underneath," she lifted her dress, flashing her white spandex. "I've learned to be prepared for anything these days."

"Feeling any better?" Kaden asked as he sat down on the bed. Andy noticed he was barely sweating at all from their training session.

"Actually, yeah. I'm feeling great." She grinned and flopped down on the bed beside him, letting herself fall back onto the comforter. "Thank you." He looked down at her and smiled back.

"Don't thank me yet, you'll probably be feeling a little sore tomorrow," he smirked. "Do you want to get some dinner?" At the mention of food, Andy's stomach began roiling again, and she was reminded of her failed attempt at eating earlier.

"Um," she sat up slowly, cringing as her stomach did a flip. "I'll come down with you," she answered, not committing to eating. He seemed to accept her answer, and they headed out of the room.

The usual buffet was set up in the dining room, but Andy couldn't bring herself to put anything onto her plate. She worried that eating anything now would just add fuel to the fire.

"Everything okay?" Kaden came up beside her as he filled his plate. She tried to nod reassuringly and took a scoop of potatoes, plopping it onto her plate for effect. She added a few other foods to her plate and followed Kaden into the living room.

Jason sat with a few other demons Andy hadn't met. They were all finishing up their dinners. Kaden took a seat on the couch and Andy took the only open seat left, which was right beside him. The couch awkwardly tilted inward, and Andy bumped against him as she sat.

"Sorry," she muttered, trying to readjust and give him some space. The other demons all stood up to leave, except for Jason, who sat across from Andy, but Kaden made no move to fill in the vacant space on the other end of the couch.

"So, how was the rest of your day, Andy?" Jason asked her. She pushed the food around on her plate to make it seem less obvious that she wasn't eating any of it.

"Alright. I just took a nap." She left out the rest, figuring he may not be as understanding as Kaden had been. The image of Jason shoving his sword through that angel's chest popped into her mind, and she had to choke down the bile that rose in her throat. Thankfully, Lily entered the room and the attention turned to her. She collapsed dramatically on the other side of Kaden and let out a long sigh, draping one leg over Kaden's knee. He didn't react, but Andy inched further away from him.

"Those damn rogue demons are going to be the death of me," she muttered. "You would think that *someone* would know where they're camping out, or have seen them at some point, but I'm beginning to think they don't even exist."

"Scouting went that bad, huh?" Jason asked. Andy let Lily's voice fade into the background, and she kept her eyes on her plate, focusing on making her food as compact as possible, so it looked like she ate something. She got lost in the process and didn't notice when everyone else stood up to leave.

"Andy," Jason said. She jerked her head up and felt everyone's eyes on her. "What are you doing?"

"I, uh, nothing. I'm done." Andy stood up and took her plate back to the dining room where the bin was for the dirty dishes. She scraped her entire meal into the trash and dropped her plate into the bin a little too carelessly, it cracked when it hit the rest of the dishes. "Crap..." she muttered.

"What's up with you, Andy? You've been acting weird all night," Jason said, placing his dish into the bin after her.

"Nothing. I'm fine, just a little distracted I guess." Since Jason was no longer an angel, she wondered if he would be able to sense the lie, but he didn't call her out on it.

"Go get some sleep," is all he said. Andy nodded and headed back to her room where Kaden leaned against the wall beside her bedroom door.

"Ready to train your mind?" he smirked, and Andy let out a groan. She forgot that he had promised to help her learn how to block her mind to other demons that night.

"I'm not feeling up to it right now..." she admitted.

"Sorry, but I promised Ronan I would train you tonight, and I don't go back on my word," he pushed. Andy sighed and opened her bedroom door, ignoring him as she walked to her dresser.

"Can't *you* just block my mind for the night, and we can train tomorrow?" she suggested. She didn't want to get lost in her thoughts at the moment.

"Are you trying to get me in your bed again?" Kaden joked, but Andy didn't have enough energy to be embarrassed or to respond. She pulled out her pajamas from the dresser, and shuffled into the bathroom, closing the door behind her.

Holly Huntress

After she showered and put on her pajamas, she spent a long time sitting in front of the mirror, absentmindedly brushing her hair. She kept her mind as blank as possible and stared at her reflection. Her stomach felt hollow, and she was having hunger pains, but she ignored them. It was nothing she hadn't felt while out in the wild with Wayne. Finally, she put the brush down and took a deep breath.

Is everything okay in there? Andy heard Kaden's voice in her head. She ignored him and opened the bathroom door. Kaden lounged in the armchair, and Andy could see the concern on his face. She wondered how she looked to him. She suddenly felt self-conscious of all the weight she'd lost while on the run, that she was still slowly gaining back. Her collar bones seemed to protrude a bit farther than normal, and she could sense his eyes lingering there. She pretended not to notice, and climbed into bed, pulling the covers up to her chin.

"I'm sorry I'm keeping you from Lily," Andy said, knowing that he would probably be with her tonight if he were not helping her block her mind.

"I told you, we're not dating," Kaden argued.

"Well, maybe you should tell *her* that," Andy suggested. Clearly, he was blind to Lily's obvious advances.

"She knows that we're just friends."

"With benefits," Andy added, and he shrugged, not denying anything.

"Why do you care so much about my relationship with Lily?"

"I don't," Andy answered too quickly, and Kaden smirked. "Are you going to sleep in that chair again?" She changed the subject.

"If you want to get me in your bed, all you have to do is ask." Andy rolled her eyes at him.

"You're hilarious." She relaxed her grip on the comforter, and let it fall to her lap. "If you would rather sleep in that chair, then, by all means, go for it. If not," Andy turned away from him, lying down on her side. She heard him sigh behind her.

"If you promise not to take advantage of me, I'll take you up on your offer," he joked, but Andy heard him stand up and he came around to the other side of the bed to lie down on top of the blankets. He kept his head propped up with the pillows and crossed his arms over his chest.

"I don't think I'll even be able to sleep tonight," Andy spoke quietly. Kaden finally looked at her.

"That's what I'm here for, to keep away the nightmares." He matched her tone, and all joking was gone from his voice. Andy could feel his mind pushing against her own, and she knew that he was there, keeping away the horrific images that threatened to fill her dreams. "I'll only block the nightmares, nothing else," he promised, and Andy nodded.

"Thank you," she murmured. Her stomach grumbled loudly.

"You didn't eat any of your food at dinner."

"I wasn't hungry," Andy lied, but her stomach grumbled again, giving her away.

"Let me get you something to eat. I can't let you starve on my watch," Kaden joked, but his voice was filled with concern.

"No. I don't want any food," Andy protested.

"Andy, you need to eat, just let me get you something," he tried again.

"No, thank you."

"Andy, come on."

"Please, stop. I can't eat," she finally admitted, her voice cracking. "I can't keep it down." She turned away from him and tears stung her eyes. She blinked rapidly to clear them away.

"Andy..." Kaden shifted on the bed, but he didn't touch her.

"It's fine. Just drop it," she huffed. Andy stared at the wall in front of her, trying to think of anything *but* the reason why she hadn't been able to keep any food down that day.

"Your anxiety isn't going to just go away," Kaden said, and Andy pretended not to hear him. "Our training today was only to help you find a way to let out some of the emotions you've been bottling up in an attempt to relieve some of the fuel for your anxiety." Andy finally turned back to him.

"I know. I know it's not going to just go away, but that isn't going to stop me from wishing that it would." He reached over and tucked her hair behind her ear. Her skin burned where his fingers had grazed it.

"We'll work on it. For now, get some sleep." He looked as if he were about to say something else, but he stopped himself and took his hand away. Andy turned away from him again and thought about the longing she felt, to feel his touch again. Her eyes grew heavier as she stared at the wall, and finally, they drifted closed.

Andy opened her eyes to the sun shining brightly through the trees. She was confused at first; Kaden had promised to keep away the nightmares, but then she realized, this was not a nightmare. Septimus was standing before her with his hand outstretched. She took it and felt a smile spreading across her face.

"I've missed you, Andromeda," he murmured and pulled her close to him. Andy draped her arms over his shoulders, and he leaned down slowly, his lips brushing against her own. She closed her eyes and breathed him in.

"I've missed you, too," she whispered. He kissed her, but it felt different; deeper, sweeter, better. *She opened her eyes to see that it was no longer Septimus that stood before her, but Kaden. He smiled down at her and she gaped up at him.*

"What?" He tensed against her.

"N-nothing," she stammered, still in shock, but she did not pull away. Instead, she leaned into him and let his warmth overtake her and settle the butterflies in her stomach.

Andy opened her eyes, back in her room, and realized that she could still feel that warmth from her dream. She relished in it for a moment and then noticed the distance that had grown between herself and the edge of the bed. The warmth she felt was not leftover from her dream, but from Kaden's chest that she had pressed herself up against.

Andy turned her head to see his eyes were closed and he breathed steadily, still asleep. Andy sat up quickly, rousing him from his sleep, and his eyes flickered open. He seemed surprised to see her so close, but he didn't react.

"Feeling better?" he asked, turning onto his back, and stretching his arms up over his head. Andy tried to pretend she didn't notice the strip of skin revealed at his waistline as he did this.

"I, uh, I think so." She scooted away from him, back to her side of the bed. The sun rose above the trees, and Andy glanced at the clock to see it was almost seven o'clock.

"Feeling up for some breakfast?" Kaden swung his legs over the side of the bed and started lacing up his boots.

"Maybe." Andy copied his movements, swinging her legs off the bed, and felt a chill spear through her as her bare feet touched the cold floor. Kaden came around to her side of the bed and leaned against the bedpost at the foot of the bed, looking every bit as mesmerizing as he had in Andy's dream. She gulped and hoped that he had not been able to see her dream while he was keeping the nightmares away.

Condemned Angel

"Well, I've got business to attend to, but we're training tonight. No excuses," he smirked. Andy stood up off the bed and came face to face with him. She could almost feel the heat coming off him, and she could imagine those arms going around her, just like in her dream...

"Are you still in my head?" she asked, almost breathless. He seemed confused, but he shook his head.

"No, why? Do you feel someone there?"

"Good, and no." She didn't want him to know what she was thinking and feeling at that moment.

"I don't have to be inside your head to know what you're thinking. You have a bad poker face," he winked and leaned in a little, almost close enough to kiss her, but then turned so his mouth was next to her ear. "If I could dream, I'd be dreaming about you, too." He turned away suddenly, and Andy almost fell forward, not realizing she had been leaning in closer to him. "See you tonight," he called back over his shoulder, and then he was gone. So, he *had* seen her dream...her body was on fire now, with embarrassment, or adrenaline, she wasn't sure. Probably a little of both.

After breakfast, Andy ran into Jason in the hall.

"Hey, Jase." She hugged him.

"Hey, what's up?" He looked like he was on his way somewhere, or she was interrupting something.

"Where are mom and dad?" she asked him. "Are they back yet?"

"They're probably downstairs. Come on, I'll take you to them." Andy followed him down the stairs. He led her to the opposite end of the hallway, to the opening with the bookcases and couches. Andy saw her parents sitting on one of the couches, each with a book in hand. They smiled as they saw Jason and Andy, and Andy felt like they had gone back in time before the war began.

"Hey, kiddos," Wayne greeted them. Andy noticed Jason roll his eyes.

"I've got to get back upstairs. Ronan needs me to work on something for him," Andy caught Jason's lie as he hurried back down the hallway. Andy watched him wondering why he didn't want to spend any time with their family.

"Come sit, kiddo." Wayne patted the couch and Andy plopped down between him and her mom. "How are you doing?" he asked, and Andy debated whether she should tell the truth.

"Not so good..." she started. They both seemed so peaceful and content, she didn't want to ruin it. She decided to keep the horrific events from the past few days to herself. "But I'm doing better now."

"Ronan told me you had a run-in with Samson," Angeline said, concern clear in her eyes. Andy could tell that Ronan hadn't given her the full replay of what happened, or else her mom would be much more upset.

Condemned Angel

"Yeah, it was pretty scary, but Kaden was there, thankfully," Andy said, figuring it was best to keep her in the dark, for now.

"Ronan mentioned that as well. I just want you to be careful, Kaden is a good person, as far as demons go, but I would prefer you don't get too close." Angeline brushed a stray hair behind Andy's ear.

"You mean because of what happened to his other girlfriends?" Andy asked, knowing that her mom was just trying to keep her safe, like Jason. "Jason already warned me about that, and it's all just coincidence." Andy didn't put any stock into the idea that Kaden had some curse when it came to his girlfriends.

"No, sweetie." Angeline gave her a sad look. "I wish it *were* just coincidence, but it's not. Unfortunately, Kaden has a complicated past," she began, looking at Wayne, who seemed to also be in the dark about whatever Angeline was about to tell them. "I knew Kaden's parents, back when I was with Ronan. They were never good people, and they never intended to have a child. When Kaden came along, they decided to keep him and use him. I only saw Kaden once, when he was still a baby. But Ronan told me, once Kaden was old enough, his parents would make him go with them on attacks, and they would use him as a diversion. When things didn't go their way, they would take it out on Kaden."

"Kaden's parents, before Kaden was even born, gave their souls over to Lucifer, to prove their loyalty to him, and eventually they started to pressure Kaden to do the same. At that point, I think Kaden was around twelve, and he didn't want to give his soul up. Ronan stepped in and told Kaden's parents that it was his right to choose, and if he didn't want to give his soul up, then he shouldn't have to. So, they let Ronan take Kaden because they didn't want him around if he wasn't going to comply with their wishes. Besides, they'd already pushed Olivia off on Ronan. But they haven't stopped trying to convince Kaden to give up his soul."

"Every chance they get, they intervene and make Kaden's life hell so that he will eventually decide there's no point in keeping his soul," she paused and let this all sink in, and then continued. "Kaden's parents killed those girls." Andy felt so much sadness for Kaden, and she couldn't find any words to react to her mom's story.

"There is no chance in hell that I am letting my daughter anywhere near that boy again," Wayne broke the silence, and Andy saw the fear and anger blazing in his eyes.

"Honey," Angeline turned to him and placed her hand on his arm, trying to calm him down.

"No. If he actually cares about her in any way, he will stay away from her." Wayne crossed his arms with finality and Angeline sighed, knowing that she could do nothing to change his mind.

Condemned Angel

"There is nothing to worry about," Andy said. "I have a boyfriend; Septimus." She decided it was time to tell her dad about the relationship, no matter how shaky it had become in her mind. He needed a reason not to worry about her and Kaden.

"Ephram's son?" Wayne looked bewildered. "When did this happen? I knew I shouldn't have left you alone in that camp..." Andy laughed.

"If I remember correctly, you were the one who chose to go, though they didn't give us much of a choice." A dark shadow crossed over Andy's mind as she recalled the result of Ephram separating her and Bo from their parents. Her thoughts strayed to Bo and what he must be going through now that she had left him too. Andy was grateful he at least had Micah and the rest of their friend group.

"What's wrong, sweetie?" Angeline noticed the change in Andy's disposition.

"I miss Bo, and Septimus," as she said it, she realized that she missed Bo more than she missed Septimus, and it made her feel guilty. "And I don't know that I'm ever going to see them again," she added, which gave her a gut-wrenching feeling.

"There was a time when you thought that you would never see us or your brother again, and here we are," Angeline pointed out, smiling. She was right, but it didn't change the way that Andy felt.

"I thought you were dead," Andy pointed out. "If I'd known you were alive, it would have been different. Dad and I would have come and found you, I would have never even met Bo or Septimus."

"I'm glad that you have found these people that you care so much for. That's what life is all about, I would hate to think you were missing out on your whole life because of this..." Angeline threw her arms up in frustration, "...this stupid war," she finished. "You're supposed to be in college, learning and meeting new friends, and falling for boys." Tears welled up in her eyes.

"I know." Andy grabbed her hand and squeezed it tight. "I would have loved to have been able to do that, but this is the way it is, and I *am* learning, a lot actually. And I'm falling for boys and meeting new friends, so it's *almost,* maybe, sort of similar."

"You said boys, plural," Angeline smirked. Andy blushed and shook her head.

"No, no. There's only been one, and there only *is* one," Andy corrected her, though she didn't specify who the one she was thinking of was, and she wasn't so sure who she meant herself. Angeline seemed skeptical, but she said nothing.

"I'm sure you will see Septimus again," she reassured Andy. "And I hope that I have the pleasure of seeing you with him, and Bo."

"Me too." Andy leaned her head on her mom's shoulder and closed her eyes, trying to imagine the day when she would see them both again. There was nothing, just darkness. In her heart, she knew that the chances of seeing either of them again were slim. They had left and gone to another angel camp, who knew where, and she was stuck with the demons for an indefinite amount of time.

"Oh," Andy snapped back into reality as she remembered her question for her parents. "I forgot, what did Ronan have you doing the past couple of days?" she asked.

"Nothing of great importance," Angeline said. "He just wanted to make sure that your dad and I were kept busy. He sent us to pick up a couple in Las Vegas with the jet and get them moved to Xavier's camp." Andy gaped at her for a moment. "What is it, sweetie?"

"Nothing, I just… was it Natalia and Thomas?"

"Well, yes. How do you know them?" Angeline's eyes were round with surprise.

"Lindy and Ace's parents…what were they like?" Andy was curious to learn about the people who had abandoned their children to help fight with the demons.

Wayne took Andy's hand. "I'm sorry, Andy. They didn't talk about Ace or Lindy. If I'd known who they were, I would have asked them more questions. Otherwise, they seemed like any other demon and human I've met. We made small talk and delivered them to their new camp."

"Oh, I guess I shouldn't have expected more. I just wish they would go back to Ace and Lindy…they need them."

"Not all people are fit to be parents. They truly believe that what they are doing is for the best. I don't see them returning to their children any time soon." Wayne squeezed Andy's hand and released it.

"I think I'm going to take a nap," Andy said, having had enough bad news for one day. Although, the fact that Ronan had sent them to personally assure that Natalie and Thomas were transported safely meant he cared. He knew that Andy cared about these people for the sake of their children.

"Okay, sweetie." Angeline kissed her forehead.

"Don't forget to stay away from Kaden," Wayne chimed in.

"Dad come on. Kaden has saved my life multiple times now," Andy said, but he didn't soften.

"I owe him for keeping you safe, but now, he needs to keep you safe by staying away from you," he remained stern.

"You'll have to take that up with Ronan. He's the one who assigned Kaden to watch out for me." Andy had no fight left in her to argue with her dad.

"Oh, trust me, I will. Now, go get some rest." He patted her arm and went back to reading his book. Andy was interested to see if he convinced Ronan to agree with keeping Kaden away from her. She wasn't too worried about it happening because she knew that Ronan didn't like Wayne and would probably do the opposite just to spite him.

12

The Request

"I need to speak with Ronan please, Cairn," Ronan heard Wayne outside his door. He rolled his eyes. Ronan had been trying his hardest not to lash out at him with all the pent-up resentment he held towards him. It should have been *him* who got to live a happy life with Angeline, raising *their* children, not *Wayne*.

Ronan took a deep breath, trying to calm himself down, yet again. He usually didn't get so worked up about things, but since Wayne had been living under his roof, he had become more irritable.

"Just a moment." Cairn slipped into the room, closing the door behind him. "Sir, Wayne would like to speak with you."

"Yes, let him in." Cairn noticed the annoyance on Ronan's face. He smirked and said, "I can send him on another errand." But Ronan shook his head and Cairn nodded, leaving the room again. Wayne entered and strode down the long aisle towards Ronan.

"Wayne, welcome," Ronan stood from his chair. "Please, come have a seat." He gestured to a chair that had been placed beside his own. Wayne made his way to the chair and sat. Ronan returned to his throne.

"I need to talk with you about Kaden," Wayne began, and Ronan nodded. He had been wondering when this would come up. "I'm sure you know about his parents killing his old girlfriends." Ronan nodded again. "Yet, you still let him near our daughter. *You* assigned him to be her bodyguard." Ronan scoffed internally.

"I understand your concern, but I know more about this situation than you do. I have been keeping tabs on Kaden's parents, Gregor and Mara, since they left this house six years ago." Ronan folded his hands in his lap. "As for those other girls, they're not dead." Wayne's eyebrows raised. "Yes, Gregor and Mara took them away, but they are still alive and well. Unfortunately, Gregor's motivation for recruiting the girls was based solely on causing Kaden pain, because he did care for them. Now, they have signed their souls over to

Lucifer and sworn their allegiance to Gregor, which is arguably worse than death," Ronan sighed. "I have learned from those incidents. With the first girl, we had no idea about Gregor and Mara's plans, so we could not have prepared for it. With the other one, I did not give her the protection that would have kept them from getting to her. Kaden is the protection that they lacked. I let them go out on legions without him. That is why I have assigned Kaden to be Andromeda's bodyguard. He is my strongest and all-around best soldier."

"But Andy isn't dating Kaden, which seems to be the trigger for his parents' actions, so why give her the protection and force them together?" To Ronan, it almost seemed pointless explaining all of this to Wayne, but he continued anyway.

"They may not be dating, but I have known since Kaden brought her here that he has feelings for her. But that is beside the point. Gregor and Mara's henchmen have been trying to get to Andy since before Kaden knew her. Lucifer wants Andy on his side, and they were his surefire way to obtain her. But now, I have convinced Lucifer to give me time to let her make her own decision."

"If Gregor and Mara want to hurt Kaden, they will still come after her. I don't want him near her. I'm sure you have someone else who is equally as capable of protecting her," Wayne argued.

"I'm sorry, Wayne. I will continue to do what I believe is best for my people, and that includes my daughter." Ronan stood and Wayne realized that was his cue to leave. "Please, Cairn, see him out." Cairn came into the room to escort Wayne out.

"I can go on my own. Don't think that I will let this go so easily. I will do whatever it takes to make sure that my daughter remains safe," Wayne snarled, and Ronan did his best not to react or respond.

Once Wayne was gone, Ronan sat back down. How dare Wayne question his judgment? He had been leading and protecting his people for over twenty years now, he knew how to protect his daughter.

"Cairn!" Ronan called out. "Bring me Zain." Cairn nodded and hurried off down the hall. As Ronan waited, he thought about the warning Kaden had given him the other day. Kaden thought the demons who attacked him and Andromeda in the clearing may have been rogue, but he also had another theory…his parents. He had been strong enough to get away, but he said they had been too powerful to be just any demons.

Zain arrived within minutes. "Close the door behind you," Ronan ordered. Zain did as he was told. Ronan waited until Zain was standing in front of him to continue. "I need an update on Gregor and Mara."

"They were last seen by one of my scouts outside of Baltimore, sir. That was two days ago," he reported, standing tall before Ronan, who nodded with satisfaction.

"Good. Get me an update on their current location and keep on them. I need to know if they take so much as a single step in this direction." Ronan paused. "And how about their followers?"

"They've been all over the place, sir. They are hard to pin down. As you know, they were responsible for that attack in Baltimore and the one on the human camp near Andromeda's angel friends. Since then, they have been moving about sporadically. I don't think they're still trying to get to Andromeda. I believe they're following Lucifer's orders and working on their own tasks now," Zain said, and Ronan tried to find comfort in his assessment.

"Good. I need you to keep this quiet, but if you need any extra bodies, let me know and I will provide trusted soldiers for you," Ronan spoke calmly, but on the inside, his muscles were tense. "Now go."

"Yes, sir." Zain left the room. Ronan called out to Cairn once more.

"What do you think, Cairn?" he asked him, and Cairn appeared confused.

"Sir?" he questioned, stepping into the room.

"Am I doing the right thing to keep her safe?" Ronan clarified, hoping that maybe Cairn would have an outsider's perspective on his current situation.

"There's no way to know, sir. Only time will tell," Cairn said, and Ronan sighed. He knew Marcus was the one to ask for any advice, but he didn't want to call for him now.

"Thank you, Cairn. You may resume your post." Cairn returned to his place outside the door, closing it behind him, leaving Ronan alone with his thoughts.

∞

Angry voices came from Jason and Kaden's room. They were so loud; they woke Andy from her nap. She opened her door and peeked out into the hallway. It was empty. She crept towards their door and could almost make out what they were saying when the voices stopped. The door opened and Kaden stormed out slamming the door behind him. Andy jumped in surprise.

"Is everything okay?" she asked, knowing this was a stupid question since he was clearly pissed off.

"It's great," he answered sarcastically and whipped around to storm off down the hall without giving Andy a second glance.

"Kaden!" she called after him, but he didn't turn back. Andy opened the door to Jason's room and found him and Wayne. "What did you do?!"

Condemned Angel

"We did what needed to be done. I'm sorry if you don't understand right now, but I will not stand by and allow you to be in danger," Wayne answered sternly. "Do not fight me on this, Andromeda." He used her full name for the first time in a long time, and then followed in Kaden's footsteps, though with less theatrics. Andy stood alone with Jason in his room. She stared him down and he rolled his eyes.

"You were in on this?" she huffed.

Jason avoided her gaze. "You're my little sister," he said as if that were enough explanation. "We just told him to stay away from you, and that I will be watching out for you from now on." Andy stormed out of the room. She headed downstairs to find Kaden. At the bottom of the stairs, she came across Lily on her way to the dining room. Lily paused and looked over at her.

"Andy," she greeted her coolly, still upset about the day before apparently.

"Hi, Lily." Andy attempted to smile, but she was not in the mood for pretending right now.

"I heard about your incident with Samson. You may want to try staying away from obvious traps and creeps," the sarcasm was thick in Lily's voice. Andy rolled her eyes.

"I don't have time for this," Andy snapped. She was already in a bad mood, and Lily's attitude made it worse. "Get out of my way." Lily put her hand on her hip and flipped her hair.

"I'm just trying to help," she sneered.

"I'm sure your motives are totally pure." Andy brushed past her and walked towards the door leading to the garden. Her heart began racing as she approached the door. Just thinking about the maze brought back all the memories of Samson and her nightmare.

"If you're looking for Kaden, I would check my room," Lily called after her. "He always winds up there in the end. Second door on the left." Andy could hear the triumph in her voice, and she tried to push away her feelings of rage towards Lily, but it was nearly impossible. The heavenly fire built up inside of Andy and her fingertips tingled.

As much as she didn't want to, she decided to take Lily's advice and check her room first. Andy went downstairs, to the second door on the left. She paused outside the room. The door was closed, and Andy knew that Lily had roommates, so she took a deep breath and knocked. No one said anything so she opened the door a crack. Kaden sat on what Andy assumed was Lily's bed with his elbows on his knees and his head in his hands. Andy's heart dropped. *He always winds up there...* Lily's words echoed in her mind.

"I don't want to hear it, Lil," he said without looking up. Andy shook her head in disbelief. She should have never gone down there.

"I should have believed you that first day when you told me you like to play with people's emotions," Andy kept her voice as calm as possible, but her emotions were on overdrive and the heavenly fire threatened to burst out of her. Kaden finally looked up, in surprise.

"Andy," he started, getting up off the bed. She turned away and stalked back down the hall towards the stairs. He caught up with her and grabbed her hand but let go instantly. The heavenly fire had burned him, and Andy felt a glimmer of satisfaction. "Let me explain."

"Why should I?" Andy turned back to him. "This shouldn't be a situation that I have to be in. I don't want this." She clenched her hands into fists, and the heat pulsed in her veins. "I should have known that you didn't actually care about me," as she said it, a weight dropped in her stomach, and all the heat dissipated from her body. "That's why you can be around me, without worrying about your parents, because if you cared about me, you would stay away..." Tears sprung into her eyes and she turned away from him again, this time she didn't turn back. Kaden didn't come after her, and she knew that whatever she thought they had or could have had, was gone, and maybe never existed.

When Andy made it back to her room, she felt lost. She knew she had not been fair to Kaden. All week she had been telling people that she had a boyfriend; Septimus. Kaden had every right to believe that there was nothing between them, but it didn't make the hurt lessen. Andy had admitted that she cared about him, and he had seen firsthand the effect that he could have on her in her dream... and seeing him there, in

Lily's bed, made her realize how stupid she'd been. She had been using Septimus as an excuse to push Kaden away.

There was a knock on her door. She hesitated, assuming it was Kaden. After a second, she decided to open it. She was surprised to find Cory standing there. He held a bottle of rum in one hand and two glasses in the other.

"I come bearing a peace offering, and an apology," he said. "Can I come in?"

"That depends, let me hear the apology." Andy crossed her arms and waited. He took a deep breath and began.

"I'm sorry I assumed that our relationship would remain unchanged after all this time. I shouldn't have put you in that awkward position before, and I shouldn't have gone off on you." He offered Andy one of the glasses and she took it.

"You're forgiven," Andy said as Cory filled her cup a quarter with rum. "What is it with demons and drinking?" she laughed as she took a sip of the rum and nearly gagged.

"A need to defy our parents and society, just like any other teenager," Cory joked, chugging the rum straight from the bottle. "Since we have a higher tolerance, it's more of a game to see how much we can drink before we start feeling the effects."

As much as Andy didn't want to be that person who got drunk every time something went wrong, she couldn't help but think about how she was possibly going to sleep that night with what happened yesterday, and today... she shuddered and bile rose in her throat again.

She took a few more sips from her glass as Cory poured himself a drink. The next sip went down a little easier and started to take the edge off Andy's thoughts and memories.

By the time she finished the glass, she felt like she was floating on a cloud and her whole body was filled with warm tingling. Thankfully, she was not usually a crier when she drank, or else she would be a mess.

"If you want any more, you know where to find me." Cory retreated to his room. Andy closed her door and went to bed. She leaned back in her bed and closed her eyes. When she opened them, she was antsy and felt the need to keep busy. She pulled on her leather jacket and left her room.

She started down the hall towards the stairs, swaying from side to side as she went. She peered over the railing to see if anyone was down below and saw a couple of unfamiliar demons walking towards the dining room. Once they were gone, she went down the stairs. Andy missed a step and nearly fell but caught herself on the railing. She snorted, laughing at herself.

She made it to the bottom of the stairs in one piece and turned to the front door. No one was around, as per usual, so she got out without incident. The gate was open, so she didn't have to figure out the code for the padlock. Andy walked right out and started down the long driveway towards the road.

At the end of the driveway, she paused. The second gate was also unlocked, which seemed strange, but she didn't question it. Part of Andy knew that she should not be out there after what happened with the rogue demons, but the euphoria from her freedom pushed away those worries. Turning left, she felt herself drifting off into her thoughts.

Andy realized after a while that she was walking through the woods. She didn't remember leaving the road and couldn't see it anymore. Darkness surrounded her, and she didn't remember the sun going down. She started to panic. She was lost.

"Take deep breaths," she told herself. "It's okay, just breathe." Andy tried to do this, but her heart raced and made it hard for her to calm her breathing. She tried to focus her eyes, but the lingering effects of the alcohol made it difficult. Andy closed her eyes and focused instead on communicating with the demon network. She knew that connecting with the angels was impossible, and there were probably none around anyway.

Hello, Andy called out in her mind, hoping that someone answered.

Feeling a little lost? she heard, and her blood ran cold. It was the same voice from her nightmares.

What do you want from me? she asked, turning every direction to try to find whoever was talking with her, but they could be anywhere.

We need you to do something for us. And don't bother saying no. You're going to do it whether you want to or not. Andy felt herself being drawn to the left and soon the mansion came into view. She hadn't strayed too far from it. *You are going to kill Ronan for us.* Her heart jumped into her throat. Andy walked towards the mansion even though she used every ounce of strength she could muster to try to stop herself. Panic set in again.

"Please, no," Andy said aloud, and she heard a laugh in her mind.

As she approached the gate, Andy realized it was locked from the inside. She felt a small bit of relief, thinking this would deter whomever it was controlling her from getting inside, but then, the gate swung open. Andy blinked in disbelief. Something was wrong. She squeezed her eyes shut, and when she opened them, she was back in her room. *I never left,* she realized, and she knew that someone was in her head playing tricks.

What's going on? she thought, and she heard a chuckle bounce around inside her mind.

We needed to wait for the opportune moment, so we kept you busy. The voice had been real, at least. Andy's breathing came in rapid bursts and her heart raced as she involuntarily swung her legs over the side of her bed and stood to pick up her sword from her desk. *Calm down, darling.* Almost instantly, her anxiety seemed to disappear, and she knew that whoever the voice belonged to was somehow responsible.

The one time Andy hoped to bump into someone, there was no one around. She found herself walking down the hallway towards Ronan's throne room. Cairn was posted outside the door as usual. Andy tried to give away her current situation in some way, but he didn't notice anything was off.

"I need to speak with Ronan, please," Andy said unwillingly. It sounded distant to her own ears. Cairn nodded and opened the door, allowing her to pass without question. She walked past the benches lined up like pews, towards Ronan.

∞

Septimus led the way to the overhang, where it would be safe for the angels to take off. They each began unfurling their wings. Bo gasped. He hadn't seen their wings yet.

"I hate to ask, but how am I supposed to travel?" Bo looked around at the rest of them.

"Don't worry, I've got you covered." Micah winked at him and swept him up into his arms, taking off into the air and flying towards the open sky. Bo felt the wind rushing past them but was shielded from the worst of it by Micah's body.

Condemned Angel

He heard everyone else taking off below them, following in Micah's wake.

Septimus flew to the front of the group and set the course. After about two and a half hours, they were flying over New York City. It was strange to see it so clearly from above. The only time Bo had seen it like that was from a plane, and it had been shrouded in clouds and smog. Nothing lay between them and the city.

"Do people still live there?" Bo shouted to Micah over the roaring wind. Somehow, he heard him and nodded. Micah pointed down, careful not to drop Bo in the process. Bo turned his head to see what Micah indicated and noticed a few cars driving across a bridge into the city. Otherwise, there wasn't much sign of life from this high up.

They flew for another hour before coming to a stop. They landed in a field of weeds on the outskirts of a small town in Connecticut. Bo had not seen the sign saying which town, but he knew they were nearing the border of Rhode Island, where the Demon's territory began.

"I think we should take a break. I want everyone fully rested and ready for anything," Septimus said. "Let's head into this town and see if we can find a place to rest." They walked through the field towards the town. Septimus had picked it because it was deserted, but they had passed several inhabited cities along their journey so far.

They stopped at the first house they came to and went inside to rest. Bo thought he had only closed his eyes for a moment when Micah shook his shoulder to wake him.

"Come on, Bo. It's time to get moving again."

Bo tried to wipe the sleep from his eyes as he sat up. "Already?"

"It's been three hours. It's almost dark, so by the time we reach Ronan's territory we will be able to get in under the cover of night."

"Oh alright," Bo said, rolling out of bed.

They took off into the sky again and flew for another hour before the sun began to set. Micah put Bo down gently on the ground. They took cover in a grouping of trees.

"I'll go keep watch," Micah offered, beginning to climb a nearby tree. Bo watched him, thinking about how the setting sun filtered through the trees, causing him to appear to be glowing. He was beautiful. As Bo watched him, he suddenly dropped to the ground, clutching his head in his hands.

"Micah!" Bo shouted in surprise and rushed over to him. A million thoughts started running through his mind as to what could be happening. Sera, Nathan, and Gabby all dropped simultaneously. Bo glanced around in confusion, fear coursing through him. His eyes found Septimus who was the only one still standing, besides himself.

"What's happening?!" Bo exclaimed, panic clear in his voice. They had come so far; they couldn't fail Andromeda that soon.

"It's a trap. There must be a demon camp nearby. They're not really in pain, they are being forced to believe they are," Septimus said, trying to stay calm.

"Why are you fine?"

"I've trained my whole life to keep my mind protected from any kind of control or invasion. Help me with them, we need to get out of here before the demons find us." Septimus hurried over to Nathan and could see the pain in his eyes. "Look at me, Nathaniel!" Septimus broke through to him, but Nathan still clutched his head in pain.

"What do we do?" He asked through clenched teeth.

"I need you to focus. Focus on blocking out all other minds; the opposite of what you do when you communicate through the network. Push away the pain and come with me." Septimus looked over to Bo and Bo started repeating his words to Micah.

"Come on, Micah. Focus. It's not real. Block them out." Bo said. He breathed a sigh of relief as Micah nodded slowly and after a few moments of struggling, he stood, putting one arm around Bo's shoulders for support. Sera stood next, she seemed to have pushed through the pain on her own. Septimus lifted Gabby into his arms and turned back to the rest of them, there was no time to get through to her.

"We need to get away from here now. The demons have probably already realized we're here and are on their way." They made their way out of the woods to the road and took off, Micah scooped Bo up into his arms wearily. Bo could tell that his extra weight was beginning to weigh Micah down, especially after the strain of the demon's trap.

Once they were flying away, Bo looked back and saw a group of demons crossing the road to where they had been only moments before. One of them turned his head up to see the angels escaping and Bo noticed a wicked sneer spread across his face.

Bo turned his face into Micah's chest, so he did not have to see the demons any longer. He felt like dead weight, and he began questioning his decision to go on the mission. He worried that he was only slowing the others down, and he knew that time was of the essence when it came to finding Andy. But he pushed away these thoughts, it was too late to turn back now.

They put a lot of distance between themselves and the demon trap. The next time they landed it was out of necessity because Micah was growing tired. The guilt formed a hard knot in Bo's stomach, knowing that they would be able to keep flying if not for him.

Once they were on the ground, everyone grouped together to talk about their next step. They all seemed worn out from fighting the demons out of their minds. Bo could only imagine what it must be like to have someone else trying to invade your mind. He shuddered.

"We can't give up on Andy," Bo stated, looking around at the group. They all nodded in agreement.

"We're not giving up," Septimus reassured him. "We are closing in on the area where Ronan's camp is said to be located."

"Is it okay if we hang out here for the night? I'm still feeling drained from that demon trap," Gabby asked and it seemed that everyone, except for Septimus, felt the same way. He was lucky that he had been trained from so early on to ward off those kinds of attacks. Bo wondered why all angels weren't trained that way.

"We can all rest and recoup for the night. I'm going to scout the skies for a while." Septimus left the group and took off into the sky again. The others watched him leave and then viewed each other, waiting to see what everyone else would do.

"I guess I'm just going to try to get some sleep." Sera shrugged heading to the nearest tree and settled into the base of it, sitting upright.

Gabby yawned. "I'm going to sleep too," she said looking at Nathan. He walked to a tree on the other side of the little clearing, opposite of Sera, and settled in as she had done. Gabby followed him, laying down with her head in his lap, and she was asleep within moments. Bo glanced over at Micah who sat on a log with his elbows resting on his knees propping his head up. His eyes were closed.

"I'll keep watch, you get some rest," Bo told him, and Micah shook his head, opening his eyes to look up at Bo.

"I'm fine. My strength was just sapped out of me by that demon trap. I'm already feeling better," he patted the log for Bo to sit beside him. "Come here." Bo paused at first, wondering if he should take a walk around first and make sure there were no unwanted guests in the shadows, but he decided that could wait a few minutes. He took a seat beside Micah and Micah took his hand. "There is something on your mind, I can tell," Micah said, and Bo let out a long sigh.

"I already lost my parents, I can't lose Andy, too," it came out as a whisper.

"I know how much you care about Andy, and I know what it's like to lose friends."

"She's not lost..." Bo cut in, but Micah put his free hand up and stopped him.

"I'm not finished. I know Andy is still out there, and we are going to find her. But in the meantime, I am here for you if you need me. I may not be as good of a listener as her, but I will try my best." Micah gave Bo one of his heartbreaker smiles and Bo melted inside, just a little.

"Thanks, but I'm worried that maybe I should have just let you all come out here without me. I have been slowing you all down, and I'm sure you would feel much better without the extra weight," he admitted, glancing at the ground. Micah laughed softly.

"That's all? You do realize I wouldn't be on this mission if it weren't for you. I wasn't going to let you come out here without me," he smiled, and the butterflies woke in Bo's stomach. "As for the extra weight; for me, carrying you is like carrying around a purse all day for a human, or something like that." Micah laughed again and Bo couldn't help but smile.

"Are you just saying that to make me feel better?" Bo asked, eyeing him suspiciously.

"Cross my heart. It's the truth. I would pawn you off on Sera if that wasn't the case." They both laughed, which seemed to disturb the others as they tried to sleep. "Come on, let's take a walk." Micah took Bo's hand as they stood and led him towards the surrounding woods which were growing darker by the second.

They walked for a little while, thankfully not coming across anyone, until they found a stream. Micah sat cross-legged on the edge. Bo stood beside him, staring off into the distance, past the stream, into the trees. The breeze blew the leaves around slightly, but other than that, there was no movement. The heat was intense, but not too stifling. Bo took a deep breath.

"It's so peaceful out here, you could almost pretend that there isn't a war going on around us," Bo said, breathing in the clean, crisp air.

"Yes, but there *is* a war going on around us. No matter how terrible the war is, I am grateful for one thing since this war began, and that is the fact that I met you." Bo looked back into the stream and he could see Micah's reflection still watching him. Those butterflies were back and putting in some work.

"Why do you like me?" Bo asked the question that had been burning inside of him since Micah first showed an interest in him. Micah glanced up at him again, concern on his face.

"What do you mean? Why *wouldn't* I like you?" he questioned Bo. He stood up and took both of Bo's hands in his. "Aside from the fact that you are more interesting than anyone I have ever dated before, you are also brave, strong, and kind. There is so much more to you than just a pretty face, as they would say," he smirked and winked at Bo.

"Am I just interesting to you because I'm human?" Bo remembered that question Micah had asked him when they first met: *what is it like?* Was this all just him trying to figure out that answer for himself?

"I'll admit that it's what drew me to you in the first place. Now, I wouldn't care if you were human or an angel. Either way, you're you, and I love you." His eyes widened as he realized what he had just said, and Bo's face grew hot. He wondered if Micah regretted letting that slip and if he wanted to take it back, but he said nothing more. Micah still gazed into Bo's eyes and held his hands. He leaned in and kissed Bo before pulling away slightly. "I mean it," he murmured against Bo's lips and then kissed him again. Bo pulled back.

"Is it okay if I don't say it back yet?" Bo asked, unsure

of his real feelings at that moment. His whole body felt electrified, and he didn't want to say something that he would regret later. Micah laughed and kissed him again.

"Of course it's okay." Bo smiled with relief and kissed Micah. He knew a part of himself was still hung up on the warning the others gave him about Micah being a heartbreaker, but a larger part of Bo was falling head over heels for him.

"We should get back to the others. We're the ones who are supposed to be keeping watch," Micah reminded him. They walked, hand in hand, back to the small clearing where everyone else still slept soundly.

Septimus had not returned yet. Micah sat resting against the log and nodded off. Bo stayed awake and alert, ready to wake him at the sign of any disturbances.

When Micah woke after an hour or so, he let Bo rest his head against him and get some rest as well. By the time Bo woke up, darkness had engulfed them, and the only light came from a fire in the middle of the clearing. Everyone else sat around it.

Bo realized that he leaned on the log now, alone, and Micah was nowhere to be seen. He stood up, and stumbled, realizing his legs had fallen asleep. He stomped his feet a little, trying to wake them, and then made his way to the fire. Septimus had returned and he had a solemn look on his face. Bo could guess that he did not find Ronan's camp.

"Welcome back, sleeping beauty. Nothing wakes you, does it?" Sera joked as Bo joined them.

"I guess I was more tired than I thought," he admitted, scanning the clearing for Micah.

"Your boyfriend is up a tree keeping an eye out for any threats," Sera guessed what Bo was looking for and he nodded in response. "Come sit." She scooted over, making room for him in the small circle around the fire.

"We decided to stay here for a couple of nights," Sera filled Bo in. "Septimus said he felt a few more demon camps nearby, and this place is nicely distanced from all of them. Tomorrow he is going to be training us all on blocking our minds from the demons' traps so that we won't be caught up in one again. Then, we can continue with a better chance of getting past the next couple of demon camps unharmed." Bo took in everything that she said. They were staying put for a couple of nights. He felt like they should keep moving immediately. Andy needed them, and who knew how much time she had. Bo looked over at Septimus who seemed to read his expression.

"We won't be able to help Andromeda if we are captured, or killed, by any of the demons along the way. It's in everyone's best interests that we prepare ourselves properly before proceeding," Septimus explained and Bo nodded, reluctantly agreeing.

"I know, you're right. It's just…knowing that Andy is

with the demons right now, all alone. Who knows what she's going through?" Bo voiced his concerns. Septimus sighed, and Bo knew he struggled as well.

13
The Good One

"To what do I owe the pleasure of your visit?" Ronan spoke casually, not realizing anything was amiss. Andy pulled on all the strength she could find within herself and tried to focus on breaking through whatever hold the demons had on her. She felt her hand moving towards the hilt of her sword, but it hesitated. Andy realized she must be breaking through and kept trying.

"I-I..." she stuttered. "P-please stop me," she broke through briefly; long enough for Ronan to understand that something was wrong. Andy pulled her sword from her belt and it was immediately engulfed in flames. Ronan was already off his throne and across the room, her warning giving him the time he needed to get away.

"Cairn!" Ronan roared. "Go get Kaden!" Andy made her way towards Ronan who left the room and closed the door behind him as if that were going to slow her down. But, surprisingly, Andy stopped and put her sword to her side.

There's the powerful Andromeda that Lucifer has been yearning to meet. The voice in her head spoke. *I enjoyed our little experiment. Until next time.* And then they were gone. Andy fell to her knees as she was released from their grip, her sword clattering to the floor. She felt as if she had been holding her breath, and it came out in ragged gasps. Kaden burst through the door and searched until he found Andy kneeling on the floor.

"D-don't come near me," she put her hand out to signal him to stop. She wasn't sure that she wouldn't be taken back over at any second. Her breathing remained heavy, and her mind whirled trying to wrap around everything that had just happened.

"Don't worry, I'm in your head, they can't get back in right now," Kaden said, and Andy realized that she could feel him there, at the edge of her mind.

"What?" Andy looked up at him from the floor.

"I'm blocking them from reentering your mind," he explained.

"So, *you're* controlling me now?" Andy's voice shook as tears trailed down her face.

"No, you're in control. I'm just making sure that no one else can get in. Like when you were sleeping, and I blocked the nightmares." Kaden approached Andy, and she did not object this time.

"I don't remember the end of the day." Andy choked back a sob. "I was walking down the road, and then I was in the woods and it was dark. But I wasn't really, I don't think...I don't even know," her voice shook, and she put her head in her hands. "Anything could have happened..." Andy was lucky that they wanted to use her or test her instead of killing her.

"Yes, but you're safe now." Kaden sat cross-legged beside her.

"Cory brought me rum. I drank it to forget you..." Andy muttered, still resting her head, face down, in her hands.

"So, you're blaming me for this?" There was amusement in his voice, and Andy wanted to slap him for it, but she refrained.

"No, I am blaming you for making me *want* to drink. Everything after that I'm blaming on the rum," Andy told him, managing a laugh. Kaden scoffed.

"I didn't even do anything wrong," he pointed out.

"Maybe not, but that doesn't change the way I feel," Andy admitted.

Condemned Angel

"We should talk about this somewhere else." Kaden stood and offered his hand to help Andy up, but she ignored it and stood up on her own. She was growing tired of feeling helpless. Her head throbbed, and she wondered if that was because Kaden was in her mind.

"If you think I'm inviting you back to my room, you're wrong," Andy said. Kaden rolled his eyes.

"Where do you propose we go to talk then?" He crossed his arms over his chest, and Andy paused, not sure where else they could go where they wouldn't be overheard.

"Fine, we can talk in my room, but no more alcohol. I don't know why I keep thinking that's a good idea." Kaden nodded in agreement. Andy led the way out of Ronan's throne room. Ronan stood chatting with Cairn as if nothing had happened.

"Thank you, Kaden," Ronan nodded to him and Kaden bowed slightly to him.

"Is that it? I try to kill you and you have nothing to say to me?" Andy asked in disbelief.

"You showed that you are loyal by breaking through to warn me, Andy. That took a lot for you, I know, and I thank you for it," Ronan said, and she realized he was right. She could have let herself kill him and then all of this would be over. Her family could leave and go back to the angels. But she would never be able to live with herself if she had allowed that to happen, and it wasn't that simple anymore.

"You're welcome," Andy responded, feeling awkward. Ronan turned back to Cairn and Andy took that as her cue to leave. She continued walking down the hall with Kaden trailing closely behind her.

"You're too good," he commented, and Andy turned her head to look back at him.

"What do you mean?" She gave him a quizzical look.

"If you were more selfish, you're right, you could have just let yourself kill him, and then you and your family could leave," Kaden repeated her thoughts. "Though, the minute you left, my parents would swoop in and claim you for their own. And you couldn't *actually* kill him, since Ronan re-forged your sword." Andy stopped and gaped at him.

"Get out of my head!" She shoved his shoulder.

"I have to make sure no one else can get in, and it's so hard *not* to hear your thoughts. Sometimes I forget not to listen," he smirked, and Andy rolled her eyes.

"Yeah, sure. You can at least *pretend* that you aren't invading my privacy by leaving my thoughts unsaid." Andy continued up the stairs and down the hall to her room. She paused at her door, took a deep breath, and opened it. Kaden followed her in and closed the door behind him. Now that they were there, Andy's nerves began to go haywire at the thought of talking about her feelings.

Before she had the safety net of having a boyfriend, now she had thrown that out the window and needed to tell Kaden how she felt. It felt ten times harder than when she'd had a similar conversation with Septimus. She fiddled with the zipper on her jacket and cleared her throat hoping it would prompt some words to come out, but nothing came.

"So?" Kaden crossed his arms over his chest eyeing her curiously and Andy stopped her stalling.

"My mom told me about your parents," she blurted out. This was not where she was thinking that they should start, but it was out in the open now.

"So that's what all of this is about? Because your dad and brother already lectured me; I'll stay away," he went to leave, and Andy grabbed his arm to stop him.

"No. That's not what I want," she said, the heat rising in her cheeks. "I know that I keep telling everyone that I have a boyfriend, but the truth is, I have no idea if I'm ever going to see Septimus again," she admitted. "And if I did see him, who knows if he would want to be with me once he finds out I'm half-demon, and I don't know if I even feel the same about him anymore."

"I don't see what this has to do with me," Kaden interrupted her, but she continued.

"Okay, so yesterday, in the stream, I felt something, and I thought that you did too... and then this morning, with the whole dream thing..." her face reddened, "...and then to see you in Lily's bed...well it hurt more than that time Cory pushed me through the glass table." Andy closed her eyes, waiting to hear how Kaden would respond.

"I shouldn't be saying this, because your family is right, I am putting you in danger being with you, but I've had feelings for you since the day I brought you here," Kaden admitted.

"But you said the day we met that we would never be friends, and you made me *hate* you by throwing a private moment between Septimus and me in my face," Andy reminded him.

"I thought it was better for you to hate me. Then we wouldn't be where we are now; with you being used as a pawn by my parents to get to me. They want you for Lucifer, but they're toying with you because of me," he sighed. "It was too hard to keep pushing you away, though."

"So, what made you fall for me that day, was it my ten thousand questions, or my throwing up on the side of the road? Both equally appealing, I know, I'm quite the charmer," Andy joked, and Kaden humored her by laughing, or maybe he actually found her funny.

"It was everything. You were sacrificing yourself for the people you care about and still managed to smile and laugh. You should have hated me, which I guess you did by the end, but instead, you blamed the war and the situation instead of the one who was actually taking you away from the people you love," Kaden finished, and Andy still had one question.

"So why go back to Lily?"

Condemned Angel

"It's safe for me to be with her – I have no real feelings for her," he explained, but that didn't make Andy feel any better.

"So, you're using her? Because she has real feelings for you." Andy crossed her arms, not sure why she felt so defensive of the girl who had been trying to hurt her just hours before.

"I made it clear to her that nothing more was ever going to happen between us, and she was fine with that. She knows about what happened with Lexi and Molly," Kaden said, and Andy realized that these were the names of the two girlfriends that he had before. No one else had used their names.

"She lied, Kaden. She wasn't fine with that, she was hoping you'd change your mind," Andy said, knowing it to be true.

"Well, how was I supposed to know that?" Kaden was exasperated. "What does any of this have to do with us?"

"I need to know that you're not going to be running back to Lily anytime something goes wrong, or you're upset," Andy explained, crossing her arms.

"Then I need to know that you're not going to keep using Septimus as an excuse not to be with me," Kaden countered, crossing his arms to match Andy's stance.

"Fine," she pursed her lips.

"Good," he smirked.

"So..." Andy fiddled with her jacket zipper again, unsure of where this was now leading. It could either end with Kaden leaving with the idea that they would take this slow, or it could go in the opposite direction...

"I vote for option two." Kaden gave Andy a devilish grin making the heat rise in her cheeks and the butterflies start fluttering in her stomach.

"Stop it! You're not supposed to be listening to my thoughts!" She pushed him playfully, laughing at her embarrassment. He caught her arms and pulled her closer, causing her cheeks to burn even hotter.

"Are you sure this is what you want?" he asked, his smile melting away any worry passing through Andy's mind. She put her arms up around him, clasping her hands behind his neck, and kissed him. It sent shivers down her spine.

"I'm sure," she murmured against his lips. He kissed her again and then pulled away.

"As much as I want to continue with this, I need to stay focused to keep anyone out of your head." He gazed at her longingly.

"Is it always going to be like this? How long are you going to have to stay in my mind?" Andy still stood with her hands clasped behind his neck and his arms around her.

"Just for tonight and then tomorrow Ronan wants me to spend the day training you to keep everyone out on your own," he said.

Condemned Angel

"Okay, so I guess you're staying in my room again tonight." Andy brought her arms to her sides and took a step back. The idea made her extremely nervous. He'd stayed in her room before, but there was nothing *real* between them then.

"The closer I am, the easier it is to keep your mind blocked, but I could do it from my room, too." Andy figured he knew what she was thinking still and was trying to make her more comfortable.

"No, that's okay. If it's easier for you, then you can stay," she said.

"We should get some dinner," Kaden suggested. Andy nodded in agreement, thankful for the change of pace.

In the dining room, Kaden and Andy grabbed food and then headed to the sitting room to eat. Jason, Lily, and Olivia were there, along with some other people Andy had not met. There was only one seat open.

"Andy!" Jason jumped up when he saw her. "I was searching everywhere for you earlier! Lily just told me what happened." He didn't mention anything about her being with Kaden and she assumed he had already realized he was not up to the challenge of keeping her safe. Andy doubted her dad would take it as well, but that was an issue for another time.

"I'd rather not talk about it." Andy glanced around and noticed everyone in the room staring at her. She started to feel extremely uncomfortable, but Kaden held her hand in his and it eased her discomfort.

"Kaden, you can come sit by me." Lily scooted over a little, leaving a small space between her and the side of the couch.

"I'm all set," he answered, sitting in the one open chair. Andy sat on the arm of the chair. She could tell Lily was upset, but she kept eating her food in silence. Olivia raised her eyebrows but said nothing.

Once they were all finished eating, Jason brought all the plates to the kitchen. Everyone else left the room except for Lily, Olivia, Kaden, and Andy. Andy tried to avoid Lily's gaze.

"So, Andy, if you don't mind me asking, what's it like to have someone take over your mind?" Lily asked, and Andy knew she was trying to get to her again as she had earlier. Kaden stood up.

"Come on, Andy, let's get out of here." Andy stood up to leave with him, and he kissed her, making her smile. But then she realized what he was doing. Lily stood up and stormed out of the room. Olivia sighed.

"You shouldn't have done that," Andy said to Kaden.

"Why?" He feigned cluelessness.

"I'm going to talk to her." Andy started walking in the direction of her room.

"Just let her be, Andy," Kaden called after her.

"Because that worked out so well when I had no one come after me," Andy called back and kept walking.

Condemned Angel

Andy knocked on Lily's door and she opened it, rolling her eyes when she saw Andy.

"Coming to gloat? You win, happy now?" She flopped down onto her bed.

"I wanted to make sure you're okay," Andy said.

"No, I'm not *okay*. All this time I thought Kaden didn't want to date me because of his parents, now I know he just never cared about me." Andy could see the hurt in Lily's eyes and hear it in her voice, and she felt terrible.

"I'm sorry," is all Andy could come up with.

"Don't be. You saved me from wasting any more time trying to be with someone who was never going to want to be with me," Lily sighed. "Just, try to keep the PDA to a minimum around me, please."

"So, are we okay?" Andy asked, hoping they could go back to the way things were before the tension of fighting over Kaden began.

"I guess," she rolled to her side, turning away from Andy. "Just don't expect us to be friends, I need some time to get over Kaden, and seeing your face is not helping."

"Gotcha. I'll go now. If you need anything, though, I'm here," Andy offered and walked back upstairs. Kaden was waiting for her at the top of the stairs with Olivia, who looked like she was giving him her two cents.

"Feel better now?" Kaden asked as Andy reached them.

"No." She strode past him towards the spiral staircase. Kaden followed behind her, while Olivia headed downstairs to comfort Lily.

"I'm sorry I don't have feelings for her," Kaden said sarcastically. "You're too good. You care too much about other people's feelings." Andy turned on him.

"Is that such a bad thing? Maybe you don't care *enough* about other people's feelings." She veered back to the stairs and started taking them two at a time. She stormed down the hallway and flung open her door walking inside and straight through to the bathroom, slamming the bathroom door behind her. She heard Kaden close her bedroom door with a soft click.

Andy splashed water on her face trying to calm herself down. She sat at the vanity and leaned her elbows on the top, putting her head into her hands. She sat there, taking deep breaths, and wondered if she had made a mistake giving Kaden a second chance. They were so different, and, as he'd said, she was 'too good' for him.

"Andy, you can't stay in there forever," Kaden said through the door. "I'm sorry about what I said. I like that you're so good, and I care about *your* feelings, isn't that enough?" Andy sighed and gazed at herself in the mirror. She took her hair out of the elastic holding it up and let her curls tumble over her shoulders. After standing, she removed her jacket, boots, and socks. She unbuttoned her pants and wriggled out of them.

Condemned Angel

She turned back to the mirror, in just her underwear, bra, and a tank top. She flipped her hair, practicing looking sexy. She couldn't help but laugh at herself. If Kaden thought she was so good, she wanted to show him that wasn't all she could be. Having no experience being sexy, it made her feel awkward. But what did she have to lose?

Andy opened the bathroom door and knew immediately that she had accomplished her goal of catching Kaden's attention. His jaw dropped for a moment before he composed himself and Andy walked past him, trailing her hand over his chest. She glanced back over her shoulder and gave him her best devilish grin, biting her lip for effect. He caught her hand and pulled her close, putting his arms around her waist. He leaned down to kiss her, and she pulled away slightly.

"You need to stay focused," she murmured, brushing her lips against his. She felt him shudder under her touch and grinned in triumph.

"You are cruel," Kaden groaned, but he released her, and she made her way to the bed. Lying down on her side, she propped her head up with her hand. "You are trying to make my job impossible, aren't you?" Kaden strode across the room towards the bed and sat down on the edge.

"Maybe I'm just trying to put your mind to the test. I need to know that I can *truly* trust that you can keep me safe,"

Andy smirked, lazily running her finger up and down his arm.

"Maybe?" he cocked an eyebrow, grinning. She nodded, sitting up, and put her arms around his neck.

"I mean, I'm too *good* to have any other intentions, right?" she teased, and he laughed.

"Darling, you are borderline evil right now." He removed her arms from around him and stood up off the bed. Andy swung her legs over the side of the bed and watched as he paced across the room. *Darling...*the word echoed through her mind, but in another voice, not Kaden's.

Before Andy could think any more about it, an itch developed between her shoulder blades and she tried to scratch it, but it only made it worse. It changed to a burning sensation. Kaden noticed her discomfort and stopped his pacing.

"What's wrong?" His eyebrows stitched together in concern. Andy shook her head, unsure of what was happening, she stood from the bed, rolling her shoulders.

"My back," she said and could tell that Kaden thought she was still trying to seduce him, so he went back to his pacing. The burning sensation was steadily worsening. Andy cried out in pain as it peaked. She fell to her knees on the floor. Kaden rushed over to her.

"I don't feel anyone inside your head," he sounded confused.

Condemned Angel

"No," Andy gasped. "It's my back." She was trying to tug her shirt off because it felt like sandpaper against her back. Once it was off, she felt slightly better, but still in pain.

Finally, the pain ceased, and the burning subsided. Andy breathed deeply, trying to catch her breath again. There was one more burst of pain. Andy cried out, and it was gone, but she realized what was happening. Her wings spanned out on either side of her, white as snow. Kaden helped her to her feet.

"I guess there's no doubt now that you're an angel," he joked. There was a tension between them.

"I wasn't sure I would get my wings. Septimus said I might not since I'm only half-angel," Andy remarked, ogling her wings in the full-length mirror. Kaden seemed to tense up even more at the mention of Septimus.

"You should put on some clothes and get to bed. We have a lot of training to do tomorrow," he said, sitting down in the chair beside Andy's bed. Andy wrapped her arms around herself, suddenly self-conscious. She drew her wings into her back where they disappeared. It was strange knowing that they were there without being able to see them. Andy could almost feel their added weight, like wearing a backpack. She grabbed a slip from the dresser. Kaden stared at the wall and Andy wondered what was going through his mind.

Only minutes before Andy had been empowered, and now she felt denied and tossed aside. She turned off the light, leaving them in darkness until she turned on the lamp on the side table. She sat on the edge of the bed facing Kaden, who still refused to look at her.

"I'm not apologizing," she said, which caused Kaden to finally look at her.

"Why would you?" he asked, confused.

"I don't know, but I just feel like you're upset with me," Andy explained, and he shook his head.

"I'm not upset with you," he said.

"Then why are you acting like I offended you?"

"I'm sorry. I just thought you should get some rest before training tomorrow." Andy knew he was holding something back.

"That's not it. Is this about Septimus?" she pressed.

"Maybe," Kaden admitted. "Now that you have your wings, it seems like you're more angel than demon. What happens now if you see Septimus again?" Andy sighed, but she understood where he was coming from.

"While I'm almost positive that's not going to happen, it still won't change anything between us," she tried to convince him.

"How can you be sure? If you choose to side with the angels, wouldn't you rather *be* with an angel?"

"I don't care about the whole angels versus demons thing. I will do what I want, be with who I want, and do whatever I think is right, no matter which side I'm on." Andy watched him visibly relax. He reached his hand out for her to take.

"Come here," he waited for Andy to take his hand and then pulled her towards him and onto his lap. Andy crossed her legs over the arm of the chair and draped one arm over his shoulders. He held her a little tighter and her stomach did a flip. "I'm sorry," he murmured and then kissed her. "I shouldn't have told you to put clothes on," he joked, and they both laughed. "But I am sorry. I was a jerk."

"I might be able to forgive you." Andy leaned in and kissed him. She pulled away and a smile spread over her face. Kaden grinned too.

"You know, this thing..." he tugged on the hem of her silk nightgown, which had bunched up at the tops of her thighs. "Is equally as distracting as what you were, or weren't, wearing before," he smirked.

"Do you remember the first night you came to my room because I woke you up with my nightmares?" Andy asked, thinking back. Kaden nodded.

"You were wearing something like this, how could I forget?" he smirked.

"Why did you really come to my door – not just to tell me off for waking everyone up."

"I may have been hoping you'd invite me in, which it seems like I finally got what I was hoping for." He kissed her again. "But really, you should get some sleep. It will be easier for you to create blocks in your mind if you're not dozing off tomorrow."

"You think it's so easy, yet you didn't even notice that you're no longer alone," Andy said, her eyes widening in horror as she realized she was not the one doing the talking. Kaden lifted her off his lap and set her on her feet as he stood, his brow furrowed. "Surprised? I hope you enjoyed the spectacle earlier; I knew she could never kill Ronan, but it was so much fun to watch it all play out."

"How..." Kaden tried to speak, but Andy, or whoever was controlling her, interrupted him.

"You thought that was the work of the rogue demons? If you really expected Lucifer to ignore what they were doing any longer, you're all fools. We took care of them. But they made a great guise for us to hide behind while we closed in on you and your lovely companion."

"Andy," Kaden gazed into her eyes. "I need you to remember what I taught you before. Imagine a wall going up, blocking off your mind." Andy nodded, or at least she thought she did, still unsure of who was in control. She tried to do as he said and imagined the wall. She could feel Kaden's presence in her mind, but there was also the new presence.

I'll go of my own accord, darling. The voice spoke in her mind. *Just give Kaden one more message – Mummy and Daddy are back in town, and we'll be seeing you all very soon.* The presence slowly receded from Andy's mind and she let out a gasp as she felt herself regain control over her thoughts.

"You don't need to give me the message, I heard it too," Kaden said. He seemed worried, which scared Andy. "I should go tell Ronan." He started to walk towards the door, but Andy grabbed his arm.

"I'm going with you," she said, but he shook his head.

"You should stay here and get some rest." Andy laughed at the suggestion.

"Do you think I'm going to be able to sleep after this? I don't think you understand. I am *terrified* right now. Do you have any idea what it's like, not to know if you are in control of your own thoughts and actions?" Andy yelled, but she didn't care. "I feel more vulnerable than I've ever felt in my whole life, and there's nothing I can do about that until *you* help me learn how to shield my mind. So, either teach me right now or take me with you," she finished, crossing her arms over her chest, forcing back the tears that threatened to spill down her cheeks. A determination seemed to take over Kaden and he stepped towards Andy, taking both of her hands in his.

"I know how you feel, I lived that way for the first twelve years of my life... but you have the strength to keep everyone out, you just need to believe in yourself. You're constantly doubting how strong you are, but I feel it when I'm inside your head. You have both heavenly fire, and hellfire running through your veins," when he said this, it was as if he had lit a spark inside of Andy. She could feel the heavenly fire, or maybe it was the hellfire. It rose inside her chest and spread out to her extremities. Kaden grinned, clearly able to feel the warmth circulating through her.

"Hold onto that fire, you're going to need it."

14

The Cage

Septimus woke up at the crack of dawn. Everyone else still slept, besides Sera, who offered to take over the watch for Micah in the middle of the night.

Septimus glanced over at Bo and Micah curled up by the dying fire, across from Gabby and Nathan. It was strange how close he had grown to each of them. They had requested he not use their full names at the beginning of the trip, and he was still getting used to it.

He headed off to find Sera at the top of one of the tallest trees. He joined her there and they sat in silence for a while, keeping watch.

"Are you ready to begin training your mind today?" Septimus asked casually, and she nodded.

"When I was younger, I received a little bit of training from my parents on how to block my mind, but they were always more concerned with me learning combat," she said.

"That explains how you recovered on your own when we were stuck in that demon trap," Septimus recalled how she needed no coaching, unlike the others, to come out of the painful stupor that the demon trap caused. "As for your parents, that was the norm before the war. Only a few demons can get inside people's minds, it wasn't a common occurrence before."

"I know. I just thought I had a better handle on it than I did… the trap still brought me down in the first place which proves that I have a lot to work on."

"But you already have the foundation, so you should pick up the skill quickly. Maybe you can help me train the others. It will speed up the process and then hopefully we can move on sooner." Septimus looked at her, hopeful.

"Okay. I can try," she smiled, and it was contagious, Septimus smiled back.

"Here, let's try something now." Septimus readjusted in the tree so he could more easily face her. Sera did the same. "Do I have your permission to enter your mind?" Unlike demons, angels needed consent to enter someone's mind. Sera nodded in agreement. "Close your eyes." She did as she was told and laughed.

"I don't think this is the best way to keep watch," she joked, and Septimus laughed along with her.

"It's fine, I can still keep watch, just keep your eyes closed." Septimus glanced at their surroundings, making sure nothing had changed and then turned back to Sera. "Imagine there is a wall in your mind. This wall is protecting your mind from any outside influence." Her brow furrowed. "Stay focused. Now, I am going to try to enter your mind, do not let me in." Septimus took another glance around and then closed his eyes. He focused on trying to enter Sera's mind. At first, he could sense her thoughts and almost heard some of them, but then suddenly, he hit a wall. Her thoughts became shrouded, and he could no longer make out any of them. As he tried to push onward, he felt a push back and he was being pushed completely out of her mind. He opened his eyes and grinned. Sera opened her eyes as well and a triumphant smile transformed her face.

"That felt amazing. I haven't had to focus so hard in a while, though. It was kind of nice to have to work at something again." Her eyes lit up.

"You did well. I have faith that you will be able to keep out the demons just fine."

"It's like all of my training came back to me when I started pushing you out. I haven't practiced that in so long, but it felt natural. It felt good."

"I think you're ready to help me train the others now." Septimus glanced around one more time to make sure that there were no unwanted visitors in the vicinity, and then began his descent to the ground. "Come on, the others should be awake by now."

∞

Bo circled the small makeshift camp that they had created. Septimus and Sera stood in front of Micah, Gabby, and Nathan as they all sat on the fallen log. They were learning to better protect their minds from invasion. Septimus figured that Bo didn't need the skill and was unsure whether humans could even use it. It was less likely for the demons to invade his mind anyway since they had access to more power through the angels compared with Bo's human body, which had too many limitations.

In the meantime, Bo kept watch while the others trained. He had his sword in its sheath hanging around his waist, but he still felt exposed. He was no match for any demons or hellhounds, but he could at least warn the others if he saw them coming. So far, there had been no activity since they arrived. It almost seemed a little *too* quiet. Bo had not brought it up to anyone else, but he wondered if they were being watched. Like how the demons had watched Andy before taking her away.

Bo heard Septimus instructing the others. "Put up a wall in your mind – an impenetrable wall." Bo walked further out, expanding his circle.

Eventually, Bo reached the stream he and Micah had found the day before. He crouched down and placed his hands in the water. It was so refreshing in the heat. He cupped his hands, allowing the water to pool into them, and then splashed the water onto his face. It cooled him down, if only for a moment.

Bo continued walking, keeping his eyes sharp, and his ears alert for any sound. He started closing his circle back in around the camp, and the others came back within earshot. "Good, now push back, push me out of your mind," Sera encouraged them. "I can still hear your thoughts, Gabby, keep trying." Bo glimpsed them through the trees and saw Gabby had her eyes closed and seemed to be trying hard to do as Sera instructed.

Bo kept circling until, after a while, he heard Micah calling out to him.

"Bo!" he turned to see Micah jogging up to him.

"What's up?" Bo hadn't forgotten that Micah told him that he loved him, and more importantly, that Bo still hadn't said it back. Micah didn't seem to be worrying about it as much as Bo.

"We're taking a break – come get some lunch." Micah took Bo's hand as they walked back to the others. There was a pot of beans heating up over the fire. Bo stayed clear of it since it was hot enough without the heat radiating from the fire pit.

"So, how is training coming along?" Bo asked, surveying the rest of the group who lounged around the small clearing. They all appeared tired already.

"Not too bad," Septimus filled him in. "They are all picking up the skill quickly, which is good since we are going to need it starting tomorrow." Bo nodded in understanding. Tomorrow they were planning on continuing their search for Andy, which involved flying past more demon camps, and possibly more traps.

After lunch, the others returned to their training, and Bo resumed his circling around the camp. They continued like that for a few more hours, and then Septimus decided that the rest of the angels were ready to face what lay ahead. Bo was thankful that he no longer needed to walk in circles, and he collapsed against the fallen log.

"It's been a long day." Micah plopped down beside Bo and rested his head on Bo's shoulder. Training had drained Micah, and the others were all looking about the same. Septimus had gone up into the trees to keep watch for the rest of the day and through to the next morning, because it was not nearly as draining for him to train them all.

"Why was Septimus the only one trained to keep demons out of his mind?" Bo asked Micah.

"Before the war, it wasn't something we had to worry about," Micah shrugged. "Most demons don't even have the power to be able to invade other people's minds, only those who are born with demon blood already in them have the ability. Even then most don't use it, or can't. All angels have the ability if they learn how to use it. Though, we can't use it unless we have the permission of whoever's mind we are entering."

"And, what about your parents, where are they now? Were they at the camp?" Bo realized that he never saw Micah, or any of the others besides Septimus, with anyone resembling a parent.

"When the war began, all of the angels were separated and divided among different areas and camps depending on skills and age. That way, every area was equally protected," Micah yawned. "My parents were sent somewhere up North. I hear from them occasionally, but we aren't as close with our parents as humans are." Bo glanced down at Micah and realized his eyes were closed. His breathing deepened as he slowly drifted off to sleep. Bo didn't dare move for fear of waking him, so he leaned his head back and tried to fall asleep against the log. It was not the most comfortable position, but he fell asleep nonetheless.

∞

"I see." Ronan steepled his hands under his chin. Kaden and Andy stood in front of his throne. Kaden had just recounted the whole ordeal of his father taking over Andy's mind. Ronan's brow furrowed and he closed his eyes. He stayed like that for a moment and Andy turned to Kaden, who looked focused and then he cocked his eyebrow in question. Andy realized they must be talking in their minds. "I am putting Andromeda under a twenty-four-hour watch and she will be moved into the basement, there is too much access to the room upstairs," Ronan spoke only to Kaden even though she was standing there too.

"What will stop his parents from making me do something, or say something to convince you that it's really me and to let me leave the room or... I don't know." Andy tried to think of everything that could happen even if she were completely protected and secluded.

"You will be fully restrained and nothing that comes out of your mouth from this point on is to be trusted or believed to be your own words," Ronan spoke matter-of-factly. Andy gaped at him, but he continued. "I still expect you to train her on strengthening her mind as planned." Kaden nodded and Ronan seemed appeased.

"I feel like I should have some say in this! I shouldn't have to be put in a prison just to be kept safe. This is crazy!" Andy glanced from Kaden to Ronan, hoping to get through to one of them, but neither of them reacted to her.

Condemned Angel

"Cairn, Jackson," Ronan called, and they stepped into the room. "Please escort Andromeda to her new room. Kaden will be accompanying you as well, and he will begin her training as soon as possible." Cairn and Kaden nodded to each other. "Once they are settled, please find Zain."

Jackson grabbed Andy's arm and started pulling her towards the doorway. She looked back to Ronan who stared at the wall with a grimace on his face. Andy stumbled but Jackson kept her upright and didn't stop. Cairn walked along beside her.

"I don't need to be restrained yet," Andy complained, trying to shake Jackson off, but he held tight to her arm.

"You forget what your father said. We are not to trust anything you say," Jackson reminded her. Andy couldn't believe what was happening.

"This is for your own good, Andromeda." Cairn appeared more sympathetic, but he did nothing to help.

"Kaden, please. Tell him to loosen up a little." Andy tried to catch Kaden's eyes, but he stared straight ahead and said nothing. Her heart dropped. Did he really not trust her? She should at least be able to count on Kaden, who knew how to get inside her head and see that there was no one else there, but he was pulling away. Andy could still feel his presence inside her mind and so she reached out to him there.

Why are you just letting all of this happen? she reached out. He turned his head to the side, away from her, and gave no indication that he had heard her. But after a moment, she heard his voice enter her mind. *Just trust Ronan.*

How can I trust him? she thought, hoping he wouldn't leave her mind, but he didn't respond. She was on her own.

Jackson led Andy downstairs into the basement. Hardly anyone was out and about since it was so late. The few people that did pass by, avoided eye contact. Andy tried calling out to her parents, but Jackson clamped a hand over her mouth before she could make too much noise.

At the end of the hall, before the sitting area, Jackson opened the last door on the right. It revealed another staircase. He lightly pushed Andy in front of him, indicating that she should go down first. She took the first few steps hesitantly. Cairn remained at the top of the stairs, standing guard. He gave Andy an apologetic look as she passed by him.

Once Jackson, Kaden, and Andy reached the bottom of the stairs, she realized where they were. She recognized this room, and as she turned, she saw a cage like the one from her nightmares. The bars extended from the floor to the ceiling, but the cage was only big enough for one person. There were shackles nailed to the floor and wall. Andy turned to run instinctively but bumped into Jackson, who caught her wrists and steered her towards her new prison. Andy gave him a pleading look to no avail, so she turned to Kaden once more.

"Please don't do this," her voice shook with fear as she recalled the hellhounds growling at her in the cage in her nightmares. "Don't put me in there, I'll do anything, you can

Condemned Angel

strap me down to my bed, whatever, just don't put me in that cage." Her whole body quivered, and her knees buckled, but Jackson continued dragging her onward. She began sobbing, and finally, Kaden stepped in.

"Let me, Jack. I can handle this. You go bring Zain to Ronan." Jackson appeared skeptical but dropped Andy's arms and headed for the stairs. Andy wrapped her arms around her legs, hugging them to her chest. Kaden put his hand on her shoulder, but she shrugged it off.

"Don't touch me," she spat the words like venom. Jackson paused on the stairs to watch. He wanted to make sure Andy made it into the cage.

"This is the way it has to be, Andy. I'm sorry. There is nothing I can do; my hands are tied," Kaden said, and Andy choked out a laugh.

"I expected more from you. I thought you cared about me, but you're letting them put me into a *cage*, and you have no qualms about it." Andy sniffled and wiped away a stray tear. Hurt flickered in Kaden's eyes, but it only angered her more. He wasn't the one being forced into a cage.

"If there was any better way to keep you safe, you know I would do it," he tried to reason with her.

"If you truly believe this is the only way to keep me safe, then fine. Throw me in the cage. But I'm not helping you do it." Andy crossed her arms over her chest and stared him down. A change came over him and he lifted her into his arms and carried her into the cage. She was so shocked; she didn't fight back.

Before she knew it, she was back on the ground, while he placed her wrists and ankles into the shackles. Then he closed the door with a deafening thud. He turned the key in the lock and threw it into the opposite corner of the room. Andy didn't know how to react.

"Are you ready to practice closing off your mind?" he asked, but he still had the hard look on his face, and Andy wanted nothing to do with him. She closed her eyes and thought she could hear the hellhounds. Her heart began to race, and her breathing became more rapid. She tried to yank her arms to her sides instinctively to protect herself, but instead, she was brought back to reality by the pain of the shackles cutting into her wrists. Her eyes flew open and she felt blood trickling down her arm. She looked up to see the scores carved into her wrists. They started healing almost instantly, but the pain lingered.

"You should be more careful," was all Kaden had to say. Andy groaned in frustration and pain. "The sooner you learn to block your mind from other demons, the sooner you can get out of here."

"I don't know why I ever trusted you," Andy snarled. "I should have known this was all just another mess-around for you." Andy was shaking again, but this time with rage rather than fear.

"Mess-around?" Kaden seemed amused by this.

Condemned Angel

"You don't care about me, you never did," she clarified for him. His amusement faded away, but he was unreadable now. The heavenly fire burned inside of Andy and she felt it flowing through her veins. She clenched her fists and the fire surged towards them. Her hands were suddenly free, the shackles melted away. Andy grinned with satisfaction and then focused, sending the fire down to her ankles which started to melt the shackles there. She stood up and took a few steps towards the cage door. Andy's wings unfurled from her back, sticking out between the bars on either side of the cage.

"The bars are forged in hellfire; your heavenly fire won't be able to melt them," Kaden pointed out, seemingly unfazed.

"You said yourself that I have both heavenly fire *and* hellfire running through my veins, so who's to say that I can't do anything?" Andy challenged, smirking, letting her anger take over her whole body. Power coursed through her and it felt amazing.

"I can't let you do that, Andy. I'm sorry." Andy felt his presence in her mind growing and she realized he was trying to control her and stop her from breaking out of the cage. Andy used the full might of her power and pushed him out of her mind, feeling a little empty once he was gone for the first time in hours. But she also finally felt like herself again and she relished in it.

"Sorry, Kaden, but I can't let you stop me." Andy placed her hands on the bars of the cage and released all the fire she felt surging through her into them. The bars disintegrated and Andy drew her wings back in so she could fit through the gap in the bars. Instead of being afraid, or at least a little worried, Kaden grinned, which confused Andy.

"It worked," he laughed. "I knew you could do it on your own." He was happy for her.

"What do you mean 'it worked?'" A realization dawned on her.

"We were never going to keep you in this cage, Andy. We just needed to get you to realize your own potential, and the only way Ronan and I knew how to do that, was to get you mad," Kaden explained, looking smug. Andy took a step towards him and slapped him. She felt a zing as her hand hit his face with the heavenly fire still coursing through her, and it left a red mark. "I deserved that I guess." He rubbed his cheek, but he still smiled.

"I can't believe you did this to me." Andy still shook with rage, and now hurt and disbelief.

"You *asked* me to help you. You know you can push people out of your mind now. You said it yourself, you can do anything," he pointed out. "Here, let's try it again." Andy felt his mind pressing against hers, but she put up a wall and blocked him out. It seemed so simple now. "See! It worked!"

"Fine. It worked. I hope that's worth it for you because I'm done. Whatever we were, it's done." He didn't react as Andy turned and walked upstairs.

"You're still under twenty-four-hour watch!" He called after her as if that were the most pressing issue at the moment. Tears sprung into her eyes. Cairn was gone from the top of the stairs. Andy found her parents' room and woke her mom.

"Can we talk in my room?" Andy whispered to her, trying not to wake Wayne. Angeline nodded and followed Andy out the door.

Andy barely made it back to her room before breaking down. She told her mom everything; what happened with Samson, Kaden's parents, Ronan, Kaden, and finished with her most recent traumatic experience.

"Oh, honey." Angeline pulled her in for a hug. "Why didn't you come to me sooner?" her voice was thick with worry.

"I didn't want to worry you, and..." Andy turned away, "I didn't want you to think less of me, thinking I was cheating on Septimus with Kaden," she admitted, feeling her face redden.

"I could never think less of you. I love you so much, Andromeda, you and your brother, no matter what choices you make." Angeline wiped away Andy's tears and smoothed her hair away from her face. "You can come to me with anything."

"I know. It just all happened so quickly..." Andy sighed. "But I guess none of the stuff with Kaden matters now anyway. What he did to me, I could never forgive him for."

"I'm so sorry about their tactics. I would have had something to say about it had Ronan consulted me, but he never does," her annoyance was clear. Andy wondered about their relationship before, had Ronan been more open with Angeline? Or had he always been closed off? There were still so many questions she had.

"I'm glad I can protect my mind now, but I wish they hadn't done it in such a traumatizing way. Ronan and Kaden *know* I had nightmares about a similar room. You told me yourself that Kaden could see my nightmares while I was in the angel camp."

"I know, sweetie. They don't have quite the same morals as we do."

"That's no excuse." Andy crossed her arms.

"I know. So, tell me more about you and Kaden. How did that happen?" Angeline changed gears, confusing Andy.

"What does it matter? I can't be with him now,"

"Can't be, or don't want to be?" Andy gave her mom a look of pure disbelief.

"He forcibly put me in a cage! How could I ever get past that?" she exclaimed, wondering what her mom's idea of romance must be. She did fall for Ronan, after all, who was the mastermind behind the cage plan.

"I understand, I just want to make sure that you aren't going to regret your decision somewhere down the road. I am all for you staying away from Kaden, he reminds me so much of your father when he was that age..." Angeline drifted away for a moment, lost in a memory, and then came back to herself. "But you told me he was doing what he thought would keep you safe. It sounds to me like he does care about you. He's just not showing it in the same way that Septimus would, in your mind," Angeline tried to explain, and Andy shook her head.

"You're right, Septimus would never lock me in a cage. Did Ronan ever lock you in a cage? Is that what made you fall for him?" Andy countered, unsure how her mom was still on Kaden's side.

"No, but Ronan's parents weren't trying to get into my mind and use me," Angeline sighed. "I know you think I am disregarding the hurt that Kaden and your father caused you, but I am only thinking of the pain they have saved you, and me, from by helping you realize your full potential. Don't get me wrong, if either of them ever hurt you again, I will make sure that they hurt one thousand times worse, but in this one particular instance, I am letting it go because I can't lose you. It would kill me." Tears spilled over Angeline's eyes and Andy took her hand to try to comfort her.

"I understand, but that doesn't mean I'm going running back to Kaden now." Andy did see her point, and as much as she hated to admit it, maybe Kaden and Ronan were right to trigger her into reaching her full potential, but she wasn't ready to forgive them just yet.

"Of course not. I don't expect you to. I want you to do whatever feels right, I just needed you to understand where they were coming from. As unfathomable as it is, your father loves you." Angeline squeezed Andy's hand. "Can I see your wings?" she changed the subject, which Andy was grateful for. She stood and unfurled her wings. Angeline's eyes gleamed with pride as she viewed them.

"My baby finally has her wings." She smiled brightly and Andy couldn't help but smile back. It felt so amazing to let her wings free from her back.

"What about your wings, Mom?" Andy asked and Angeline glanced away.

"They were taken from me when I chose to be with your father," she admitted, almost looking embarrassed.

"I'm so sorry, Mom. I had no idea." Andy pulled her wings back in and sat down beside her mom.

"It's fine." Angeline placed her hand over Andy's, reassuring her. "I never told anyone, not even Ronan. I didn't use them that much around Ronan anyway, so it wasn't unusual to him that I never used them after I decided to be with him. It all happened so quickly, but I made my choice knowing that there would be consequences." She lifted her head, her eyes gleaming. Andy had never realized how much her mom had given up to be with Ronan and to have her and Jason.

Condemned Angel

"Why did I get wings, if you don't have yours?"

"You wouldn't be punished for my choice. Once you make your own decision, then you will either be allowed to keep your wings or have them taken away. Just like your brother," Angeline explained.

"Jason had wings?" Andy had wondered whether Jason had received his wings, or if they just never showed up.

"Yes, he received them before he chose to side with the demons. Unfortunately, they were taken away from him. It's a very painful experience and I wish I had been there for him, but I was too caught up in my own distress because of his decision." Her guilt was plain on her face, and Andy hugged her, trying to comfort her again.

"You can still be there for him now. He needs you," Andy told her, but she looked unsure.

"You should get some rest." Angeline stood and kissed the top of Andy's head. "I'll talk to you tomorrow." Andy watched her leave, and when she opened the bedroom door, Andy noticed a shadow in the hallway. "Marcus," Angeline nodded to the figure, and then shut the door behind her. Andy assumed Marcus was the demon assigned to her watch for the night.

Andy curled up underneath the blankets. It didn't take her long to fall asleep, and by some miracle, she had no anxiety and no nightmares.

15

The Traitor

Jackson and Cairn led Kaden and Andromeda out of the room. Anger rose inside of Ronan, igniting the hellfire in his veins, as he began to understand what had happened. With all the precautions and extra measures he had taken to be sure he would know when Gregor and Mara came within fifty miles of the mansion, they slipped past his defenses. That could only mean one thing.

He knew there was at least one person in this house who should have warned him about Gregor and Mara's presence, and he failed to do so. He would be held accountable for his actions.

Ronan couldn't sit and wait for Cairn to bring Zain to him. He strode out of his throne room and down the hall. Making his way down the stairs to the basement, he could hear Andromeda's protests coming from the dungeon. She would probably hate him for the actions being taken to help her, but it was a cost he was willing to pay to ensure she was safe and able to defend herself.

Refocusing on the task at hand, Ronan knocked on the first door on the left and the door almost immediately swung open. He stood face to face with Harvey. He looked shocked to see Ronan standing on the other side of the door at first, but he quickly composed himself and bowed slightly.

"Sir, to what do I owe this visit?" his voice trembled and Ronan smirked. He would never get over the sheer power and authority he held. It truly made everything else he had to go through worth the hassle. It starkly contrasted his life before taking over for his father, when everyone thought he would amount to nothing because he had fallen for an angel. Thankfully, his father knew better than the rest of them.

"I am looking for Zain," he told Harvey, who appeared confused.

"He told me that you had assigned him to another camp, Sir. He left this morning." Harvey's confusion turned to fear as if he himself had done something wrong. Ronan rested a hand on Harvey's shoulder to try to calm his nerves, but it seemed to only make him antsier.

"Thank you, Harvey. That's all I needed to know." Ronan nodded to him and walked back up the stairs. He remained calm for the benefit of all the sleeping bodies. He knew for sure now what had occurred.

Zain had betrayed him. He had been sucked in by Gregor and Mara's charm and decided to realign his allegiance to them. Ronan had put his faith and trust in Zain, and he had completely shattered that. Ronan imagined that Gregor promised Zain protection in exchange for the betrayal. What Zain didn't realize was that there was no such thing as protection from Ronan. He controlled all the demons in North America. Gregor and Mara were the exceptions, along with a few others who were specially recruited by Lucifer. But Zain was Ronan's. He smirked, thinking of his plan for him.

Let Zain think that he had made a clean getaway. Let him believe he was safe. When he least expected it, Ronan would be there, hellhounds and all, to reclaim him and send him where he belonged. Lucifer would be thrilled to have a new being to torture for eternity.

Ronan stepped outside and let out a long, low whistle. He heard crashing through the woods off to his right and smirked. A moment later, two hellhounds crouched in front of him, awaiting a command. Ronan could almost see the tortured souls beneath their transformed and mutated shells. No one truly knew what they were signing up for when they promised their soul to Lucifer, some ended up losing more than they bargained for.

"Find Zain. Watch and wait," Ronan gave them the simple command, and they took off, bounding over the gate and on past his line of vision. He knew they would find Zain quickly, and would sit and wait until Ronan gave them the order to attack. Ronan turned to go back inside and closed the front door behind him. Jackson and Cairn were walking towards him.

"Sir?" Cairn looked to him for an explanation, he had obviously found out that Zain was not where he should be as well.

"I'm taking care of it, Cairn. Not to worry. Resume your posts." Ronan strode towards the kitchen, while Cairn and Jackson made their way back to his throne room to stand guard outside the double doors.

Of course, now that Zain was gone, Gregor and Mara would be looking for another inside man. Ronan must keep his eyes and ears open for any whisper of betrayal. He would not be fooled again.

He felt Kaden's mind pressing against his own. Ronan allowed him to pass his wall, but only to communicate. He trusted no one to enter his mind fully, not even Cairn.

It's done. She's ready. There was a sense of melancholy to his voice. Ronan knew that though Andromeda was now armed to protect herself, Kaden had cost himself her trust.

Ronan felt no guilt for his decision to have Kaden be the one to put her in that cage. It had to be him for the plan to work. Ronan didn't doubt Andromeda's ability to forgive, and he knew that her anger would not last.

Thank you, Ronan responded. *I will send Marcus to keep an eye on her. Take some time for yourself and get some rest.* Ronan closed his mind to Kaden and grabbed an apple off the kitchen counter.

∞

Andy woke to a knock on her door. She opened it to find a demon with shoulder-length blonde hair standing there with his arms crossed. She recognized him as the demon who had helped with the rescue of Wayne and Lindy. He had a similar chiseled body to Kaden, but he was a little shorter. Andy was beginning to think that Ronan had purposefully chosen only muscular, attractive demons to live in this house. Which, she guessed, on his part, was smart since it probably made it easier to lure in humans for their souls, and all the better to defend the premises.

"Good morning, Marcus," Andy greeted him, still half-hidden behind the door.

"Ronan would like for you to join him for breakfast," he said.

"Of course he would. Just give me a few minutes to get ready." Andy closed the door and hurried to her bureau to grab some clothes. She stuck with her familiar outfit from Sera since it brought her comfort and pulled her hair up into a high ponytail. She went back to the door and found Marcus in the same position she'd left him.

"Good, let's go," he said, turning away from Andy to walk down the hall to the stairs.

When they reached the dining room, Ronan already sat at the head of the table. Plates were set up just for the two of them and food set out on the table. Andy took her seat to Ronan's left.

"Where does everyone else eat when you have breakfast in here?" Andy asked, curious as to how all forty or so of the other demons were supposed to be able to have breakfast when Ronan decided to have a sit-down meal.

"There is a buffet set up outside in the gardens for them," he explained. "How are you feeling?"

"If you are referring to what happened last night, pretty pissed off still," Andy snapped and he smirked, causing her blood to boil.

"But it worked, did it not?" Andy rolled her eyes and put fruit onto her plate. "Do not blame Kaden for his role in it all, it was my idea. I planted it into his head while the two of you were talking with me last night. He agreed that it would probably do the trick, and so it did."

"Next time you could at least try not to be so cruel about it. You *know* I had nightmares about that room since

Kaden was messing around in my head while I was with the angels," Andy snapped.

"You're right. Knowing that you had nightmares about a similar room, I knew it would further trigger your emotions that would lead you to uncover your abilities. Which, I admit, are even greater than I imagined. You remind me so much of your mother when she was your age," he smiled.

"She's the only reason I'm even talking to you right now," Andy told him. "She convinced me that what you and Kaden did was in my best interest, even if it was cruel." Ronan looked surprised.

"Your mother is a smart woman. We did not always see eye to eye, but she understood where I was coming from. That is one of the many things that made me fall in love with her," he admitted.

"Do you still love her?" Andy asked, assuming that the reason he disliked Wayne so much was because he was jealous of him.

"We have both changed in many ways, but I will always love your mother." Ronan paused for a moment, thinking, and then continued talking. "Enough about me. Let's test out your new skills." His mind pressed against her Andy's. It felt different than Kaden's, a little heavier somehow, but less invasive than Gregor's mind. Andy easily pushed him out with the wall Kaden taught her how to create. Then she felt another mind pressing in, along with Ronan's, presumably Marcus'. Andy's focus switched, and she felt Ronan's mind slipping past her defenses. She imagined putting up blinders on both sides of her mind and forced them both out. The pressure dissipated, and Ronan grinned.

"Nicely done," he clapped his hands once. "I don't doubt that you will be able to keep Gregor and Mara out now." This brought Andy some relief. "Just keep practicing and you'll only grow stronger."

"Do you think that Kaden's mind is strong enough to keep them out?" Andy asked, recalling how he was unable to keep Gregor out of her mind.

"Truthfully, I'm not sure. Kaden has one of the strongest minds I know, but his father is also a very powerful man. Only time will tell." Ronan's face reflected the worry that Andy felt.

"Where is he now? I want to talk to him." Andy was ready to possibly forgive him, so long as he had a good apology ready for her.

"He's out with a legion. I wanted him to be your guard after resting, but he requested to go out with Lily's legion this morning instead," Ronan said, causing Andy to cringe. "Marcus is equally capable of protecting you, though, now that you can keep people out of your mind on your own."

"When will they return?" Andy kept her voice steady, even though it irked her that Kaden chose to go out with Lily rather than stay close to her.

"Probably sometime this afternoon. Jason is around here somewhere if you need some company, though Marcus will be with you as well. I, unfortunately, have a few meetings to attend at other camps today, or I would offer my company." Ronan stood, pushing his chair back from the table, and Andy realized that was her cue to finish up.

"I'll go find Jason." Andy took her last bite of breakfast and then left the dining room, Marcus trailing along behind her. As she walked towards the living room, she heard Jason talking with someone. Andy rounded the corner and saw him standing with Cory and another demon she had not met yet. The first thing Andy noticed was his bright red hair cropped close to his head. He was another demon with the tall, muscular build that seemed to be the factor that brought them all to this mansion.

"Hey, Jase," Andy said as he noticed her.

"Hey, Andy. This is my other roommate, Travis. He just got back from visiting another camp up north." He pointed to the redhead, and Andy nodded to him. "Trav, Cory, and I were just about to go for a walkabout, but we can catch up later," Jason offered.

"Yeah, that's fine," Andy said. "Unless; can I join you?" Jason looked to Cory and Travis and they both shrugged.

"I don't see why not." Jason waved Andy on as they all left the room. She followed along behind them with Marcus at her side. They walked down the front steps towards the fountain and Olivia appeared from around the side of the house. Andy watched as Jason saw Olivia and tripped over his own feet. His face reddened as he waved to her and she waved back, strolling over to them.

"What a crew!" Olivia greeted them. "I just sent the hellhounds to patrol the grounds, if that's what you were planning on doing."

"I- uh, yeah. Thanks," Jason fumbled over his words and Andy couldn't help but giggle. She noticed Marcus smirking as well.

"Well, I'm not just sitting inside doing nothing all day. Come on, Trav, let's take a drive." Cory started walking in the direction of the car lot, and Travis followed. Cory turned back, continuing to walk backward. "Wanna tag along, Andy?"

"Um, no thanks," she said. It didn't seem like a good idea for her to leave the grounds, even if she was able to keep people out of her mind.

"Suit yourself." Cory turned back around, and they disappeared into the trees.

"Do you want to take a walk, Liv?" Jason asked, and she nodded. They left Andy standing alone with Marcus in front of the fountain.

"Well. That was short-lived," Andy sighed, taking a seat on the edge of the fountain. Marcus sat down beside her. "I guess I never thought that Jason would have found someone here."

"He has been trying to win over Olivia since day one," Marcus chuckled. "She clearly likes him too, but he has yet to step up and ask her out. It's almost like a reality show around here some days."

"Is there anyone that Cory likes?" Andy asked, hoping that he would have someone to keep him away from her.

"Besides you? Nothing serious. Lily and Olivia are the only other ones here who are the same age as all you kids," Marcus reminded Andy of her dad when he talked like that.

"How long have you been working for Ronan?" she asked, and he laughed.

"Too long. Before he was even a twinkle in his mother's eye, I worked for his father," he said, and Andy gaped at him. She would never guess he was that old. "It's the same for Cairn and Jackson as well. We've been through it all with your father."

"That's crazy," Andy said.

"Enough about me. How about you, you don't seem happy to be reunited with Cory," he commented, and Andy shook her head.

"That obvious, huh?" she laughed bitterly. "Word must travel fast around here that we used to date."

"Unfortunately, yes. There are no secrets when you live in one house with forty other people. Not to mention Cory has no filter. He let everyone know the situation."

Andy groaned. "Of course he did."

Condemned Angel

"I was a therapist at one time in my life, a long time ago, in between working for Ronan's father and him. If you ever need to talk about anything, I will be happy to listen. And don't worry, I still stick to the doctor-patient confidentiality thing most of the time, so long as it doesn't impact my people in any way, your secrets are safe with me."

"Thank you. I appreciate that," Andy said. "Can I ask you for some advice?" Marcus nodded for her to go on. "Kaden and I just started dating, kind of. And, then last night...well you know what happened. He betrayed me," Tears welled in her eyes, and a lump formed in her throat.

"You would like my advice on whether you should forgive him?" Marcus filled in, and Andy nodded. "Well, that depends. In any normal, human relationship, I would say not. But this is far from any normal human relationship."

"I know, but it didn't hurt any less..."

"If you're hurt, let yourself feel that. Don't discount your feelings to placate anyone else. I want you to think about what came out of last night's transgressions, and whether you can accept that he did what he thought would *save* you."

"You sound like my mom," Andy choked out, laughing.

"Good. Your mother is a smart woman," he smiled. "Now, if you think you can forgive him and want to forgive him, then do it for yourself, not for anyone else. After that, you have to decide whether you can trust him again." Andy thought about it and wasn't sure whether she would be able to do that. She did want to forgive Kaden, and she still cared about him. But she wasn't sure if there was any trust left after what he had done.

"Thank you, Marcus." It was quiet between them for a few minutes, until Marcus spoke again.

"Now, don't be upset, but Kaden did mention that you were having some anxiety…"

"Of course he did."

"Is it still as bad as it was when you first arrived?"

Andy sighed. "No. It's been better since Kaden had been helping me."

"That's good."

"Though, there are some things that are still bothering me…" she paused, but Marcus just sat silently waiting. "One of my memories that keeps coming up…" she shuddered, and Marcus nodded for her to go on. She took a deep breath. "When a man was holding a gun against my head…" Andy couldn't bring herself to recount the rest of the story.

"I was there that day, Andy," Marcus said what Andy had already suspected. "That man was originally planning on just killing you both. I was able to change his mind to let you go. From a distance, it's hard to completely change someone's mind. It was easier to lead him to a similar, but different path."

"Wow, that makes me feel so much better," Andy choked out, her voice thick with sarcasm.

"There is something you need to know, that may help. You wouldn't have died then, Andy. You are an angel and a demon. He would have had to kill you with a weapon forged in either hellfire or blessed with holy water. Even then, who knows if it would work. There haven't been too many others like you."

"I guess that *does* make me feel better," Andy admitted. Knowing that her fear was irrational only helped slightly, the original gut-wrenching terror that she had experienced in that moment was still too vivid to just push aside.

Andy dropped the subject of her traumas. They spent a few hours making small talk in the garden, getting to know each other. Marcus even shared a few stories about her parents. Eventually they returned to the living room to eat lunch while Andy waited for either Jason or Kaden to return.

Kaden and Lily were the first ones to walk through the front door. They were laughing about something and Andy felt her jealousy flaring up even though she knew it was unwarranted.

"Here we go," Andy took a deep breath and stood. Kaden noticed her before she reached him and Lily. He seemed unsure of how to react, so he remained neutral. Lily greeted Andy casually and had enough sense to leave them alone.

"Did you enjoy your outing?" Andy asked, not sure if that was the best way to begin their conversation, but it was already out there, so she let it go.

"I guess. Are you here to reprimand me some more? Because I stand by my decision to go along with Ronan's plan." He was already on the defensive, which Andy knew was not a good start.

"I have a right to be upset." Andy was about to go off on him, but she reeled herself back in and took a deep breath. "But no. I wanted to say...I understand why you did it, and I'm not over it, but you did what you thought was best." It was hard for her to say, she was not usually one to admit that she was wrong. Kaden seemed to know this, and he looked surprised.

"Well, I'm glad that you can see it from my point of view." He was still on edge. "I'm surprised you didn't have something to say about me going out with Lily today."

"*Should* I have something to say about that?" Andy crossed her arms, unable to believe he was trying to push her right after she just admitted that she was wrong.

"I don't know," he crossed his arms over his puffed-out chest, and Andy cracked.

"Why are you doing this?" She threw her hands up in exasperation and he didn't respond. He regarded her as if she were the one being difficult. "Say something! Why do you keep doing this? I am trying to make things right, and you keep trying to push me away." It was his turn to crack now.

"Don't you realize, Andy? We shouldn't be together! If Gregor made anything clear, it's that I am putting you in danger just being near you. He's using you to get to me. I am trying not to be selfish with you! You make it impossible... I just...," he paused, his breath finally catching up with him. "I can't bear the thought of losing you because I was too selfish to stay away from you."

"I can take care of myself. Ronan even tried to get into my head this morning, and I blocked him and Marcus out at the same time," Andy said. "You don't need to worry about me anymore. I'm more worried about you, honestly."

"I don't want you to worry about me. I'll be fine. Gregor may be strong, but I learned to block him out a long time ago," Kaden explained.

"Good. I'm willing to give us another try –"Andy said, and Kaden smiled. "But I can't make any promises that this will work. You broke my trust last night, and you're going to need to rebuild that."

"Fine. I can do that."

"I have Marcus on my twenty-four-hour watch, but maybe you should relieve him of his duty for a little while. He's been with me since last night, I can only imagine how tired he probably is," Andy smirked

"Marcus!" Kaden called out to him, and he appeared in the doorway to the living room. "I think I can take over for a little while. Go get some sleep." Marcus nodded and headed towards the basement stairs. Just as Kaden and Andy were about to leave the entryway, Jason, Olivia, Trav, and Cory, came strolling through the front door. Andy felt a wave of nausea wash over her.

"Trav, you're back," Kaden grinned at him. Andy tensed as Cory noticed her holding hands with Kaden.

"Cory, there is something..." Andy began.

Cory interrupted. "So, Kaden's good enough to be your side piece? Am I not damaged enough for you? Not enough daddy issues, or girl problems?"

Everything that happened next was a blur. Kaden had Cory pinned up against the wall and was hissing something into his ear. Andy couldn't make it out over the roaring in her ears and Jason and Travis yelling at Kaden to let Cory go.

Olivia's voice broke through them all. "Kaden, let him go." He gave her an incredulous look, but then dropped Cory. "Get out of here, Cory." Cory paused, sneering at Andy, and then retreated outside. Andy debated whether she should go after him, but her guilt won out and she followed.

Cory paced in front of the fountain.

"Cory, I – "

"Save your breath. I know why you're out here. I don't want your pity."

"That's not what – "

"You think I don't know what everyone thinks about me? Demon through and through. No matter how hard I try, I can't control it...not like Kaden."

Condemned Angel

"Cory, just let me talk for a second, okay? I'm sorry. I should have been more honest with you before. I had been dating Septimus, but since I've been here, things have changed. *I've* changed. I'm not the same person I was two weeks ago, let alone all those months ago when I knew you," Andy leaned against the fountain, taking a deep breath. "I'm sorry I don't feel the same way about you anymore."

"I'm sorry, too. I'm sorry that you gave up on us so easily. I thought we could become close again," he scowled, "but I was wrong." Andy could tell there was going to be no getting through to Cory. He was not a reasonable person, and she saw that now more than ever.

"I hope someday you can forgive me," Andy turned to go inside.

∞

"What is she doing?" Kaden looked worried as Andy ran out the door after Cory.

"Don't worry about her. She can take care of herself," Olivia reassured him. "I'm worried about *you*."

"Why does everyone keep saying that? I'm fine."

Olivia shook her head. "No, Kaden, you're not. Our parents are yet again threatening someone you care about."

"And?"

"And it's okay for you to be upset, or worried. But it's not okay to take out your anger on Cory. He gets in enough trouble on his own," Olivia smirked.

Kaden scoffed. "That wasn't about me, that was about Andy."

"Sure, Cory was pointing out all of *your* flaws, and you attacked him for *Andy's* sake. That makes sense."

"Your sister has a point," Jason chimed in. Kaden cast a withering stare at him, he put his hands up in surrender. "Just saying."

Olivia shooed Jason away and turned back to Kaden. "You don't have to talk to me about it, but you should talk to someone. Andy, Jason, Marcus, anyone. Marcus helped *me* get through my abandonment issues, for the most part."

"I'm not you, Liv. You were lucky that our parents left you here." Kaden had always been a little jealous of Olivia for that reason. He wondered why he had been the one his parents chose to torture.

"You keep telling yourself that. Our parents love you in their twisted way, and still want you to join them. They've never even said a word to me. Not even when they were working for Ronan. It was as if I didn't exist," her voice cracked on the last word. Kaden had never realized how much his sister had been hurt by their parents. He had always considered her to be the one they loved more because they gave her up instead of forcing her into a life of horror and mistreatment.

Condemned Angel

He reached out and took her hand. "Liv, the only reason they want me to join them is because they can't stand that they wasted so many years training me to be just like them, and they failed. They want me to give up my soul so I can become just like them. That's not love, that's narcissism."

Olivia nodded. "I know. I still think you should talk to someone, though."

Kaden sighed. "Fine. I'll think about it," he caved, and Olivia smiled.

16
The Game

As Andy passed by Cory to head inside, he grabbed her arm.

"You can't just walk away from me," his voice was hard and his eyes distant.

Andy smiled. "Yes, I can, Cory. And if you ever touch me again, I will make sure you never step foot back in this house." She let the fire burning through her veins send the message. He leaped back and Andy saw the pain in his eyes as he looked down at his hand, now bright red from the burn.

Condemned Angel

Andy went inside, leaving Cory behind. Kaden waited for her just outside of the sitting room.

"You were right, you can take care of yourself. I was wrong to ever doubt you." He took her hand. Andy's heart raced, and the adrenaline from finally standing up for herself coursed through her.

Kaden and Andy went upstairs to her room. Andy stopped before going inside.

"I just need a minute alone," she said.

Kaden nodded, and Andy closed the door behind her, slumping down to the floor. Just as quick as it had come, the adrenaline left her body and she felt exhausted. She wished Bo were there to talk to. She missed him more at that moment than she had all week. She had been so busy; he had been pushed to the back of her mind. Talking with Marcus earlier had reminded her of her talks with Bo. A tear escaped her eye and rolled down her cheek.

If Bo had been there with her, she wondered how things would have been different. Would she have fallen for Kaden? Would Bo have kept her focused on Septimus? He would know what to do about Cory, too. Andy hated thinking that Cory would never forgive her, even though she didn't want anything to do with him anymore.

Your mind is so interesting. You care so deeply about so many people, it weakens you. Gregor spoke in Andy's mind, but she had no sense that he controlled her.

How are you doing that? I blocked my mind off; you can't get inside anymore.

You let your walls down, worrying so much about other people. I can't get inside, but I can talk to you. I may not be able to hear your thoughts anymore, but I know enough to know what haunts you at night, and during the day. Andy could almost hear him smirking. *Congratulations on your achievement. It took Kaden years to learn to do what you accomplished in one night. He thinks his mother and I didn't know what he was doing, but we played along because we wanted him to become stronger.*

What do you want? Why are you even talking to me? Andy knew there must be some motive other than to reminisce.

Oh fine. I admit it, I have a burning question for you. How does it feel knowing that if you choose to be with Kaden, your bright shiny wings and angel abilities will be ripped away, and if you choose to side with angels, you'll probably never see Kaden again?

We're done talking. I won't let you get into my head.

I think that's exactly what I just did. Think about it. Goodbye... for now.

There was finally silence in her mind. She wouldn't let his words get to her. Who was to say that she even had to make a choice? Maybe Ronan would let her remain neutral, or maybe she could convince Kaden to run away from it all with her... she shook her head to clear it. No need to worry about it yet anyway.

Condemned Angel

Andy pushed herself up off the floor and opened her door. Kaden stood guard outside and she couldn't help but smile when she saw him.

"You can come in if you want." She held out her hand for him to take.

"I have to stay out here to keep watch. Who is going to protect you if I'm in there, getting distracted?" he smirked. "Do you not remember what happened the last time I let my guard down?"

Andy shuddered. "Okay, fine. Though, I feel like I'm perfectly capable of protecting myself."

"I don't doubt it, but orders are orders," Kaden said, and Andy knew he was right. Ronan would not allow Andy to be unguarded until Kaden's parents were dealt with.

That night, after dinner, Kaden went back to his room to take a nap, while Marcus resumed his post outside of Andy's room. There was a knock at her door.

"It's me," Jason said.

"Come in," Andy called back to him, and he opened the door, stepping inside and closing the door behind him. "What's up, Jase?" He sat next to Andy on her bed.

"I just needed to get out of my room," he sounded annoyed. "Cory and Trav are playing a drinking game, and I'm not in the mood for their crap tonight."

"What about Kaden? Isn't he still in there?" Andy asked, wondering if he got to take his nap or not.

"Yeah, he was still passed out when I left. He'll probably be able to sleep for a little while longer. They don't get too obnoxious until they're drunk," Jason said. Andy nodded in understanding; she'd seen Cory drunk.

"So, what do you want to do?"

"Well, first I wanted to say that I'm sorry for trying to keep Kaden away from you. Dad put it in my head that he was only going to be putting you in danger, but I've known Kaden for a while now, and I know how skilled he is. He taught me everything I know. If anyone can keep you safe, it's him."

"It's okay, I understand why you did it. But I can take care of myself. I don't need you, or Kaden to keep me safe, I can do that on my own." Jason looked like he didn't quite believe her. So, she felt the need to demonstrate. Walking to the middle of the room, Andy allowed her wings to unfurl from her back. She picked up her sword from beside her bed and needed to focus only for a moment before it was engulfed in flames.

Jason laughed. "Alright, point taken." There was a hint of longing in his eyes when he observed her wings. Andy had forgotten what their mom had told her about Jason's wings being taken away and she felt insensitive. She put the sword down and pulled her wings back in. "I guess you did get your wings!"

Condemned Angel

"Yeah, just the other night." Andy looked away sheepishly.

"I remember when I got mine. It was before the demons brought me here. Mom was still hiding our real identities from us." His repressed anger was coming to the surface, and Andy understood because she had felt it, too.

"Did you understand what was happening? Or had you already guessed what you were?" Andy asked, curious because she had never really had any kind of suspicion about what she was, just that she felt different.

"It was scary. I had no idea what was happening. The extreme vision came first, and I thought I was going crazy. Then came the voices in my head, and I *knew* I was crazy. I tried to talk to Dad about it, but he always seemed preoccupied with some project or another. When my wings appeared, I pieced it all together. I thought back to those stories that mom used to tell us when we were little, about the angels and their adventures. I always thought they were made up, but in that moment, I knew they were real," Jason sighed. "I don't have my wings anymore, but I'm sure you already knew that."

"Mom told me," Andy said awkwardly. "She lost her wings too; did you know that?"

"I guessed as much, though she never told me herself. She hasn't talked to me much since I chose my side." His eyes held sadness, but they hardened. Andy knew that he was pushing his feelings back down, just as she did when they were too hard to confront.

"Did it hurt?" Andy asked, and he seemed confused, and then he realized what she was asking.

"It was the worst pain I've ever experienced in my life." The pain was clear on his face as he remembered the day it happened. "I came back from helping with my first legion and felt like I was making a difference. Like I finally had a purpose. I was alone in the garden thinking about my decision to join the demons when it happened. I could have sworn my wings were literally ripped out of my skin. It burned and itched, and I could barely stand it. I passed out for a few minutes, and when I came to, they were gone." His shoulders slumped in defeat. "Just like that, I was no longer an angel."

"I'm so sorry, Jase. I should have been here with you." Tears welled in Andy's eyes. Had she been there, would Jason have chosen a different path? Would she have done as he did, and chosen to side with the demons already?

"Don't be sorry. It's not your fault. I made my decision and I stick by it. I have no regrets, and I don't think I ever will." He took her hand. "I just hope that someday you can say the same."

"I still haven't made up my mind yet." Andy bit her lip, trying to stop it from quivering. She felt so sad for Jason but couldn't blame him for the decision he had made. Before, she knew that she wanted to side with the angels, but now...she had no idea what she wanted.

Condemned Angel

"You haven't seen dad, Wayne, since last night, have you?" Andy worried about how he would react to her hanging around with Kaden again.

Jason sighed. "He blames himself for what happened," he spoke quietly as if this would break her, and he was not entirely wrong.

"Why? *I* drank and let my guard down. I chose to forgo my safety." Andy shook with anger at herself. *Why had I been so stupid?* she thought.

"You and I both know that Wayne won't let himself off the hook that easily. He's going to hold onto his guilt until he feels like he has redeemed himself."

"We should go see him and let him know that he is faultless. I have to at least try to make him see that." Andy stood up off the bed, but Jason grabbed her hand.

"There's no point. He's not here. He went out with some demons. He should be back sometime tomorrow, though," he said. Andy let out a huff of air. He was off trying to redeem himself already. If only he realized that it was unnecessary.

Jason appeared thoughtful and then said, "if Ronan had raised us, can you imagine how different everything would be? We would be more powerful than any of the other demons here."

"If Ronan had raised us, we wouldn't have had the privilege of having a choice. We would be different people, and who knows if Mom would have stayed in the picture. I can't imagine my life without her and Wayne."

"Yeah, I guess. I just think sometimes it would have been much better to know what I was sooner." Jason stifled a yawn. "Do you mind if I just close my eyes for a few minutes?"

"Feel free." Andy motioned to the bed and he kicked off his shoes and crawled under the covers, closing his eyes as his head hit the pillow. He was asleep within minutes. Andy could almost pretend he wasn't a demon, as he lay there with his eyes closed. In her heart, she knew the truth, and it hurt.

There was another knock at her door. Andy wondered who it was this time. As she opened the door, she was surprised to find Kaden on the other side. He leaned with one arm against the door frame and his eyes were heavy. Marcus still stood guard, and he cocked an eyebrow at Andy.

"What's up?" she asked Kaden, and quickly realized as he lost his balance and stumbled forward, forcing her to steady him, that he was drunk.

"Can I com'n?" his words ran together, and Andy couldn't help but laugh. She never thought she would see the day when Kaden wasn't in complete control of himself.

"If you promise to be quiet, you can come in. Jason is sleeping," she spoke to him as if he were a child because that seemed to work best in her experience when people were that drunk. He nodded and stumbled inside. Andy turned to Marcus again.

Condemned Angel

"Let me know if you need any help with him. I will be out here all night," he offered.

"I will, thank you." Andy closed her door, turning back to find Kaden nodding off in the armchair already. "I take it you didn't get your nap," she stated the obvious and he snapped back awake.

"Cory n' Trav were playing a game," he slurred. His eyes drifted closed again, but he fought to keep them open.

"And you joined them, I presume?" Andy laughed and walked over to sit across from him on her bed. He sat forward in the chair and leaned his elbows on his knees.

"I 'ad to. Cory wasn't gonna win." Even though he slurred, he sounded serious and Andy found herself laughing, unable to take him seriously in his current state. "Cory's an ass."

"I will agree with that," Andy said. "So, who won?"

He smirked. "I did." Kaden leaned back in the chair and closed his eyes. Jason stirred on the other side of the bed and Andy turned to check on him. His eyes blinked open and he seemed confused for a moment when he saw Kaden in the chair.

"What's he doing here? I thought he was sleeping in our room?" Jason yawned and stretched his arms up over his head.

"Apparently he joined Cory and Trav's drinking game," Andy informed him. "And Kaden claims that he won."

"Oh crap. I should go check on the other two. If they were trying to out drink Kaden, and Kaden is this drunk, then they are probably much worse off." Jason laughed and jumped up and left the room.

Kaden dozed in the chair, so Andy was alone. She sighed and headed into the bathroom. She showered and put on the silk pajamas that she was getting sick of. For once she'd like to just have some normal cotton pajama shorts and a t-shirt. She turned off the main light in the room but left the side table light on. Kaden snored lightly.

There was yet another knock on the door, but this time they came right in. It was Jason again, he was laughing.

"Kaden won alright. When I went in there, Cory was knocked out cold on the floor. Trav was just drinking alone on his bed, waiting for Cory to regain consciousness I guess."

"He drank that much?" Andy gaped at Jason, but he shook his head.

"I guess Kaden punched him out before the alcohol did him in." Jason jerked his head towards Kaden who still slept soundly in the armchair. Andy looked at him too, wondering why he would have punched Cory. She thought Olivia had talked him down earlier.

"Why would he do that?" Andy looked to Jason again, but she could see that he had no answers for her.

"All Trav said was that he was staying out of it, and if I wanted to know, I had to talk to Kaden or Cory." Jason walked over to the bed and crawled back under the covers.

Condemned Angel

"I guess you're staying in here tonight, too, then?"

"I'm not going back in there until Cory is sober, and maybe not even then." Jason yawned and closed his eyes. "Thankfully, Marcus is out there. I told him not to let Cory anywhere near this room."

"Thanks, Jase," Andy said, but he was already sleeping again. Andy turned off the light on the side table and closed her eyes, drifting off to sleep.

Andy woke to a soft thud. She looked over at the clock, the numbers glowing softly in the dark. It was four in the morning. Reaching over, she turned on the light, nearly jumping out of her skin, as she saw Kaden looking back at her.

"Sorry, I didn't mean to scare you. I just woke up, too," he sounded completely sober now, which seemed impossible. Andy rubbed the sleep from her eyes.

"It's okay. I just forgot you were there." She glanced over at Jason who was still snoring on the other side of the bed. "How are you feeling?"

"I'm fine. Demons have a higher tolerance for alcohol, and it processes through our systems much faster." Andy knew it was similar for the angels as well, though, apparently from her most recent experiences, she did not have the fortune of inheriting that trait.

"What happened between you and Cory last night? Jason said you knocked him out." Andy eyed him suspiciously, wondering if he would try to lie to her.

He crossed his arms. "I'd rather not talk about it." Andy knew he wasn't going to budge easily.

"You know, I could always ask Cory what happened," Andy fished, and he cocked an eyebrow, knowing she would probably never do that. "Fine, you don't have to tell me. But I *will* find out. Jason will get the details from Cory and relay them to me. The joy of having a brother." Kaden sighed in defeat.

"You're not going to like it..." he began. Andy took his hands in hers, encouraging him to continue. "When I woke up, Cory and Trav were already drunk, and Cory was ready to fight. Trav suggested we diffuse the tension with a drinking war. Whoever drank the most without passing out, would win, and then that would be that," Kaden paused, gauging Andy's reaction. She said nothing and hoped her face wasn't giving away any of her emotions. She wanted him to continue. "So, we did it. We started going shot for shot. Big surprise, Cory couldn't keep his mouth shut in between his shots. He kept making comments... about you," he paused again.

"What did he say?" Andy asked through gritted teeth. Kaden shook his head and squeezed her hands, still in his.

"It doesn't matter," he tried to avoid finishing his story, but now he was too far in, and Andy needed to hear the ending.

The heat rose in Andy's cheeks. "I have a right to know what he was saying about me."

Condemned Angel

Kaden sighed. "Fine. He was making jokes about how much of a tease you always were when you were dating. He said that you never put out for him, but he knew that you were screwing other guys on the side while you were together." He closed his eyes and Andy pulled her hands out of his, balling them up into fists. She jumped out of bed and started towards the door, meaning to go straight over to Cory's room, but Kaden was up, and he grabbed her hand, pulling her back towards him.

"That's why you knocked him out?" She looked up at him and he nodded. "I feel like I shouldn't be condoning that, but I hate him so much right now." There were hot, angry tears in her eyes. She laid her head against Kaden's chest and after a few moments, she pulled away. "You know that none of what he said is true, right?"

"Of course! Cory was just trying to get me riled up." Kaden's arms were around her and all the warmth coming from him soothed her. She remembered when Cory used to hold her like that, it never felt quite as welcoming, and there was a coldness in his heart that seemed to radiate out through his body. But it was that same coldness that was so compelling, it made her want to know more about him. That was the reason she stayed with him for as long as she did.

"I'm so sorry I dragged you into this mess."

"Cory and I are always butting heads. This will pass, and everything will go back to normal. Just wait," Kaden tried to reassure her, but she wasn't so sure. Cory could be *very* stubborn. For now, though, she let it go. "Come on, you should get back to bed." Kaden inclined his head towards the bed where Jason slept.

"What about you? Are you going to go back to your room?" Andy asked, selfishly hoping that he chose to stay with her, even though that meant sleeping in the chair for him. He grinned. His arms were still around her waist.

"Are you thinking about sharing the chair with me?" he teased, sliding his hand up her back, pulling her even closer. Andy put her hands on his chest and smiled up at him.

"As tempting as that is, I think it's best if I sleep in my bed," Andy said reluctantly. She longed to stay in his arms all night, but Jason was still there.

"I think I'm going to have to pass on sleeping alone in the chair." Kaden traced her jawline with his thumb. "I don't think I would be able to fall back asleep anyway. I have some things I need to take care of." He leaned down and kissed her. "I'll come back and check on you at a more reasonable hour." He went to leave, but Andy pulled him back in for one more kiss.

"Promise?" She smiled coyly and he nodded in agreement.

"Sleep well, darling." He left the room and Andy climbed back into her bed. *Darling*...the word that both Kaden and his father called her. The more Kaden used it, the less it made her skin crawl. Jason rolled over in his sleep and started snoring. Without much effort, Andy fell asleep again.

∞

The day was a complete waste. They had found nothing. Bo was beginning to think that there was nothing out there. He had no idea how the others were keeping it together; he was beyond frustrated. He almost wanted to give up and go home, but he could never give up on Andy.

Gabby kept watch, while the rest of the group racked their brains for some idea to keep them going. Septimus had been God knows where since they'd returned from their failed attempt at locating Ronan's camp. Bo had been watching Sera draw maps in the dirt as she tried to pinpoint any possible location that they hadn't searched yet.

"Sera." Bo looked up to see Septimus standing over her, he seemed just as frazzled as the rest of them felt. "Can I sit?" Sera nodded and he took a seat on the ground beside her, examining her dirt map. He sighed and leaned back, lying on the ground with his hands folded under his head like a pillow.

"I'm sorry, I haven't thought of anything," Sera murmured, looking defeated.

"Me neither." He closed his eyes. "I searched...I flew every which way, and nothing."

"I know." Sera rubbed her hand over her dirt map, erasing it from the Earth. "I know. Let's just take the rest of the day to regroup."

"We've done that, and we've come up with nothing every time." Septimus was frustrated. "Ronan's camp is here somewhere. Everyone knows this is where it is. I just never imagined it would be this hard to find."

"They must be cloaking it somehow. We will find her. Don't give up just yet." Sera gave his arm a reassuring squeeze and he managed a halfhearted smile. "Trust me." Bo finally turned away from them and strode into the woods.

17

The Field Trip

When Andy woke up later that morning, Jason was gone. There was knocking on the door, and she realized that was what had woken her. Andy rubbed the sleep from her eyes and swung her legs over the side of her bed, yawning. She ran her hands through her hair a few times, taming it slightly.

Opening her door a crack, she saw Kaden chatting with Marcus in the hallway. She opened it fully and Kaden turned to smile at her. She couldn't help but smile back. He appeared fully rested and in good spirits, too.

"Good morning, sunshine." Kaden nodded to Marcus, who resumed his post beside Andy's door, and then he swept Andy off her feet, walking her back into her room. She wrapped her legs around his waist and closed the door behind him.

"Well, good morning indeed," Andy laughed and kissed him. He hugged her tight against him and placed her back on her feet. "To what do I owe for this pleasurable wakeup call?"

"I got permission to take you on a field trip." He grinned triumphantly and Andy raised her eyebrows, wondering where they could be going.

"A field trip?" She gave him a questioning look and he nodded.

"Yes, we should get going soon so we can be back before dark." He took his arms from around her and Andy took that as her cue to start getting ready.

"Well, I have to shower first," Andy said, walking to the dresser to grab an outfit for the day.

"Is that an invitation?" He cocked an eyebrow and smirked playfully. Andy grabbed a pair of jean shorts and a green tank top out of the top drawer and turned back to face him.

"You wish." She started towards the bathroom and he stepped into her path.

"Oh, yes I do." He kissed her and then stepped out of her way, making his way over to her bed. She watched him, biting her lip to keep from giving in to her want to be near him. "Hurry back." He plopped onto her bed, crossing his legs out in front of him, and put his arms behind his head. Andy turned away from him and forced herself to walk into the bathroom, closing the door between them.

After Andy showered, she dressed, and tousled her hair, letting her natural waves have their way. Today she decided to wear makeup for the first time since her birthday. She used just mascara, some blush, and lip gloss. She knew that Kaden wouldn't care either way, but this was how she always prepared for a date before the war began, and she was grasping at anything to make her life feel somewhat normal.

She opened the bathroom door. Kaden whistled from the bed and Andy strolled over. He was in the same position that she left him in. She lifted one knee onto the bed and swung her other leg over, straddling his hips. He looked surprised for a moment, and then he grinned as she leaned down to kiss him. He put his arms around her and trailed his hands along her arms, ending with his hands holding her face. He pulled away from the kiss for a moment and regarded Andy.

"You are so beautiful," his voice came out low and raspy and it made Andy want him even more. He kissed her deeply. Lost in his embrace, she felt as if she were floating.

Their moment was shattered by a knock on the door. Andy groaned in annoyance and Kaden chuckled. She hopped out of bed and quickly checked herself in the mirror, fixing her hair and reapplying the lip gloss which had all come off. Kaden beat Andy to the door and opened it.

"The car has been brought out front for you," Marcus announced, and Kaden looked back at Andy.

"Ready to go?" he asked. She would much rather stay in bed with him all day, but c'est la vie. She took his hand and he led her down the hallway.

After they ate a small breakfast, they headed outside. The car that waited for them in the driveway was a four-door pickup truck. Andy stifled a scream as she saw what was in the bed of the truck, and found herself hiding behind Kaden, even though she was probably more powerful than him now.

Two hellhounds sat in the bed of the truck, eerily calm. Andy avoided making eye contact with either of them thinking that they would sense her fear and attack. Taking deep breaths, she tried to calm herself down.

"It was the only way Ronan would let me take you on our field trip. I had to agree to bring hellhounds. Plus, Cairn and Marcus are going to be tailing us in a separate car the whole time," Kaden said. Andy stood beside him again but did not take her eyes off the hellhounds. "There is no reason to be afraid of them, you can control them."

"How?" Andy looked at him incredulously. They had been *hunting* her before, what made them decide that she was worthy of not being eaten? Kaden gave a quick whistle, causing both hounds to stand on all fours at attention. Andy shuddered. Kaden inclined his head and they both sat back down, but they were ready to react to his next command at a moment's notice.

"Try it," he encouraged, and Andy stepped forward shakily. She gave her best impression of Kaden's whistle, and the hellhounds stood at attention again. Andy was taken aback that it worked. "They will listen to actual commands, too, but sometimes it's best to keep things as simple as possible." He turned back to them. "Sit," he commanded, and they did as he said. "Are you ready to head out?"

"Ready as I'll ever be." Andy was still wary of the hellhounds, but it was a little comforting to know that they would listen to her. Kaden opened the passenger door for her, and she let him help her up into the cab of the truck. After shutting her door, Kaden made his way around the driver's side and hopped up onto the seat effortlessly. Andy slid over into the middle seat so she could be closer to him and he draped his arm over her shoulders, kissing her forehead. It *almost* felt like a normal start to a date – minus the hellhounds and the chaperons.

"So where are we going?" Andy finally asked as they left the driveway and turned onto the main road.

"You know I would never ruin a surprise," he smirked, and Andy rolled her eyes but couldn't help but smile too.

"I have another question if you're not going to give me an answer for that one."

"Alright, ask away."

"When you came into my room last night, drunk, Jason said that if you were that drunk, then the other guys could only be worse off."

"Fine, it's not a question, but I'll give you an answer anyway. Demons in general process alcohol differently than humans, and we have a higher tolerance. I used to drink *a lot*, starting when I was thirteen. It was the only way I could cope with my memories of my parents. They had left by then, but I kept having flashbacks, and I couldn't shake the feeling that they were still there, watching and waiting," he said. "Though, I wasn't totally wrong about that."

"I'm sorry, I shouldn't have brought it up." Andy clasped his hand and squeezed it.

"It's fine. I'll tell you anything you want to know. But you should also know that I don't drink like that anymore. I only drink on special occasions." His mouth pulled up slightly.

"Special occasions, or when someone challenges you to a drink off," Andy added, nudging him playfully.

"Your turn," he said. "Tell me one of your deep, dark secrets," he teased, keeping his eyes on the road.

Andy gazed up at him. "You already know most of mine. My life was much less noteworthy. I grew up thinking I was human. I had human friends, and I *thought* I had a human boyfriend. Turns out I was wrong on most counts. Cory and I were together until the war started, and then he disappeared.

Condemned Angel

After that, I thanked my lucky stars I never had to see him again, but I didn't wish anything bad happened to him, I just hoped he had moved on. A few months after that, the demon, Xavier, broke into our house and caused my dad and me to go on the run. We were thinking that both Jason and my mom were dead," the words tumbled out. Andy's eyes started to well with tears as she reflected on when she thought that half of her family was dead and gone. She wiped away the tears quickly.

"It's okay, I know the rest of the story." Kaden put his arm around her again, rubbing her arm to comfort her. Andy leaned her head on his shoulder and realized that there were no longer trees surrounding them, but fields. There were some farmhouses along the road, but they all appeared abandoned.

They kept driving until they entered another forest. This time they veered off the main road and down a dirt road. At the end of the road sat a small cabin overlooking a river. Everything was overgrown and wild. Vines climbed up the sides of the cabin, and tall grass surrounded the dirt driveway on either side. Kaden parked the truck and they both got out, leaving the hellhounds in the bed.

"What is this place?" Andy asked, coming to stand beside Kaden at the foot of the stairs leading up to the front porch. There was once a railing, but it had rotted and fallen off.

Holly Huntress

"It used to be a vacation home, but it's abandoned now. Come on, let's go inside." Kaden took Andy's hand and ascended the stairs. The door was unlocked and led into a small living room kitchen combo. The interior of the camp was in no better condition than the outside. There were two open doors off to the right, one revealed a bathroom and the other a bedroom. Opposite the door they just entered was a sliding glass door leading out onto a back porch that overlooked the river. Andy left Kaden's side and went to the porch. Two Adirondack chairs faced the water covered in cobwebs and dirt. Andy put her hands on the railing, leaning slightly, and it creaked. She pulled back quickly. Kaden came up beside her.

"It's not the most up to date cabin, but there is never anyone here when I come, so that's a plus," he laughed. "It's the view that I come for."

"It's beautiful here. It feels so...separate. From everything that's going on in the world."

"I thought you might like it." Kaden leaned back against the railing, crossing his arms over his chest. The whole railing groaned and leaned back with him. It gave way, breaking off from the porch. Andy lunged, grabbing Kaden's arm to keep him from falling with the railing. Thankfully she had full use of her extra strength now. She pulled him against her and stumbled backward with the force of it all. "Nice save." He gave her a knee-weakening grin, and Andy couldn't help but kiss him. He pulled away slightly. "Don't forget that we have an audience," he murmured. To the side of the house,

Condemned Angel

Cairn stood on the ground, looking out over the river. Andy turned the other way and saw Marcus doing the same. She blushed.

"We're never really going to be alone, are we?" Andy leaned her head against Kaden's chest and the whole porch seemed to groan in answer. They hurried inside so that they weren't taken out by the porch.

"Wait here a minute, I'm going to check on the hounds." Kaden walked out to the front porch. Andy almost sat down on the futon in the middle of the room but thought better of it. It probably had mice living in it.

She wandered towards the bedroom to see if there was anything of interest in there. The only two objects in the room were the bed and an old, cedar dresser. Andy began to wonder whether this place was even inhabited before the war began. It seemed like no one had been there in a very long time.

Andy approached the dresser and wrenched open the top drawer. It screeched against its tracks, but she was able to pull it out enough to see inside. There were a couple of yellowing books and some stacks of paper inside. The books were just some old trashy novels. But there was one unmarked brown journal that sparked Andy's interest.

Andy opened it and read the date scrawled across the top of the page. *November twelfth, 2000.* The journal was almost twenty years old now. So, this place had been uninhabited for at least a decade probably. Andy read on.

Today I watched as Bella used her wings for the first time. It was absolutely beautiful. The sheer delight that comes over her face when she's flying, it makes me wish I could join her up there. I have no regrets about my decision to stray from God's grace. Morgan may never understand my choice. I can't believe it's been almost fifteen years. It all seems like a lifetime ago now.

Morgan...I miss him most days. I wish he had stayed by my side longer than the few years after I transitioned, maybe he would have seen the reason I chose the path I did, and maybe he would have joined me.

It does no good to think about these things. I have my babies and that is all that matters to me. Iz has been helping me train Bella.

Andy let out a gasp as she realized whose house this once was. There was no way that this was a coincidence. Kaden must have known... Andy looked back at the journal now shaking in her hand. She flipped to a new page and read the next date. *January twenty second, 2001.*

Morgan spent Christmas with us. He keeps filling the children's heads with ideas of the grandeur of being an angel, and the fairy tales of God's good deeds. I don't try to sway them to believe differently, it will be their choice in the end, which side they wish to join.

Bella has been sneaking around with a boy. She thinks I don't know, but I can see it in her eyes that she's in love. He's an angel, and I know he will sway her to his side. I'm scared that I'm going to lose her.

"Andy?" Kaden's voice came from the living room. She dropped the journal back into the drawer and walked out of the bedroom. His face lit up as he saw her.

"Did you know the people who used to live here?" Andy questioned him.

"I did. Morgan, Deirdre, and the girls. Izzy helped train me," he said. "That's not why I brought you here, though. I truly just wanted to get you out of the mansion for a little while."

"I believe you," she said, closing the distance between them and taking his hand. "Their mother has a journal in the dresser in there. Why would she leave that here, unless..." Andy couldn't say it, but Kaden understood where she was headed.

"Their father, Morgan, turned on her. She was killed by the man she once loved, and it broke the girls." Andy gaped at him, not wanting to believe the story. "It was over ten years ago now. Izzy defected to the demons immediately, while Annabella took a little more time. I'm not sure what held her back, but I guess it doesn't matter now. She chose the demons in the end." Andy shook with anger at a man she never knew.

"How could he turn on her like that?" Andy's voice came out as a whisper. Her heart hurt for the poor woman whose last moment in life was spent suffering the betrayal from a man she once knew as a partner and the father of her children.

"He was carrying out an order." Kaden pulled Andy closer. "I'm sorry this day took such a turn. I wanted to lift your spirits today, not drag them back down." He gave her a sad smile and brushed her hair back from her face. Andy did her best to remain cheerful, despite the feeling of sorrow she felt for the family who had been torn apart.

Kaden pulled away and beckoned for her to follow him out to the front of the house. They walked around to the river. The hellhounds were no longer in the bed of the truck and Andy glanced around, half worried that they would jump out at any moment. Cairn and Marcus circled the property, keeping watch.

"Do you want to try out your wings?" Kaden asked, and Andy realized that she had not tried to fly with them yet. She nodded and he took a step back so she could unfurl them. They spread out on either side of her and the wind blew softly through the feathers. It tickled and she couldn't help but giggle.

"Want a ride?" she offered, waggling her eyebrows at Kaden, but he shook his head.

"I prefer the ground, thank you." He motioned for Andy to go ahead without him. She focused her thoughts on pumping her wings. Slowly but surely, they began to come together and spread apart and she lifted off the ground. She climbed higher into the air until she was above the treetops.

Andy could see Cairn and Marcus, but she could also see the hellhounds sniffing towards the road. She started to move forward and then tried veering left, and right. It was the most incredible feeling in the world. Flying with Septimus had only been a taste of what it was like to fly on her own.

Andy was reminded of the passage Annabella's mother wrote, about watching her daughter flying for the first time, and Andy wondered if she looked the same. She certainly felt the sheer joy that came from soaring through the air. She laughed again and tried to let go of everything that tried to drag her down that day.

When she returned to the ground, her body felt so much heavier, and cumbersome, whereas in the air she had seemed light as a feather. She furled her wings into her back.

"That was amazing!" She couldn't keep the smile off her face and did a spin with her arms out and her head tilted back, letting her hair whip around her face. Kaden threw a rock, skipping it across the river.

"It looked like you were enjoying yourself," he commented, his face impassive.

"Are you sure you don't want me to take you up there?" Andy offered again.

"I'd rather not." He turned away from her and walked to the river's edge, bending down, and picking up another rock to throw. Andy could tell he was holding something back from her. She walked up beside him and took his hand.

"Is everything okay?" she asked, hoping he would fill her in. He didn't look at her but continued surveying the river. A shadow came over his face.

"Everything's fine," he said, but Andy sensed he was not being truthful. He had lied to her in the past and she hadn't sensed it, but this time was different. Andy was stronger now, and she had much more confidence in all her abilities.

"You're lying to me," she said, and he glanced at her, cocking an eyebrow. He let out a sigh and then turned to face her, holding onto her hand.

"Watching you flying... it reminded me that you still have a choice to make. If you choose to be with me, and side with the demons, you will lose your wings." He searched her face for a reaction, but she had already been thinking about this.

"Who says that I can't choose to be with you, but side with the angels?" Andy argued, knowing that this wasn't a plausible option from her mom's experience. Kaden laughed at the suggestion.

"What happens if I'm sent out on a legion to eliminate a group of angels, and you happen to be in that group?" he painted the picture for her. "I can't fight off the other angels *and* make sure no one else in the legion kills you, because they aren't going to willingly let you live." Andy buried her face in her hands, letting out a groan of frustration.

"Are you giving me an ultimatum, right here, right now? I have to choose?" Andy asked him to clarify. She still had no idea what she wanted, and this was not helping her situation at all. He threw his hands up.

"I don't know." He ran his hands down his face. "You're making it sound like you've already decided to side with the angels."

"I have no idea what I'm going to do! I still have a week left to make my decision." Andy didn't want this to come between them, but she knew that Kaden was right. If she *did* side with the angels, they would not be able to stay together.

"I can't believe it's only been a week..." Kaden mused, and Andy shared the sentiment. It seemed more like a lifetime. So much had happened. "But you're right. You still have one more week to make your decision, and in the meantime, I'm not going to let what may or may not happen ruin the time that I have with you." He finally smiled again, and Andy put her arms around him, pulling him close. She wished they could just stay in that moment forever. If only she never had to go back to Ronan's house or make any life-altering decisions.

"Thank you," her voice came out muffled against his chest. He tilted her head up so he could gaze into her eyes.

"I should be thanking you. I have no idea what I did to deserve you." He kissed her softly, then pulled away and left her standing alone. She watched as he turned away from her, pulling his shirt up over his head, and tossing it to the side. He unlaced his boots and kicked them off. He looked back at Andy, standing just in his jeans now, mischief on his face, and she cocked her head, crossing her arms. He turned away and started wading out into the river. When he reached the point where he was waist-deep, he dove into the water.

While she waited for him to resurface, Andy unlaced her boots, kicking them off and wading into the river after him. Kaden finally resurfaced on the opposite side. Andy continued into the water, not wanting to go under because she had to wear makeup that day. She kicked herself for not just going without.

The water became deep enough so Andy could no longer touch and had to start swimming. She flipped onto her back and chose to float for a while.

She glanced up at the sky and realized that clouds had overtaken the sun, and they didn't look happy. She felt Kaden's arms around her and leaned into them. He was a good six inches taller than her, and he could touch in the middle of the river. Andy turned around in his arms, wrapping her legs around his waist and draping her arms over his shoulders.

"We should probably head back; it looks like a storm is coming in," he said. He trailed his hand down her spine, sending shivers through her whole body. Rain began to sprinkle down around them as if on cue.

"What's a little rain when we're already in a river?" Andy traced the muscles along his back and up his shoulder absentmindedly. Lightning flashed, followed by a crack, and a huge roll of thunder.

"I think that's our cue." Kaden kissed her briefly, and then started walking, with her still wrapped around him, towards the shore. He set her down once they were back on dry ground and grabbed his shirt and boots. Andy grabbed her boots as well and went to the front of the house. Cairn and Marcus were climbing into their car. Kaden whistled and the hellhounds came crashing through the brush to get back to the truck. Andy shuddered. By the time they were in the cab of the truck, the hellhounds had made their way into the bed.

Once they were back at the mansion, the storm was fully upon them. It was down pouring so hard they could barely see out the windshield. The lightning was striking all around them, and the thunder was loud enough to drown out any conversation they may have thought of having. Andy was still soaking wet from their swim. Her jean shorts were plastered to her legs, and her tank top clung to her.

Kaden pulled up to the front gate. He looked at Andy and squeezed her hand.

"Are you ready for this?" he asked, referring to having to leave the nice warm truck and step out into the sheets of rain coming down. Andy was already shivering.

"I guess so, and just when I was beginning to dry off a little from before," Andy sighed. Kaden braced himself and opened his door hopping out into the rain. Andy waited for him to enter the code to open the gate, and then followed him out into the downpour. She was instantly soaked through again. So much for not wanting her makeup to run. She started laughing as she splashed through a giant puddle that had taken over the whole driveway. She wiped away the mascara she assumed ran down her face and may already be completely washed off.

Once they were inside the gate, Kaden and Andy ran inside. There were towels just inside the door, and they grabbed them, trying to soak up the worst of the rain. They headed straight for the dining room to get some food. They were still drenched, but Andy was starving. After grabbing plates and filling them up, they went to the sitting room to eat. Lily was already there, eating with Jason.

"Hey, Lily. How's your day been?" Andy greeted her.

Lily smiled. "I've been keeping busy, but today is shot. I hate the rain." She shook herself as if there was some rain lingering on her, though she appeared thoroughly dry. Kaden sat on the couch and Andy plopped down beside him.

"I love the rain. It clears my head," Andy said.

Condemned Angel

Jason laughed. "When she was little, she used to like to jump in puddles right next to me, splashing me. That's probably why I have an aversion to the rain." He nudged her with his elbow. Andy had forgotten about that. Cory strolled into the room with his plate of food and took a seat next to Lily.

"She did that to me a few times when we were dating," Cory jumped into the conversation and Andy felt Kaden growing tense beside her. "Didn't you, Andy?" Andy set down her empty plate on the coffee table and placed her hand on Kaden's knee.

"I guess I probably did," she answered vaguely. She knew what he was trying to do, and she wished he would just leave her alone.

"So, what did y'all end up doing today?" Lily cut in and Andy gave her a look of gratitude.

"I had the day off, so I took Andy out to do some exploring," Kaden answered, but Andy knew he was still on edge with Cory there.

"Liv and I had the day off too, but we just hung around here," Lily said.

"Where is Olivia?" Jason tried to sound casual, but the anticipation on his face gave him away.

"She's reorganizing our room. You can come back with me and help if you want," Lily offered, and Jason proceeded to wolf down the rest of his food and practically throw his plate down onto the coffee table. They both stood up to leave and Andy realized she and Kaden were about to be alone with Cory. "Do you guys want to come along?" Lily added as an afterthought. Andy gave her a grateful look.

"Yeah, sure." Andy glanced over at Kaden who glared at Cory, who stared at her. "Kaden, why don't you go with them, I have to talk to Cory, and then I'll meet you all downstairs." Andy would rather never be alone with Cory again, but she knew that she needed to try talking to him again if she ever wanted this extreme awkwardness to go away. Kaden looked at Andy like she was crazy.

"I can stay." He folded his arms over his chest, and Andy shook her head. Lily and Jason started walking towards the hallway that led to the stairwell.

"I'll just be a couple of minutes, if I'm longer than that, you can come back," she reassured him, glancing back at Cory who appeared disinterested.

"Fine," Kaden agreed reluctantly, standing up from the couch. He kissed her and left the room.

Cory smirked. "Trouble in paradise?" He leaned forward, resting his elbows on his knees. "Am I causing a rift between the two of you?" Andy rolled her eyes.

"Hardly," she scoffed. "I just wish you could act like a normal human being and stop being so petty." She crossed her arms and he laughed.

"That may be easier if I were a *human being*," he pointed out and Andy realized her mistake. "I am so much more than that, and you've always known it. That's what drew you to me in the first place isn't it?" He cocked an eyebrow, almost like a challenge.

"What can I say? I've grown up a little since then. My taste in guys has improved." Andy countered, and he threw his head back, laughing.

"Oh, gorgeous, you have no idea what you are getting yourself into." He stood up off the couch and at first, Andy thought he was going to walk over to her, but he stayed where he was. "I waited for you. I'm not just going to let this go. Kaden can't hide in your room forever; I still owe him a little payback."

"You got what you deserved for telling him all those lies about me." Andy stood, her fists clenched.

"I never lied to him. You were a tease." His eyes flashed with anger. "I wasn't lying when I told you that I loved you." All the fire left Andy's veins, and she let out a huff of air. She was taken back to the memory that Cory was talking about. They had spent the day at the beach, and when he brought her home, they got into a huge argument. Andy was on the verge of ending things when he said the words. *I love you.* She was so taken aback that she turned away from him and went inside, saying nothing. She left him standing alone in her driveway. He drove home, and the next day he was gone. The war began shortly after that and Andy tried her best not to think back on that moment.

"I'm sorry, Cory," she said. "I shouldn't have left you like that, but I didn't know how to tell you that I didn't feel the same way. I didn't love you." Tears stung her eyes, but she blinked them away quickly.

"Got it." Cory gave her a thumbs up. "If you wanted things to be okay here," he motioned to the space between them, "it is far from okay." He turned on his heel and strode out of the living room leaving her alone. Andy collapsed back onto the couch, feeling exhausted all of a sudden. She did not want to go downstairs. Out of the corner of her eye, Andy noticed Marcus enter the room. She turned to him.

"If you need to talk," he said. Andy nodded slightly and turned back to stare at the ceiling.

"I don't think this is going to end well," Andy commented, and Marcus remained silent, so she went on. "Cory isn't going to let this go, and he has quite the temper."

"There is no need for you to worry about him hurting you. He won't get past me," Marcus offered reassurance.

"It's not me I'm worried about," Andy explained, and Marcus nodded in understanding.

"Kaden can take care of himself. Cory has always liked to stir up trouble, ever since he came here. Usually, it's pretty harmless. I wouldn't worry too much," he said. It was probably true, but it did nothing to ease Andy's worrying.

"I should get to Lily's room..." With an effort, Andy stood from the couch and went to the basement. Marcus followed along behind her.

18

The Watcher

Septimus knew something was off.

They spent another night in their makeshift camp. The others were all drained from a day of walking through fields and forests, and he could tell they were losing hope of ever finding Andromeda. Septimus felt a little worse for the wear as well.

He could not sleep again last night. Bo mentioned that all day he had felt like he was being watched. He chalked it up to the heat and paranoia, but Septimus could feel it from then on. He had sensed it before but had figured it was just from being in demon territory. Now, he knew it was real. They were being watched. The question was, why were they being watched instead of attacked? If demons watched them, they should have already tried to either kill them or run them out of their territory.

Septimus left his spot where he had been keeping watch and walked to where the others were gathered. They had all just woken up and were letting Bo snack on whatever provisions they had left. Their supplies were running low. They all looked up at Septimus as he approached them.

"Clearly our rescue mission has not gone as we had hoped," he began. "But we cannot give up. I need everyone's help to think of anything we have missed. We cannot stay out here much longer." They all nodded. He turned to Sera. "Can I talk with you for a moment?" She stood to follow him away from the others.

"What's up?" Her brow furrowed and he wondered if she already knew what he was about to tell her.

"Act normal, but we are being watched," he murmured to her so as not to be overheard by anyone who may be listening.

"I can feel it," she admitted, stretching her arms out, pretending everything was fine. "What do we do?" Septimus glanced from side to side, seeing nothing out of the ordinary, but he still *felt* a presence.

"It seems like whoever it is doesn't want to hurt us, but they are probably the reason we haven't been able to find

Andromeda yet," he said. "They must be demons, so everyone needs to be on their guard. But do not let on that we know they are out there." Sera nodded in understanding.

"I'll tell the others." She left to go back to the rest of the group, and Septimus decided to take a walk around their camp. He kept his ears and eyes strained for movement or anything out of the ordinary, but there was nothing. He was beginning to think he had made a grave mistake and that he had led these angels into a death trap.

Later that day, a storm blew in and it down poured. Thankfully, they had put up a tent, so they were able to stay somewhat dry.

By the time the sun set, the rain had stopped. They started a fire to cook the last of their canned foods. Their packs were considerably lighter, but it did not bode well for their mission. Everyone chatted, trying to keep things light, and trying to keep their minds off the fact that they were waiting for the other shoe to drop.

No one could fall asleep. Septimus kept watch over them, again. He had not slept in two days, but he felt as awake as ever. He wouldn't allow anything to happen to any of them.

As the sun began to rise the next day, Septimus felt some relief washing over him with the daylight. They made it through the night. Maybe the demons would leave them alone long enough for them to escape their watch. As Septimus walked back into the camp, he heard a commotion off to his right. Everyone else was on their feet in an instant. A demon burst out into the clearing, his black eyes gleaming and his hands covered in blood. He grinned wickedly as his eyes landed on the angels. Septimus motioned for everyone to stay back, and he unfurled his wings from his back. Gabby, Sera, Nathan, and Micah began to do the same.

"Well, well, well, Andy's little rescue party. Too bad you lot are going to be the ones needing the rescuing," the demon snapped his fingers and then they were surrounded. There were six demons that Septimus could see. Two of them, a man and a woman, appeared older than the others, and they stood out among them, seeming to be in charge. The man stepped forward.

"We'll take it from here, Cory."

∞

After making her appearance in Lily's room and showing Kaden she was 'fine,' Andy excused herself to go dry off. A chill had settled into her bones from sitting in wet clothes for so long.

"I'll meet you in your room in a bit, I want to change, too," Kaden said.

"You mean, you're going to your room?" Andy asked, thinking about Cory's threat. Kaden cocked an eyebrow.

Condemned Angel

"Well, yeah, that *is* where my clothes are," he chuckled, not understanding that she was asking because she was worried about him.

"Well, Jason, don't you need to change, too?" Andy prompted, trying to give him a look that said *go along with it.* He nodded slightly, letting Andy know he understood.

"Yeah, I guess I should. I'll see you ladies later." They all headed up to their rooms. Jason caught Andy's arm as they were walking and pulled her aside. Kaden kept walking, giving them a moment alone. Marcus hung back as well.

"What was that about?" Jason asked, eyeing Andy curiously.

She twirled her hair around her finger. "It's probably nothing, but I just worry about Kaden and Cory being alone together." Her heart hammered in her chest.

"I think Kaden can hold his own against Cory. Don't worry about him," Jason reassured Andy and continued on ahead. Andy followed and Kaden fell back to walk with her. He took her hand as they walked. When they reached his and Jason's room, Jason walked right in, but Kaden hesitated, still holding Andy's hand. She didn't want him to let go. Jason popped his head out of their room.

"Just an FYI, Cory is not in the room, so you're safe, Kade," he said. Andy gave Kaden a quick kiss before going to her room to shower.

Holly Huntress

When she finished showering, she threw on her pajamas. She opened the door to her bedroom and realized Kaden wasn't there yet. She shrugged it off, figuring he was probably talking with Jason. Andy turned off the main light and turned on her light on the side table, then climbed into bed.

There was a knock on the door, and Kaden stepped inside. He was wearing jeans and a t-shirt, not quite the attire she would expect him to wear to sleep.

"Going somewhere?" she asked, and he sighed.

"Ronan needs me to help out with an errand tonight." He made his way over to the bed and sat down on the edge. "Believe me, I would much rather be staying here, with you, but I have to do this."

"It's fine. I have Marcus watching out for me." Even knowing this and knowing that she had complete control over her abilities, Andy still felt a small twinge of fear at the thought of Kaden not being there with her. She knew it was irrational, though, and pushed the feeling down. "What does he have you doing tonight?"

"I can't say..." he glanced away, and Andy crossed her arms over her chest. "I'm sure Ronan will fill you in later, but for now, it's best you're kept in the dark." He turned back to Andy and took her hand. "I have to go, but I'll see you tomorrow." Andy took her hand back and pulled her knees up to her chest, hugging them tightly.

Condemned Angel

"Fine, then. Leave." Hostility rose inside of her. It was towards both Ronan, for leaving her in the dark about whatever it was he was sending Kaden to do, and towards Kaden for siding with Ronan, yet again. They were still trying to keep her out of whatever it was they were doing, to protect her, but she no longer needed protecting.

"Don't be mad at me, please." He leaned towards her, and she switched off the light and turned onto her side as if she were going to sleep. He took the hint and stood off the bed. "Goodnight." Andy heard him walking across the floor and then the door creaked open and closed.

All around Andy were people staring blankly ahead. She tried to wave her hand in front of them, they did not even blink. She walked around in a circle, trying to get someone's attention, but they were all as still as statues.

"Hello?" Andy called out, wondering if there was anyone else there with her. For once, no one answered. This was a nightmare of her own making. Andy pushed through the crowds of people and finally came to an edge. She kept walking past them all and then she heard it. Screaming. She turned around to see the entire group of people had fallen to the ground.

Andy turned back and ran to them, but their eyes were glassy, and their mouths hung open, blood trickling out.

"Someone please, help!" Andy called out, but there was no response. "What is happening?" She carefully stepped over the

bodies and their faces began to change, to people she recognized, people she cared about. Andy screamed out in agony as she fell to her knees beside the closest body to her, Micah. She gathered him into her arms. His eyes flickered to her and she shrieked in surprise.

"What have you done, Andy? Why did you do this to me?" His voice was thick and came out a little garbled from the blood that coated his throat.

"I'm so sorry…"

"Andy!" she woke to someone shaking her shoulders. Her eyes felt like they were glued shut, but she forced them open. Marcus stood in front of her, concern in his eyes.

"W-what time is it?" She looked out the window, but it was still dark outside.

"It's three in the morning. You were screaming bloody murder and flailing in your sleep," he explained, and Andy's cheeks began to redden.

"Sorry… nightmare." She smoothed down her hair self-consciously. "I thought they would go away since Gregor can't mess with my head anymore, but I guess not."

"Everyone has nightmare's Andy. It's nothing to be ashamed of, or to apologize for. I just didn't want you to hurt yourself." He took a step back and leaned against the bedpost at the foot of the bed. "Do you want to talk about it?"

"Not really… I'd rather never think about it again…" she could still see the bodies laid out before her in her mind.

"It might help."

"Well... I guess I can try," Andy sighed, going into the description of her dream.

"It seems to me like you're afraid you're going to hurt the people that you love. You are discovering your new abilities, and to be as powerful as you are, it's a likely possibility that you could hurt someone," Marcus analyzed the dream.

"I guess... but I hadn't even thought about that." *Now* it was something she was going to worry about.

"Our mind has a mysterious way of pulling out our deepest, darkest fears, even ones we don't realize are there." Marcus gave her a sympathetic look.

"Great..." Andy murmured. "Well, thanks for all your help. I think I'm going to stay awake for the rest of my life now," she joked.

"You have the ability to block out any dreams or nightmares now, just know that you can't pick and choose what to block out, it has to be all or nothing," Marcus said. "I taught Kaden to block them out when he was just five years old. Ronan brought him to me while his parents were away on a mission. I don't even know that Kaden remembers it, but he was suffering terribly from nightmares at the time, so much so that he could barely sleep, or eat, and we thought he wouldn't make it much longer if he continued like that."

"Kaden did mention to me that he doesn't dream, but he didn't know why."

"Don't tell him that I told you any of this, I just want you to know that if you want to get rid of your nightmares, you can."

"Thank you, I'll think about it. But, for right now, I'll just suffer through the nightmares." Andy leaned back against her pillow, and Marcus turned to leave. "Thank you, again. For everything."

The next morning, Andy went downstairs to find her parents. She knocked on the door of their room and waited patiently until the door finally opened. Angeline stood on the other side, and when she saw Andy her face lit up and a smile crossed her face. Andy threw herself into her arms.

"Oh," Angeline let out a puff of air as Andy squeezed her. She put her arms around Andy and kissed the top of her head. She stroked her hair softly and pulled away slightly so she could take in Andy's face. Tears streamed down Andy's cheeks. "Come in, sweetie." Angeline pulled her into the room, closing the door behind them. Wayne wasn't there, and Andy wondered briefly where he could be.

They sat on a small couch at the foot of the bed, facing the door. Angeline curled her legs up under her and pulled Andy down beside her.

"Why can't we go back to normal?" Andy said, sniffling. "I just want to go back to before the war ever started, before Jason and I knew about any of this supernatural world." She wiped away her tears with her sleeve, though they kept coming.

"I'm so sorry I brought all of this upon you both. I wish I had told you who you are sooner and taught you more about what it means to be an angel or a demon," Angeline shook her head. "There's no going back to the way things were before, but maybe we can make a *new* normal for all of us." A glimmer of hope sparked in her eyes, and Andy wondered if that were possible, if what they had now could ever truly feel *normal*.

"How can you stay cooped up in here all the time?" Andy changed the subject.

"I go outside sometimes. It's just...I've been doing a lot of thinking and planning lately. Ronan is always sending your father on errands with the other demons, and I am trying to keep my mind off the danger he could be in." Angeline's eyes widened as if she had revealed some dark secret. "I shouldn't have told you that, I'm so sorry sweetie. I don't want you to be worrying about anything but yourself right now." She took Andy's hand, but it was too late. Andy's mind raced with thoughts about what kind of 'errands' Ronan could be sending Wayne on.

"Do you know what the errands are?" Andy asked.

Angeline avoided the question. "You're with Kaden now, right?" Andy remembered that the last time she had talked with her mom, she was still fighting with Kaden. She felt a twinge of guilt for not keeping her mom in the loop.

"Yes, I am with Kaden now," Andy sighed. "But, if I choose to side with the angels, we can't be together..." A lump caught in her throat.

"Don't think about that now, honey. There is so much on your shoulders, I just want you to enjoy yourself and be happy for a little while. Soak it all in," she tried to smile.

"What would happen..." Andy paused for a moment, wondering if she should continue with her thought, and decided to power onward. "What would happen if I *didn't* side with the angels?" There was a flash of something in Angeline's eyes, possibly fear. "Not that I'm going to side with the demons. I have no idea what I want to do right now, it's completely hypothetical," Andy clarified, and Angeline seemed to calm down a bit.

"I can't say what will happen to you. All I know is what has happened to those of us who have chosen not to side with the angels in the past," she sighed. "I won't say that I regret my decision, because it gave me you and your brother, but I do often wonder what my life would be like had I chosen a different path for myself. No matter which side you choose, I can guarantee you will think back once or twice and wonder the same. As for your brother, he is perfectly content with his decision for now, and as far as I know, he has no regrets. I never officially chose a side."

"I thought you chose the demons, and that was why you lost your wings."

"I chose to be with Ronan, yes, but not to become a demon. I am considered a fallen angel. Not quite here, not quite there," sadness filled her eyes. "I never told Ronan this, because I never wanted him to feel at fault, or worry that I would ever blame him. He still believes that I am fully an angel."

"Septimus mentioned fallen angels to me once, but I assumed that they all wound up becoming demons." Angeline shook her head.

Someone knocked on the door and they both glanced up, startled. Angeline stood up off the couch and went to the door, opening it slightly. Andy heard muffled whispers and saw her mom's body stiffen. "I have to go," Angeline said, without turning back, and then she was gone. Andy could see Marcus through the crack in the door, standing with his arms crossed and a serious look on his face. She jumped off the couch and ran to the door peering down the hall, but her mom was already up the stairs.

"What's happening?" Andy asked Marcus, but he simply shook his head slowly and remained silent. "If you won't tell me, I'll find out for myself." Andy went to walk towards the stairs, but Marcus cut her off, placing himself as an impenetrable wall in front of her. "Marcus, please. I need to know what's happening!" She tried to weave around him, but he was faster than her. She could feel her temperature rising, and the fire beginning to lick through her veins. "I am going to ask one more time, Marcus. Please, tell me what's going on? Or else get out of my way so I can find out for myself." She didn't want to hurt Marcus, but her parents were far more important to her. Jason's head popped out from Lily's doorway, and then he stepped out into the hall.

"What's going on out here?" He scrutinized Marcus and Andy, obviously noticing the tension.

"Andromeda needs to remain here until I am advised otherwise," Marcus said, and Jason's brow furrowed. Andy realized he was now torn between helping her and following orders.

"Can she at least come in here to be with me and her friends?" Jason asked, trying to find a middle ground. Marcus shifted slightly, allowing Andy to pass by him. She ran to Jason and into Lily's room. Lily sat on her bed while Olivia lounged on the top bunk.

Andy turned to Jason once he stepped back into the room. "Something's wrong. Mom was called off to help with something, and dad is doing an errand for Ronan. No one will tell me anything, and apparently, I'm a prisoner down here until further notice." Everything came out in a rush. Jason's face was stoic, giving away no hint of his emotions. He had always been Andy's rock.

"Everything's going to be fine, Andy. Just calm down," his voice soothed her. "Ronan will take care of whatever's going on. Don't worry." He seemed to believe this wholeheartedly, and while it did ease some of her anxiety, Andy didn't have the same blind faith in Ronan that Jason had, and she still feared that something had gone terribly wrong.

19

The Scheme

"Seize them," Gregor commanded. He attempted to invade each of the angel's minds, but they were blocked to him. Cory got a hold of the human, while Zain and Trent were able to grab the golden-haired angel and the raven-haired girl standing beside him. Two of the others were able to ascend into the sky, but Gregor sensed weakness in the girl who'd escaped.

    He gripped her mind and brought her crashing back to the Earth. Her friend descended on his own to return to her side. Gregor laughed at the weakness of angels. He stepped

Condemned Angel

forward and in one swift motion pulled the descending angel the last few feet to the ground and forced him to his knees.

"You should have left her..." he sneered as he reached to his baldric and withdrew a dagger forged from hellfire and plunged it into the angel's heart. A scream ripped from the weaker girl's mouth and echoed through the trees around them. Gregor relished in the sound.

The remaining angel, the seeming leader, pulled his wings in of his own accord and stepped forward.

"Take me and let the rest go," he commanded.

"That's not how this works. *I* decide who lives and dies," Gregor motioned to Mara who stepped forward and tied the angel's hands behind his back. He could easily break free of the restraints, Gregor knew, the angel cared too much about what would happen to the others if he did that.

Once they had the remaining angels wrangled up, they brought them out of the clearing to hide them from sight. Gregor nudged the dead angel on the ground with his boot, the body would remain until he lifted the veil shrouding them from prying minds. A hiss sounded behind him.

"Don't touch him!" one of the angels growled at him, which only made him guffaw. She was being dragged out of the clearing with the others. He ignored her and set about the next part of his plan: reaching out to Andromeda.

∞

Holly Huntress

A wave of nausea crashed over Andy, accompanied by a pounding headache. The effects of someone trying to force their way into her head. She doubled over and squeezed her eyes shut. She heard Jason saying her name, and felt his arms around her, but she couldn't bring herself to move or open her eyes. No one could get inside her head anymore, but she felt a new presence, nonetheless. Her worry about her parents had distracted her and left her vulnerable.

Andromeda, dear. The time has come for us to meet. Please, there is a car outside, your parents are already there, waiting for you. If you do not come with them, there will be dire consequences. So, hurry along, we do not have all day. Gregor's voice was in and out of her mind before she could respond. The nausea and pain were gone, and Andy stood up straight.

Everyone around her appeared bewildered, but Andy couldn't explain herself now. She knew she must do as Gregor said. Andy ran past Jason before he could stop her and out the door. Marcus was caught off guard, and Andy was able to slip past him and up the stairs before he started after her. She used all her strength to put on an extra burst of speed and was outside in front of the house in seconds.

The car Gregor spoke of was pulling away and Andy ran out in front of it. Cairn, who was driving, slammed on the breaks. Ronan rolled down his window, concern clear on his face, but also frustration. They were in a hurry as well.

Condemned Angel

"What do you think you are doing?" he yelled to Andy. "You are supposed to be inside." She ran to him and opened the car door, panting, as the more than normal energy she had exerted caught up with her.

"I need to come with you. Please, just let me do this." Andy glanced from Ronan to Angeline, pleadingly. She dared not tell them the reasoning behind her urgency, knowing that they would *never* let her go with them if they knew. Ronan glanced at Angeline who nodded slightly.

Ronan agreed. "Fine. But you are staying in the car with Cairn when we get there." Andy nodded and slid in beside him. As Andy closed the door, Jason and Marcus came running towards the car. Angeline rolled down her window and yelled out.

"We are leaving now, either get in or stand back," she warned. Jason hopped in the passenger seat, leaving no space for Marcus, who stood with his arms crossed at the gate.

"I will be here when you return," he called out to them, and they were off.

"What happened back there, Andy?" Jason turned to face her in the backseat. Everyone's eyes were on her now. She couldn't tell them the truth, or she risked them sending her back home. She tried to calm herself down and slowed her breathing to a normal pace. She needed to believe what she was about to say, or else they would guess she was lying.

"I was just trying to distract you so I could get away." Andy lied, even though that was how it ended up working out. No one questioned her answer.

"You shouldn't be here." Angeline shook her head. "This is far too dangerous..."

"Jason, you will remain in the car with Andromeda while Cairn, Angeline, and I face whatever waits for us at this angel camp," Ronan instructed Jason, who nodded, always the loyal son.

"Why was our dad at an angel camp? He can't help with a legion; he has no powers." Andy found it odd Ronan would send Wayne with a legion unless he intended for him to be killed.

"This was not a legion, but a surveillance mission. Your father volunteered for this task; he went willingly. I did not choose him for this," Ronan said.

The car had been speeding along at almost eighty miles per hour, but now they began to slow down. Cairn pulled the car off to the side of the road, and they came to a complete stop. Angeline was out of the car and running into the woods before anyone else could move.

"Remember, stay here. No matter what. If we are not back in ten minutes, leave without us." Ronan spoke only to Jason. Andy discreetly reached out inside her mind towards Gregor. She knew he was there, and she needed him to know she had listened and no dire consequences needed to occur. Andy closed her eyes, focusing her mind on communicating.

Condemned Angel

Gregor? she called out in her mind.

Andromeda. You have arrived. Good. I have something of yours that I think you will be wanting back. If I don't see you in five minutes, well, you know the drill. Then he was gone again. Five minutes. She had five minutes to get away from Jason and into the woods to wherever Gregor was. She opened her eyes to face her brother.

"Are we really just going to stay in the car?" she asked him, knowing he would rather be out there fighting.

"Yes," he said, and Andy groaned.

"You do realize who's out there, don't you?" she asked, leaning forward in her seat.

He turned away from her gaze. "It doesn't matter. But I know you're about to tell me who it is."

"Gregor and Mara. Our parents need our help."

"All the more reason for you to stay here," Jason glanced out the window. Andy sighed and realized she was going to have to fight her way out. She had already wasted two precious minutes. She casually slid over to the door farthest away from Jason and pulled on the handle. Flinging open the car door, Andy jumped out, but before she could take off into the woods Jason was there, standing in front of her.

"You're *not* going out there." He gazed down at her, and Andy closed her eyes for a moment, letting her fire build up. She knew she could win this fight. His hands were on her arms, as he held her in place, and Andy pushed the fire out of her veins and through her skin. She opened her eyes and saw the pain in Jason's eyes.

"I'm sorry, but I have to do this." He dropped his hands when he could no longer stand the heat and Andy shot off into the woods like a rocket, using all her power. She could sense the path that Ronan and Angeline took, and she followed it. As she closed in on their location, she slowed down and came to a stop just as they came into view.

Andy could see them standing side by side, with Cairn and a couple of other demons who must have come earlier. Opposite them stood two demons who Andy could only assume were Gregor and Mara. She realized that Kaden looked almost identical to his father, just a little younger and less cold. Mara was beautiful, with shoulder-length black hair and a petite, lean build.

Andy gasped as she realized who hovered close behind them: Cory. He had a sneer on his face. She should have known he would do something as traitorous as this just to get back at her. She stepped forward into the small clearing that appeared to have been a makeshift camp for some angels. Ronan whipped around and when he registered Andy had arrived, fear flashed in his eyes.

"Where is Jason? Why aren't you in the car?" he demanded. Normally Andy would be afraid of him if she were not more afraid of Gregor.

"She is here because I asked her to come." A smile spread across Gregor's face as he said this and everyone turned back to him except for Angeline, who went to stand protectively beside Andy. "Now, come a little closer, darling. I don't bite." Angeline held tightly to her as she tried to move forward, and she didn't let go.

"No, sweetie. Don't listen to him," Angeline sounded as if she were begging.

"Mom, what if he has Dad? That's why you're here isn't it?" Andy looked into her eyes. Inside them, she saw a deep sadness that shook her, and Andy knew what she was going to say. She braced herself.

"Honey, your dad..." Angeline turned away for a moment. "Your dad is dead. They already killed him." Tears filled her eyes and Andy could tell she was unraveling. Andy could feel herself crumbling as well. Her head started to spin, and she wondered if she was going to pass out, but then Gregor spoke again.

"Now, now. In Mara's defense, she didn't know he was your dad, though that may not have changed the outcome if she had." He smirked and Andy realized how truly evil these demons were. She stepped away from Angeline who was too weak from her grief to continue holding onto her and walked past the others to stand in the middle of the two groups.

"Why did you want me to come here if you already killed my dad?" Andy's voice caught as she spoke, and she almost broke down right there. "You said that if I came, you would let him go." She tried to sound confident, but her voice shook, and her body trembled.

"Stop." Kaden stepped out from the trees behind Gregor and Mara, who both grinned and Mara even clapped. Andy gaped at him, a sharp pain radiating through her gut as she took in the sight. First Cory, and now Kaden…

"It's not what you think, Andy…" Kaden began, but Gregor cut him off.

"Kaden here is the only survivor of a terrible skirmish this morning. We didn't want him to miss this moment." Gregor reached out to Kaden, who recoiled away from him.

"Why can't you just stay out of my life?" Kaden snapped, but Gregor shook his head.

"Not everything is about you, my boy. This time, we are here for the girl." Gregor ogled Andy, causing her to shudder and take a step back.

"No. I will not allow you to take her." Ronan stepped up to Andy's side and put his arm in front of her protectively. Gregor grimaced. "Lucifer promised I had two weeks to convince her to voluntarily join us. I still have time."

"Lucifer was getting impatient, and he foresaw the outcome not going in his favor. Besides, we're not taking her; you can keep her body. Lucifer only wants her soul," Gregor explained, and Andy's heart dropped.

"Well, he can't have it. Why on Earth do you think she would ever give up her soul?" Andy could see in Ronan's eyes that he already knew the answer to his question. Gregor

Condemned Angel

snapped his fingers and Cory disappeared into the woods behind them for a moment. When he reappeared, he dragged a body alongside him. He pulled the body upright, and Andy gasped, lunging forward, while Ronan pulled her back.

"Septimus?!" she called out to him, and his head snapped up.

"Andromeda," he mouthed, and Andy saw him shaking his head. "Don't..." he began but Cory pushed him back to the ground, covering his head with a bag. Andy screamed in protest and fought against Ronan to try to get to Septimus, but it was no use. Ronan was stronger. Andy couldn't focus long enough to muster the strength needed to break free of him. Three more demons came out of the woods behind Gregor, dragging more bodies along with them. Andy recognized them as Sera, Micah, Gabby, and... Bo. Andy's heart dropped out of her chest. His jaw was set, and he showed no fear. They were all hauled upright. Andy's guilt weighed her down as she realized that they were only in this situation because of *her*.

"It was so kind of Cory to inform us of your angel friends' camp out here. It gave us just the leverage we needed. Now, Andromeda, here are the terms. You must agree to give your soul over to Lucifer, or we kill your friends." Gregor grinned maliciously, delighting in the pain that he was causing them all.

"No. It's not happening." Kaden spoke up. "You wanted me to give my soul up; take mine. Leave her out of this."

"No! Kaden, you can't!" Andy reached out to him, but Ronan still held her firmly in place. Kaden didn't look at her.

"As tempting of an offer as that is, unfortunately, we are here for her soul and her soul alone. If you still want to give yours up later, Lucifer will be more than happy to take it, I'm sure." Gregor grabbed Micah from the demon who dragged him out there. "Now, ten seconds for a decision my dear."

"No. She is not giving up her soul. This is all ridiculous," Ronan growled. "Cairn, you know what to do." Cairn went to make a move, and faster than Andy could comprehend what was happening, a glint of light appeared over Micah's throat, and he crumpled to the ground, blood spilling out around him. An inhuman sound escaped Bo as he managed to wriggle out of his captor's grip and threw himself down onto Micah's body.

Andy screamed. Bo was hauled off the ground, and tears cascaded down his face. Everyone stopped and Andy realized she had broken free of Ronan's grasp. She moved towards Gregor, who grabbed Sera and held a sword up to her neck.

"What is it going to be?"

"I will give my soul to Lucifer," Andy spoke loud and clear and was surprised to hear no waver in her voice.

Condemned Angel

"No!" Kaden yelled, but it was too late. Gregor released Sera, who dropped to the ground, sobbing over the spot where Micah's body lay. Gregor nodded to Cory who pulled the bag off Septimus' head.

"There's another…well…" Gregor sneered and nodded to a demon on his left. The demon dragged another body out of the woods. *Nathan.* Andy saw the complete despair in Gabby's eyes. She had missed it before, mistaking it for fear. "And I brought a gift for you, Ronan." Gregor grabbed the demon closest to him and shoved him forward, and the rest of them disappeared into the woods, leaving the carnage behind. After they were gone, Micah and Nathan's bodies each vanished in a beam of light that shot into the sky. Andy dropped to the ground and her eyes drifted closed. When she woke, she was in an unrecognizable room.

20

The Devil

Ronan jolted forward, but Kaden was faster, crossing the small clearing, and catching Andromeda before she hit the ground. Ronan's heart raced. He hadn't felt this worked up in a *long* time. His only daughter had condemned herself in swearing her soul to Lucifer. Granted this would mean that she was on the demon's side of the war by default, so he should be happy. However, he had seen what giving over your soul could do to a person, and he feared for her sanity and her humanity.

Condemned Angel

Ronan realized he was frozen, everyone around him watching and waiting for him to give them orders. The angels on the other side of the clearing all stood, facing them, also unsure of what to do. They had just lost two of their own, and Ronan could tell it was taking its toll. He stood tall and cleared his throat.

"Cairn, seize Zain." Gregor's *gift*. Zain stood rooted to his spot, terrified. Ronan knew that Gregor gripped his mind, preventing him from running. "I'll deal with him." Cairn did as he was told. "Find Wayne's body. Once I return home, I will send a car so you can bring it back to the mansion. We will bury him there," Ronan commanded to no one in particular. He found Angeline, who trembled behind him. He gestured to Jason, who stepped up to her side and took her arm. "Bring her back to the car. I will be along as soon as I diffuse this situation," Ronan said and Jason nodded, turning his mother away from the scene before her. Her face was blank, betraying no emotions, and it seemed like it took everything she had just to follow along with Jason. Ronan knew that she was slowly breaking on the inside.

"Ronan..." Kaden knelt on the ground with Andromeda in his arms. Ronan turned to them and understood what was happening. Andromeda was inside her mind, meeting Lucifer for the first time. This was something he had seen before. Most of the time people who gave up their souls could do so simply by communicating with a demon, but others were called straight to Lucifer himself.

"She is going to be out for a while," Ronan said. "Take her back to the car and stay with her there." Kaden nodded and stood, cradling Andromeda against him.

"Wait." One of the angels stepped away from the others and made his way towards Ronan. "Is she going to be alright?" His voice shook. Ronan recognized him as Septimus, the angel that Andromeda was involved with before she came to stay at the mansion.

"Physically, yes. She will be fine," Ronan answered him, knowing that he need not voice that mentally, she may very well never be fine again. Septimus nodded in understanding.

"May we accompany you to make sure that she wakes up? The only reason we were out here in the first place was because we were trying to help her," he said. Ronan had his men watching them the entire time they'd been out there.

"You will have to make it there on your own, we only brought one vehicle, but yes. You may stay with us until she wakes." Ronan saw relief wash over Septimus. Ronan turned back to those remaining around him.

"Search the surrounding woods. Cory was not alone when he came out here, I sent him with a group to keep watch on these angels. He turned on them at some point and I want to know if any of them are still alive. If you come across Cory or any of Gregor and Mara's group, cut them down. I will not have traitors roaming around in my territory," he growled. Ronan would not rest until Cory was brought to justice for his betrayal.

He watched as Kaden carried Andromeda back towards the car and the angels followed along behind them, halfheartedly.

"Sir?" Cairn stood beside Ronan with Zain's arm gripped in his hand.

"Right." Ronan let out a long, low whistle.

"I-I'm s-sorry," Zain tried to plead with Ronan, but he ignored him. Branches breaking and leaves crunching signaled the fast approach of the hellhounds. They had been on Zain's trail.

"Leave him, Cairn," Ronan spoke with no emotion. "The hounds will deal with him now." Cairn dropped Zain's arm and Zain took off running. Neither Cairn nor Ronan moved to go after him, he would never be able to outrun the hellhounds.

They turned to walk back to the car. In the distance, they heard the garbled scream of Zain as he was ripped apart. The hellhounds had found their target.

That took care of everything, for now. Ronan could hear some of his men running through the woods, still searching for survivors. He knew they would come up with nothing. Gregor and Mara were merciless and would have killed them all, but there was a slight chance someone escaped them, and Ronan would not leave any man behind.

At the car, everyone else was waiting and ready to go. Ronan climbed into the passenger seat. Kaden sat on one side of the backseat, and Angeline on the other with Andromeda's head in her lap. She stroked Andy's hair mindlessly, her eyes filled with grief. Ronan knew she was far away in her mind. Behind the car, the angels waited with their wings unfurled, ready to fly.

"Let's go home, Cairn," Ronan said. The car pulled away from the side of the road and made a U-turn. Ronan glanced in the rear-view mirror to see the angels taking off from the ground and into the sky. It was a marvelous sight. If they were not enemies, he would envy them.

When they arrived back home, Kaden carried Andromeda up to her room. Angeline sat, unmoving, in the backseat. Ronan helped her out of the car and to her room. She acted as if she were a zombie, going along with the motions, but not truly aware.

Once Ronan made it back upstairs, he directed Cairn to go back to the clearing to pick up Wayne's body. The other demons had their own car to get back, but there was not enough room for all of them plus a body in the car. The angels were all waiting in the living room.

"Nice place you've attained here…" Septimus commented, and Ronan understood what he was suggesting;

that Ronan had acquired it after the war broke out and people had abandoned their homes.

"I'm sorry some of us demons choose not to hide away in the woods like the angels. The comfort of a solid home does wonders for morale," Ronan countered. "But I acquired this home long before the war began." Septimus remained quiet after that.

"We do not have many empty beds here, but feel free to take over this room for now. I will have a bedroom for you this evening." Ronan said. They all appeared exhausted. He went to his throne room to be alone for a while after that. He needed to refocus his mind and figure out his next move.

∞

Gazing around in wonder, Andy took in the room. It appeared as if she were in a castle. The walls were made of stone, and there was a fireplace with a fire crackling within. It gave the room a nice, warm glow. A tapestry rug laid in the middle of the floor with two armchairs on it, angled so that they were facing the fire. Andy was drawn to them. She could sense someone else with her, and as she neared the armchairs, she saw that one of them was occupied.

"Hello, Andromeda," a male voice greeted her, and she could finally see who sat in the chair. He was tall, taller than Kaden, and he had bleach blonde hair that just curled over his ears. His eyes were pitch black, just as any other demon Andy had met, but somehow, they seemed even darker and more menacing. He was of average build, not too muscular, but certainly not lacking in that department either. "Please take a seat." He gestured to the chair beside him and Andy sat without hesitation. It caught her off guard, almost as if she had no control over her movements, but she didn't feel anyone inside her mind controlling her.

"Where am I?" her voice sounded small and mousy in such a large and echo-y room. The man grinned and gazed into her eyes. She felt a chill, but she also felt safe. All her fears and worries seemed to have left her mind. Everything was fine. She felt completely at ease and wanted for nothing but to be there, in that moment.

"We're inside your mind, Andromeda. Beautiful, isn't it? I may have helped out a little with the interior designing, but most of this you have created." He inspected the room, admiring it, and then his eyes settled back on Andy and he smiled again. "Do you know who I am?" he asked, and suddenly she knew the answer.

"You are Lucifer," Andy said. He nodded and gazed at the fireplace, the glow lighting up his beautifully sculpted face.

"I am." He clasped his hands in his lap and continued staring into the fire. "You and I are here because you have promised me something," as he said it, Andy was slammed with memories from the day. She remembered going to the angel camp to find that her dad had been killed, and her friends were captured. Micah's lifeless eyes swam before her in her mind and then a vision of herself...offering her soul to Lucifer to save the rest of them. She closed her eyes and leaned back into the armchair, which seemed to fold around her. She pushed away her emotions for the moment.

"Does it matter that I was forced into this?" Andy whimpered.

"Unfortunately for you, no. Gregor and Mara used methods much more...brutal than I would have preferred. I would much rather have you come to me on your own accord. They were only supposed to steer you in my direction, but it seems they have given a much more forceful push. Though, it did speed things up quite nicely." Lucifer smirked, not too shaken by his minion's actions. Clearly, all he cared about was that Andy was there, no matter the cause.

"So, in fairness, I will allow you one request. But I should preface that with the knowledge that I cannot change the past, which means that I cannot bring anyone back from the dead." Andy gaped at him for a moment, unsure whether this was a trap. Why would he allow her a request when he had already won? But Andy would not push her luck, so she accepted that there was no alternate agenda.

"Can I think about it and ask you later?" She had no idea what to ask for at the moment.

Holly Huntress

Lucifer shook his head. "I am a busy man, Andromeda. I will give you a minute to think, but then I need your request," he said nothing else, and Andy realized he was waiting for her. She closed her eyes again and thought about what had happened. She could request a punishment worse than death for Cory for the part he had played in all of this, or something even worse for Gregor and Mara, but she didn't want to waste her request on them. Her first instinct was to try to help Bo, but she couldn't bring back his parents or Micah. She realized there was someone else that she *could* help.

"My request is that Gregor and Mara have to stay out of Kaden's life, in every way, forever, as long as he wishes it to be that way. Their actions can have no impact on his life. They cannot talk to him unless he chooses to talk to them. He deserves to be happy," Andy said and was satisfied with her request. There was no way to save herself now, so the least she could do was help Kaden to finally be free of his parents.

"An interesting request, but I will grant it." Lucifer stood from his chair and turned to Andy. "From here on out, when I call, you answer. If I say jump, you say 'how high?' There is nothing you can refuse me, and there is nowhere you can hide from me. I own your soul until I choose to relinquish it. Do you understand?" Andy felt scared now. All ease had left her mind, and she quivered. She nodded, and then Lucifer cocked an eyebrow, expecting an actual response.

Condemned Angel

"Y-yes. I understand," her voice cracked, but he seemed satisfied. "Just one more thing…" He paused as he was about to leave and gave Andy an intrigued look.

"You are in no position to be making any further requests," he remarked, and Andy nodded but continued anyway.

"Just, please, let me tie up some loose ends before you take my soul," she pleaded with him, needing just a little more time before she would no longer have complete control of her actions. He appeared thoughtful for a moment and then he smiled.

"I could very easily deny this request, but for some reason, I am feeling generous today. Maybe it's because I'm on a high from finally winning my prize." Andy knew that the prize he was talking about was her. "So, fine. I will allow you until midnight tonight. At the end of the day, your soul will be mine." He snapped his fingers, and then he was gone. Andy was alone in the abnormally large room, and the fire had died. She put her face in her hands and began to sob. She wept for her soul, her dad, for Nathan, and Micah. Her whole body shuddered, and she couldn't stop crying.

"Andy?" she heard Kaden's voice and opened her eyes to realize she was in her bed at the mansion. Sitting up, she noticed real tears spilled down her cheeks. She knew that her dream was real. At midnight, she would no longer have control over her soul. "You're okay," the relief in Kaden's voice was clear, and he threw his arms around her. "I thought I lost you." Andy hugged him closer and sobbed into his shoulder.

"M-my d-dad..." she choked out, praying that some part of that day had been a dream.

"I'm so sorry, Andy." Kaden stroked her back.

"And... M-Micah?" she tried one more time and felt Kaden shaking his head. She sobbed even harder and Kaden readjusted, slipping into the bed to lay beside her so that she could continue crying on his shoulder. He kissed the top of her head and warmth spread through her.

"There is something else you should know..." Kaden began but before he finished, there was a small commotion outside of the door, and Bo burst into the room. He ran over and jumped onto the bed on Andy's other side. Andy gaped at him in shock and smiled, which she thought would have been impossible after everything that had happened. She threw her arms around him and he squeezed her tightly.

Bo shuddered as he wept. Andy knew that he was mourning the loss of Micah.

"I'll give you two a minute," Kaden said, and he left the room, closing the door behind him. *A minute...*

Andy realized every minute mattered now that her count down was on. She glanced over at the clock on her side table and saw that it was already six-thirty. She had five and a half hours until midnight.

Condemned Angel

"Bo..." Andy was not sure what to say as tears streamed down his face. She tried to wipe them away, but they just kept coming.

"Don't. There's n-nothing you can say," he managed through the tears. Andy nodded and pulled him in close again.

"I've missed you so much." She decided to just talk while he grieved. "I've missed all of you. I can't believe that you all came out here to find me." Bo breathed heavily as the sobs reached a peak. Andy continued talking.

"There has been so much going on here. Kaden has helped me with my abilities and figuring out how to protect myself." Bo finally took a deep breath.

"B-but he's the one who took you away from us to begin with," he protested.

"He was only following orders. Ronan's the one who made him bring me here, but for my protection. He's the leader here, and he's also my real father. I'm not the same person I was when I last saw you. I found out that I'm not only an angel, but I'm also a demon."

"The demons are the ones who attacked us and *killed* Nathan and M-m-m," his whole body shuddered again.

"That was Gregor and Mara. They are loyal only to Lucifer, not Ronan. Cory betrayed Ronan by leading them to you all." Andy held a cold hatred in her heart for Cory. "I don't know why my dad and the legion were there when it happened, but Cory was with them, and he turned on them and now they're all dead." Andy choked back a sob.

"I'm sorry about your dad, Andy," his voice was hoarse from crying, and he sounded defeated. "Tell me about Kaden." Even amidst his own grief, he tried to alleviate Andy's through distraction. She smiled through her tears.

"Well, Kaden brought me here, taking me away from you guys and I hated him for it...at first. But I've gotten to know him over the last week, and he is...amazing." Her heart fluttered. "I may be in love with him..." she didn't mean to say it, but it came out and she covered her mouth as soon as it did. Bo smiled sadly and took her hand.

"Micah told me that he loved me," Bo choked out. "I was too scared to say it back." He broke down and Andy gathered him back into her arms. "You h-have t-to tell him. Tell Kaden."

"I will. I'll tell him," Andy promised, her heart breaking for Bo. There was a knock on the door, and it opened. Kaden was there.

"I'll go," Bo whispered, but managed a small smile as he hugged Andy.

21

The Countdown

Bo could barely breathe as he somehow managed to make his way back downstairs to the sitting room. All the angels were still there. Sera attempted to console Gabby, but she was ignoring her as she laid on the couch, her body trembling from her sobs.

Sera's head bobbed up as she heard Bo approaching. Before he knew what was happening, she had her arms around him and was hugging him so tightly, what little breath he had left in his lungs left him. When she released him from the embrace, tears rolled down her cheeks. She and Micah had been best friends.

"I don't know what to do," Bo managed to say.

"It's going to take time. We all need to grieve," Sera stated the obvious, but he knew there was nothing else to say. "How is Andy doing?" she changed the subject. Bo shrugged, unable to will himself to speak.

A demon strolled into the entryway. She leaned against the wall opposite them, crossing her arms over her chest. "I'm Lily. I'll be your escort while you're staying with us."

"Why do we need an escort?" Sera asked, eyeing her warily.

"Some of the demons here do not agree with Ronan's decision to let you all stay. So, I'm here for your protection." She glanced down at her watch. "You must be hungry. There's food in the dining room if anyone wants anything."

"We already ate but thank you," Sera said just as another demon entered the room. Bo noticed that his eyes were different, though. They were not completely black. They were blue, like Andy's, with a ring of black around them.

"I hope you're all comfortable." He glanced around at the others. "I'm Jason, Andy's brother," he introduced himself and Bo's jaw dropped. She seemed to have left out that tidbit of information. Her brother was *alive*.

"I-I'm Bo," he stammered, still in shock. Jason nodded in recognition.

Condemned Angel

"Andy mentioned you a few times," he said. "Glad to finally meet you." It was strange that they were being so...nice. Bo had only ever known demons who had been trying to kill them, and this was a very stark contrast to that.

"Good to meet you too...but, I thought you were dead," Bo couldn't help but say, and Jason laughed.

"Yeah, I'm not. I am very much alive." He swept his hand down his body as if to say, 'I'm all here.'

"Well, this is a happy ending," Lily interjected. "But, what do you need, Jase?"

"I'm helping you out, but Ronan wants to see you first."

"I guess I'll see y'all in a bit." She gave a little wave and then headed off down a long hallway.

∞

"Are you still feeling alright?" Kaden asked as he approached Andy's bed. She did feel a little better after talking with Bo but she was emotionally drained.

"I'm not sure how I'm supposed to feel right now," Andy admitted. Kaden sat down on the bed and pulled her close.

"Your parents just killed three people that I love..."

"I'm sorry, Andy. If there was anything I could do..."

"You were there. Why?" Andy couldn't forget that gut-wrenching pain that she had felt, seeing Kaden standing opposite her in that clearing.

Kaden sighed. "The task that Ronan had me doing last night was to watch over that angel camp. He's had people watching out for them since they arrived a few days ago."

"They've been out there for a few days?" Andy gasped. "Why didn't anyone tell me? Oh wait, no don't answer that. No one told me because me choosing to side with the demons is far too important than a few angels' lives," she spat.

"No one could have known what was going to happen. Cory betrayed us all."

"How could no one guess that? He literally hates me. He would do anything to hurt me, especially by hurting people I love!" Andy realized she was yelling and brought her voice back down. "He should have never been out there with you."

"He offered to take Lily's place because she wasn't feeling well."

"I can guess who caused that." Andy rolled her eyes. "I can't believe you kept this from me..."

"I'm sorry, Ronan asked me to wait to tell you."

"You promised you would try to *regain* my trust..."

"I know..."

"Is there anything else you've kept from me?"

"Well..."

"Oh god..."

Condemned Angel

"The day we went to the cabin, it wasn't exactly a spur of the moment trip. Ronan needed me to get you out of the house while they had a war meeting in the throne room. He didn't want you stumbling upon it," Kaden explained.

"I can't believe this," Andy wiped the tears away that rolled down her cheeks. "What on Earth could they be talking about that they didn't want me to overhear?"

"The tides are turning in the war. The demons are winning," Kaden said. Andy took this in and realized the urgency that had caused Gregor and Mara to approach her before her two weeks were up. The tides were turning, and Lucifer wanted *her* to help make sure they stayed that way.

"Is that everything?" Andy asked, praying there was nothing else Kaden had kept from her.

"Yes. That's everything."

"I forgive you," Andy ground the words out.

"What?"

"You don't think you deserve forgiveness?" Andy glanced at Kaden and he shook his head. "I don't know what's coming next for me, and I don't want to lose you when I need you the most," a sob wracked through her, and Kaden wrapped his arms around her. Andy leaned into him.

There was another knock on the door, and Andy stiffened. Who could it be now? Marcus opened the door, but Septimus stepped in front of him. Confusion and hurt filled his eyes as he took in the sight of Andy in Kaden's arms.

"Septimus..." Andy felt a wave of guilt and knew that she should talk to him but didn't know what to say.

"I heard you were awake, and I just wanted to make sure that you're okay, before I left," Septimus said, no emotion showing on his face. He turned stoic.

"You're already leaving?" Andy asked, her voice wavering. Seeing him brought back so many emotions and Andy couldn't sort them all out.

"I only came out here to bring you back to the angels, thinking that was what you wanted. But I can see now that you are exactly where you want to be." There was no accusation in his voice, it was just a simple statement.

"I need to get out of this bed," Andy announced. Kaden moved off the bed and offered his hands to help her up, but she stood on her own. Her body was fine, it was her mind that felt like it had run a marathon. "Let me help you." Septimus' brow furrowed.

"Help me with what?" there was a sharpness in his voice, and it made Andy wince.

"I want to help you get back to the angel camp safely," she said, and he shook his head.

"I can make it back on my own. I'll have Sera, Gabby, and Bo with me." He crossed his arms over his chest.

"No. You risked your life for me, and Nathan and Micah died because of me. I want to help and make sure the rest of you make it home safely," Andy spoke with authority.

Condemned Angel

She knew that it wouldn't erase all the harm that she had caused, but it was a good place to start.

"Fine. I don't know what you think you can do to help but do as you please." Septimus stepped back as Andy walked past him and out the door. She made her way down the stairs and on to Ronan's throne room. Cairn was surprised to see her but opened the door without asking any questions. Septimus and Kaden followed behind her. When Ronan saw her, his eyes lit up.

"Andromeda, you're awake." He clapped his hands together. "Your mother and I were so worried about you."

"I need a favor," Andy said, and he seemed surprised. "And you owe me."

"What kind of favor?" He glanced behind her to Septimus.

"Septimus and my other friends need to return to their camp, and I want to make sure they get back there safely," Andy said, and he clucked his tongue, seemingly thinking about her request.

"You're looking for an escort?" He eyed Septimus, and Andy quickly shook her head.

"No. This is *my* request. Septimus wants nothing," she clarified, though she figured Ronan already knew that.

"Fine. You and your brother will be their escorts. Kaden and Lily can join you as well," Ronan said.

"Thank you." Andy let out a sigh of relief.

"Sir, do you think it's a good idea..." Kaden glanced at Andy and she knew he was worried about whether she would be able to handle herself now that Lucifer owned her soul.

"If Andy thinks she'll be okay, then I trust her," Ronan's words didn't match the strange weariness in his eyes.

"Where's Mom?" Andy asked, changing the subject.

"Here." Andy turned as she heard what sounded more like a shell of her mother and saw her walking into the room. Her eyes were glazed, and Andy couldn't tell if she even really knew where she was. But she made her way to sit in the chair besides Ronan.

"Do you need me to stay and help with preparations?" Andy asked her.

"Preparations for what?" the hollowness in her voice sent a shiver down Andy's spine.

"Well, Dad's funeral," the words came out as a whisper. Angeline shook her head with vigor, surprising Andy.

"No. No funeral," she rasped. Andy gaped at her incredulously.

"What do you mean? Dad deserves a funeral." Angeline just stared at the wall and shook her head. "You're being selfish! Just because you can't handle what's happened..." anger built up inside Andy that she'd never felt before. "This is all your fault. Dad would still be *alive* if it weren't for you, and you can't even be bothered to have a funeral for him?"

Condemned Angel

"Andy..." Kaden's voice barely broke through the buzzing that filled her ears.

"No... you're too wrapped up in your own sorrows and failures to do one last thing for the man you claimed to love all these years."

"That's enough Andromeda," Ronan's voice boomed through the room and Andy clenched her fists at her sides.

"Fine. I was done here anyway," she snapped and stormed out of the room. She stalked towards the dining room and paused looking around for Kaden, but he had not followed her. Instead, Septimus walked up behind her.

"You must be hungry," Andy said, wondering how long it had been since he last had a meal. Or maybe he had eaten while she was asleep.

"I lost my appetite," he said. Andy cringed, knowing this was a jab at her. She turned to face him finally. There was no one else around, so she didn't have to worry about anyone listening in.

"I'm sorry." She was unsure where to start, so this seemed like the best place. "I honestly thought I was never going to see you again."

"I half hoped that to be true at first." Septimus ducked his head in shame. "I couldn't accept the fact that your father was Ronan. But, Bo, convinced me to come out here and bring you back to the angels." He reached out and brushed a stray hair behind her ear. She felt her skin tingle where he touched her.

"I was worried that you'd never want to be with me once you found out the truth, that I'm half-demon."

"I don't know that I *can* get over that, Andromeda. I care about you, and I always will. But it's different now." Andy's breath caught in her throat.

"I still care about you, too," Andy whispered, her face growing hot as it turned red with her admission. She opened her eyes and gazed up into his, which were burning a fiery gold color. She bit her lip, and he leaned down, putting his forehead against hers.

"I'm sorry, Andromeda," he spoke softly, and Andy trembled under his touch.

"I'm sorry, too. So much has happened in this last week, everything has changed for me." He nodded in understanding.

"I have to go tell the others that we are leaving in the morning." He left Andy standing alone in the dining room, her heart racing. She let out a shaky breath and felt a weight lift off her. That had gone better than she'd expected.

Glancing at the clock on the wall, Andy saw that it was nearly eight o'clock. She only had four more hours remaining. She left the dining room to find Kaden. He was her last loose end. She needed to make sure he knew how she felt. She reached out to him in her mind but received no response. She groaned in frustration.

Condemned Angel

In the meantime, Andy headed upstairs to her room. She kept reaching out, but every time, she hit a wall. She didn't know whether Kaden was specifically keeping her out, or if he was safeguarding himself against all communication.

The clock kept ticking, and every time Andy looked at it, she felt as if time had sped up. It was already almost ten o'clock, and she couldn't waste any more time waiting for Kaden to come to her. So, she went into the hall where Marcus stood guard.

"Marcus, I need a favor."

"Anything you need."

"I didn't tell anyone else this, but I still have control over my soul until midnight tonight, and I wanted to spend some of that time with Kaden." He understood what she was getting at and closed his eyes. Andy knew he was reaching out to Kaden.

"He's in the maze, but he will not let me into his mind to communicate with him," Marcus told her.

"Thank you, Marcus." Andy hugged him quickly and then ran down the hall to the stairs. She took them two at a time and nearly crashed into Jason at the bottom of the stairs.

"Woah, where are you headed in such a hurry?" His hands were on her arms, steadying her, and he was laughing. Andy hugged him tightly. "What's this for?"

"I don't know what is going to happen once my soul is no longer mine." Andy pulled back from him and saw the concern on his face. "I love you, Jason, and if mom ever snaps out of her pit of despair, I need you to tell her that I love her too. Can you do that for me?"

"Of course, I can," he nodded. "But what's going on right now?" He glanced around, expecting something to jump out and take her.

"I'm going to spend my last two hours with Kaden before Lucifer takes my soul," she said, and his eyes widened. He pulled her into another hug.

"I love you too, Andy. We're not going to give up on finding a way to get your soul back, I hope you know that." He pulled away and kissed her forehead. "You're my little sister, and I'll be damned if I let Lucifer take you away from me." He put on a fake grin to try to give her confidence, but they both knew that there was no chance of her getting out of her deal with Lucifer.

"Thank you, Jason. I have to go, though." She squeezed his hand and took off towards the back door.

"Kaden!" she called out after crashing into the garden. "Kaden, where are you?" She raced towards the entrance to the maze and stopped just as she was about to enter. She flashed back to the last time she had stepped foot in the maze and came face to face with Samson. Taking a deep breath, she put one foot in front of the other and pushed herself forward.

"Kaden, please," she nearly whimpered. "I don't know what's going on, but I need to see you." She took a left and started walking faster.

"I saw you with Septimus…" Andy finally heard Kaden's voice, and she nearly cried out in relief.

"This is ridiculous, can you just find me so we can talk, face to face?" Andy stopped moving and waited for a moment.

"Fine." Andy heard as Kaden rounded the corner in front of her. She ran to him on impulse and threw her arms around him. He seemed surprised at her reaction and she knew he was still hung up on whatever he thought had happened with Septimus.

"Septimus and I both agreed that things have changed and we're better off friends," Andy clarified for him. "I told him that I've changed since I've been here and that there's someone else I want to be with." She didn't take her arms from around him, and he finally returned the gesture.

"I'm sorry." He placed his forehead against hers and closed his eyes. "I was stupid, I shouldn't have acted like a jealous idiot. But after everything I kept from you, I just thought that maybe you'd changed your mind about me…"

"No," Andy sighed. "I…I only have until midnight," it came out as a whisper. Kaden opened his eyes and they frantically searched Andy's.

"What do you mean?"

"Lucifer gave me until midnight tonight, and then he will claim my soul," Andy nearly choked on the last word, still unable to fully comprehend the weight of her statement.

"Why didn't you tell me earlier? I wouldn't have left your side." He held her a little tighter, and Andy smiled up at him.

"Because I didn't think you'd run off and hide in the maze," she joked. "I tried to reach out to you earlier, but..."

"I'm so sorry, Andy," he groaned in annoyance at himself. "I should have been with you this whole time."

"There's nothing we can do to change it now. Let's not waste any more time talking about it, okay?" Andy requested, knowing that they were probably down to an hour and a half by now.

"Yes. Okay. Tell me what you want to do; I'll do anything." He kissed her and then pulled away to wait for her response.

"Hmmm... anything huh?" she smirked and took his hand in hers, leading him deeper into the maze.

Twenty minutes later, Andy was pulling her shirt back over her head and picking grass out of her hair. Kaden still laid beside her, his head propped up on his arm, watching her with a grin on his face.

"What?" she asked, sticking her tongue out at him. He laughed and leaned forward to kiss her.

"Do you know how much I love you?" he asked, and his grin widened.

"Hopefully as much as I love you," Andy responded, feeling a blush creep up her neck. This was the first time they had said those three words, and it felt perfect in that moment. "And, I can't believe I'm saying this, but you should put some clothes on." He laughed and kissed her again. "I just have a few more things I want to talk to you about…and I'd rather do it in the comfort of my room."

"Oh, fine." He kissed her one more time and then stood up to pull on his pants and shirt. Andy watched him, and then followed suit.

Once they were both fully dressed, they headed inside. Andy dismissed Marcus from outside her room and led Kaden inside, locking the door. She glanced at the clock on the side table and saw it was just past eleven now. Tears sprung into her eyes at the thought that all of this would come to an end in less than an hour. Kaden's arms came around her from behind and she let herself lean back into him.

"I love you," she said again. She loved how it sounded, and how it felt to be able to use those words.

"I love you, too." He kissed the top of her head and the tears broke loose. Andy turned around to face him.

"Please don't ever give up on me," Andy blurted out. Kaden's eyes widened, not realizing that she'd been crying, but then his lips were on hers and he lifted her in his arms, carrying her over to the bed.

"I will *never* give up on you, Andromeda." He set her down on the bed and sat down on the edge. "I will fight to get your soul back forever if I have to." Andy realized what it was that she had asked him to do, and how selfish she was being, but she couldn't take back the words.

"I'm scared that I might lose myself. I'm s-so s-scared." She could barely get the words out as the sobs wracked her body. Kaden's arms tightened around her.

"I'll be with you every step of the way. I will never leave you; I promise." He kissed her forehead, then her nose, then her lips. She pulled him further onto the bed and crushed herself against him.

Andy woke up in the dark. The clock read one thirty in the morning. Her deadline had passed. She turned on the side table lamp and realized she was alone. Kaden must have left after she fell asleep, probably to prepare for their departure. Andy was still trying to work through why Ronan was sending her away to the angel camp but couldn't make any sense of it. She was a liability and a danger to any angel since Lucifer controlled her soul.

Andy was just about to reach out to Kaden in her mind when she heard a voice inside her head. She immediately snapped out of her grogginess from sleep and her whole body stiffened. All she could think was that Gregor was back, but it was not Gregor who spoke to her.

Andromeda. You have your first task, was all the voice said. It was not Lucifer himself, but she knew that the direction came from him. Though he had not stated the task, she knew it instinctively.

Condemned Angel

There was a commotion outside of her room. Andy pulled on one of her silk slips from the floor and ran to her door. She threw it open to find all hell breaking loose.

Holly Huntress

Books by Holly Huntress

Haunting Memories

The Broken Angel Series
Broken Angel
Condemned Angel

Social Media Handles
Twitter: @HollyAHuntress
Facebook: livingthroughwriting
Instagram: @livingthroughwriting

Blog and Author Website
Livingthroughwriting.com

Made in the USA
Columbia, SC
11 May 2021